Waking Lisa

Waking Lisa

Judith DeVilliers

Book Design by Judith DeVilliers
Cover art by: Enrique Meseguer from Pixaby

ISBN 978-1-0878-8495-0
Printed in the United States of America

To my son, Jeffrey, who said,
"You can do it Mom."

"The truth." Dumbledore sighed. "It is a beautiful and terrible thing, and should therefore be treated with great caution. [J.K. Rowling, Harry Potter and the Sorcerer's Stone]

CONTENTS

Chapter 1

"I walk across the dreaming sands under the pale moon: through the dreams of countries and cities, past dreams of places long gone and times beyond recall." [Neil Gaiman, *Brief Lives*]

Lisa slumped over on her desk with her head in the middle of a book. Caroline, the girl sitting in the desk behind her, reached out and poked her in the back. She didn't get a response. When the teacher turned her back, Caroline got up and walked around to Lisa and shook her and whispered, "Hey, wake up," Still no response. She turned to the girl in the desk across the aisle, "I think she is dead."

The other one let out a shriek and all heads turned to the commotion in the back of the classroom. Mrs. Leonard, the teacher, headed towards them. "What is going on?"

Caroline again whispered, "I think she is dead."

When the other girl screamed again, half the class stood and headed toward them.

As Mrs. Leonard approached them, she firmly said, "In your seats." She shook Lisa vigorously, then took her hand feeling for a pulse. She turned to the classroom. "She is fine," and walked back to the front of the room and sat at her desk. She addressed the class, "Lisa Longford has a mental disorder that causes her to fall asleep during the day. I will have the nurse come and check on her. Back to work now."

She picked up the phone on her desk and pushed the button to the office and asked for the nurse's office. "Could you please come to Mrs. Leonard's room Five-B? I believe Lisa Longford is having one of her episodes we were warned about. Please come as soon as possible to check on her."

In about ten minutes the nurse, Mrs. Barnes, arrived. She walked over to the sleeping Lisa, repeated the teacher's action and measured her pulse rate. She also shook the girl in an attempt to wake her. Lisa did not awaken.

The nurse and teacher then whispered together a few minutes. Mrs. Barnes turned and spoke to the class, "As your teacher told you, Lisa has a rare sleep disorder that causes her to fall asleep. When she does this, she can't be awakened until she comes to on her own. This may take a few minutes to several hours. Are there any questions?"

Andy asked, "Why don't her parents make her go to bed and sleep at night?"

"Her sleep disorder is a medical condition, not caused by a lack of sleep."

The bell rang and students began shoving books and contents from their desk into backpacks; but remained at their desks until the teacher dismissed them. The teacher then turned to the nurse. "What am I to do now? A math class will be meeting in here in minutes." Even as she was speaking, the math students began pouring into the room. "Can you get her to walk to your office?"

The nurse shook her head.

"You explain it to Mr. Gates, I have an English class in Seven-C." As she left she turned and said, "This is a problem. Maybe she should be in a remedial class."

The nurse looked down at the sleeping Lisa. The girl was average height, perhaps a bit thin for a twelve-year-old. All she could see was the back of her head. Her medium brown hair was pulled back into a ponytail with a rubber band. She mumbled, "Poor kid," and left the classroom.

Later Lisa sat up, opened her eyes and looked around the room. Things had changed. She picked up the social studies text book and notebook on her desk and quietly put them into her backpack. She noticed all heads in the room turned toward her. She stood and walked to the front of the room where the man, who she knew was the math teacher, turned and watched her approach.

Lisa immediately began, "Good morning. What is your name?" She saw a puzzled look on his face.

"I am Mr. Gates, the math teacher…"

Before he could say more she added, "I am Lisa Longford, Mister Gates. Pleased to meet you." She held out her hand, and he automatically took it. "Please excuse the interruption to your class. I am sure you have been told about my sleep disorder, but now I am late for my social studies class." She gave him a large smile. "I hope we may have time to talk sometime."

She turned, flung her backpack over her shoulder, and walked out of the room. She heard Bobby Moore, who was sitting by the door, snicker as she walked out, "Sleep freak." Just as the door closed, she also heard the voice of Mr. Gates, "Bobby ..." She guessed he would be reminded he was being rude. Bobby was in her sixth-grade class in her old school. She was sure Bobby already knew he was being rude. Lisa thought perhaps he said those things to get others to laugh, which they often did.

Lisa headed to the school office. She remembered the long list of rules for junior high included hall passes and late slips. The short plump woman at the counter in the office looked up when Lisa approached. "I am Lisa Longford. I need a late slip for my social studies class please."

The woman nodded her head, "Yes we were expecting you. You are the girl who falls asleep in class." She turned and sorted through a file folder and pulled out a small blue form.

Lisa added, "I have a medical sleep disorder, ma'am. If you check with the nurse's office you will find the information you need so that I can be excused if one of these episodes occurs during school hours."

The woman's face turned pink and she quickly filled out the blue form and handed it to Lisa without looking back at her.

Lisa took the slip and headed for her social studies class, which would only last another fifteen minutes. At least she would get the homework assignment. She had been told that homeroom was supposed to be a place to do homework, not be given homework. Even so, that morning Mrs. Leonard gave the class an assignment to write out in one hundred words their response to the question 'who am I?'

As soon as Lisa got home from school she ran up to her room, dumped the contents from her backpack onto her desk, and turned on her laptop. Junior high combined three elementary schools, which meant over sixty percent of the kids didn't know her. After her sleep episode today they would, and her reputation would follow. She thought it was interesting that this morning her homeroom teacher had given the assignment to write a paper answering the question, "Who am I?"

Lisa sat at her computer and quickly typed out two versions. The first she printed and put into her backpack to take to school. The second, the real answer, she deleted once it was completed. No need for a printed page. Lisa knew exactly who she was.

The first paper described Lisa Longford as a quiet shy girl (everyone knew that), a fairly good student, an avid reader. It described where she lived, what her parents did for a living, stuff most people knew. She also added that she had a sleep disorder and was known to fall asleep in class and unable to be awakened, sometimes for hours. Again, everyone knew this, at least those from her old school. And now her homeroom class did, and probably the whole school.

The deleted version was different.

I am a freak, a noun, a person regarded as strange because of their unusual experience or behavior. I fall asleep in class and can't be awakened for hours. Most kids don't use the word, but they treat me like a freak. Also, I wear a bracelet so anyone who sees it will know I am not a normal girl. It has inscribed a phone number to call if I have one of these sleep episodes. When they call, they will be told to leave me alone, or take me to the school nurse. If I were a normal girl and did not wear this symbol, someone would be concerned and call 911, and people would come and check on me and drive me to the hospital where doctors would be concerned and do tests to make me better. No one does that any longer. They leave me alone where I am.

I am a freak, a verb, to behave or cause to behave in a wild and irrational way, typically because of the effects of extreme emotion, mental illness (nice word for crazy), or drugs. I don't use drugs.

Who I am is a person with a great secret. I can't be awakened from a sleep episode because I have gone into the book I am reading. When a book calls to me I go into the unwritten pages. I can't enter the story if I am not called. When I come back, I remember my adventures in the story, not like a dream all muddled and sketchy. I remember them clearly because I was there. I have wandered through castles listening to servants and cooks talk and gossip. I have wandered through a market in China filled with strange fruits and beautiful colored silks.

I am wherever the story takes me, places the author knew about but didn't choose to put in the pages of his book. The book opens the door and lets me come in and wander among the unwritten pages. When I was young I tried to tell my parents and doctors, back when they cared and wanted to help me. They all said I had a wonderful imagination. My father said I should become a writer. Of course, he would say that since he is the dean of the English Department at the University.

We are book people, my family. We have a large library in our house, my father has more books in his study, my mother has books in her study. I am allowed to buy as many as I wish, and I do. My father is having our basement remodeled so he can store his rare books in special protective cases. Soon there will be more room for my books in the library. We are book people. That is why the books invite me to come into the unwritten pages.

Who am I? I am Lisa. I can go into a story when a book calls me. I am Lisa. I am a freak. I am Lisa, and I like who I am.

———

Lisa's care team consisted of her family's physician Doctor Aubry, Doctor Lilly Hilton who specialized in sleep disorders, and Doctor Schwartz a psychiatrist new to the team. They all sat at a round table in Doctor Jamison's office. He agreed to a consultation meeting concerning the case of an adolescent girl with a sleep disorder because it intrigued him even though now he rarely saw patients.

Doctor Hilton appeared to be the spokesperson for the team. She began, "Sorry the girl's father, Richard Longford could not be here. And thank you Doctor Jamison for seeing us on such short notice. We all recognize your research and expertise in the field of hypnotherapy as well as your research and work in the area of brain disorders."

He cut her off as she began reciting all of his credentials. "Yes, I understand that is why you have come to me." He realized his intolerance for banality was one of many reasons why he no longer saw patients and limited his practice to consulting in his field of hypnotherapy, teaching, lecturing, and writing articles for textbooks and professional journals.

He looked down at several pages of notes in front of him. "The facts you presented to me are that occasionally the patient falls asleep and can't be awakened for hours. She has been given frequent medical and sleep disorder tests since she turned seven. These tests indicate normal sleep patterns for her age, except for these occasional episodes. During an episode the records show she is in deep sleep cycle (REM sleep) and not unconscious or in a coma. Doctor Schwartz, who I understand is new to her care team, observed that the patient had been reading a book whenever she had one of these episodes."

Schwartz was leaning back nodding his head in agreement as Jamison went over Lisa's case.

Jamison continued, "Doctor Schwartz theorized the reading process might somehow create a hypnotic trance which put her into the deep sleep mode. I understand you are here for my professional assessment regarding his theory."

Now Doctor Schwartz spoke up, "Doctor Jamison I recall one of your lectures where you suggest patients can help in their treatment with some tools of self-hypnotism and you provided a few examples. Is it possible the child puts herself into a hypnotic trance as her eyes rapidly scan the words and lines in a book?"

Jamison nodded his head, "That is a possibility. However, her sleep disorder appears to be something other than a trance according to the medical records you provided me."

Schwartz continued, "We are considering a unique situation here; that is why we are coming to you, because of your extensive research on the brain. My hypothesis is that once her brain has put her into this deep sleep mode some unconscious part of her brain puts up some kind of lockdown that prevents her waking until her dream in this cycle is finished."

Jamison would not have used such terminology, but got the gist of what Schwartz was thinking. He would keep in touch with this man who seemed to know how to use his own brain. Jamison gave him a slight nod, which indicated Schwartz may be on to something, although out of his area of expertise. Instead he answered, "I am intrigued by your hypothesis Doctor Schwartz." Then he looked around at the other two at the table. "However, I can offer no opinion unless I have her complete file and talk with the girl. What is your wish?"

Aubry and Hilton suddenly looked pleased. Doctor Aubry responded. "She has been in my care since a baby. Lisa is a very intelligent girl, friendly, though sometimes a little outspoken."

Doctor Hilton frowned. "She is challenging. Even though she is only twelve-years-old, she demands to see all the results of any tests we give her. Doctor Aubry has allowed her access to many of these, though not to any of our notes or analysis."

"Before I take her case I will need parental consent; then with their authority will need to see all of her files. I take it she has had some psychiatric evaluations?"

Doctor Schwartz nodded. "I have not yet seen Lisa personally, but was given her evaluations from the two psychiatrists who have. I am sure their analysis will be made available to you."

Lisa's care team left the office. Jamison declined an additional meeting Doctor Hilton seemed to think was necessary. He had the impression she had more interest in him than in her patient. Jamison realized early on in his career he would not be a good therapist. He had never treated children, and quickly found treating most women patients difficult. A colleague told him that was because he was too damn good looking for women to deal with. He shrugged that comment off. He was a scientist and valued reality and the truth. He thought many people live their lives in self-deception. He had a sign in his office from a quotation from Hamlet. "This above all: to thine own self be true, and it must follow, as the night the day, thou canst not then be false to any man."

It was a month before he got Lisa Longford's files from her medical team and scheduled a meeting with her.

———

Lisa walked into Doctor Jamison's office, looked around, and dropped her olive-green backpack on the floor at her feet. She held out her hand and smiled, "I am Lisa Longford."

He thought her beautiful smile exuded confidence. Although she was dressed in what he considered rather shabby clothing, he considered the young girl to be very pretty, perhaps it was the smile. She was wearing oversized jeans, a baggy sweater and red sneakers with holes in the top. Her hair was tied back into a ponytail.

He responded to her greeting as he took her hand, "Doctor Jamison."

"Where do you wish me to sit?"

"Wherever you like."

He watched her look around the room, her gaze moving from the arrangement of a small round table with four comfortable looking chairs, to a grouping of two small couches facing each other, to his desk with two chairs in front, then to a large red leather chair and ottoman near a window alcove. No one ever selected the red chair since it clearly looked like the doctor's personal chair. Lisa went to the red chair and sat. "This is good." She smiled again.

Jamison pulled his chair from behind the desk and wheeled it to face Lisa in the red chair. She kicked off her shoes and pulled her feet off the floor and tucked them under her.

"Do you know why you are here Lisa?"

He was startled with her response. "I am a freak, a noun, a person regarded as strange because of their unusual experience or behavior. Sometimes I fall asleep and can't be awakened for hours."

"Freak, did you come up with that word on your own?"

Lisa looked pensive. "Not really. Kids in grade school call me that, anyway a few boys do and I think the others think it even if they don't say it."

Jamison asked, "Do you think that is because of your sleep disorder?" with the intent of adding advice about recognizing childish name calling. But then he didn't as he thought Lisa already knew.

She continued, "Also because I am different and I don't know how to talk to them. They talk about television programs and movies and music I know nothing about. I have never experienced those things; my family are book people."

Jamison never took notes when talking with patients, but later he would note from her comment that Lisa lacked the normal socialization for children since she had not experienced the same cultural entertainment. Also noted she appeared to be rather observant to have come to that conclusion.

"Did your doctors tell you one of their theories about your sleep disorder, that you may self-hypnotize yourself into a deep sleep state?"

Lisa grinned at him. "Yes, they did. You are to hypnotize me so I don't have what they call the sleep episodes."

Jamison nodded, "That is right. Do you know anything about hypnotism?"

"I do know something. I bought two books on the subject and found three articles you wrote in two psychiatric journals, and three in medical journals." She gave him a very large grin. "I did research on you as you probably did on me."

Jamison smiled back at her. He realized he could no longer think of her as a juvenile, regardless of her looks. "What we will do here Lisa, you and me as a team, is to create post hypnotic suggestions that will help you recognize if an episode is about to occur and a way to wake you within a very short time. The theory is that if your sleep episodes occur because of a hypnotic trance created by your eyes moving over the lines in a book, then it may be possible we can prevent that."

Lisa sat pensive for several minutes before speaking.

"I need to tell you a great secret Doctor Jamison."

Jamison sighed to himself inwardly while keeping his concerned doctor face toward Lisa. In the past patients would tell him their dark secrets. These generally resulted in a display of tears or other emotional breakdown. He had no interest in a patient's feelings. He never asked them, 'How do you feel about that?' He was a scientist and interested in reality and facts. His question at those times was, 'What did you do?' It seemed to him most patients didn't want to discuss their actions. Actions imply responsibility.

What she said next surprised him. "Doctor Jamison do we have something like client confidentiality?"

"What do you mean?"

"I mean that you will not tell my secret to anyone else, ever, cross your heart! The secret is between you and me."

"Lisa I can keep your secret between us as long as it is not harmful to yourself or someone else."

"What does that mean?"

He hesitated, thinking if he told her what he meant would she now not confide in him as it seemed she was about to do. "Lisa, I will tell you what I mean because we need to trust each other. To do that we need to be honest. What I mean is if you were to tell me that someone harmed you or molested you, I would need to report it to protect you. Do you understand?"

Again she surprised him as she gave him a delighted laugh. "I understand. My secret is nothing gross like that. Doctor Jamison, I am going to trust you." She looked at him intently and continued, "What you need to know is that I am experiencing an adventure in a book during what the doctors call a sleep episode. Sometimes a book calls to me with an open door and I enter and experience parts of the story the author did not include in his book for one reason or another. I am actually there. The characters don't see me, but also I am not like a ghost. I can't walk through walls. I open doors, unless they are locked of course. I listen to the conversations of characters not in the book like servants and others generally not included in the main plot. I have seen wonderful things in mansions and castles. I have walked through a market in China and saw magnificent printed silks and fruits I don't know the names of. That is why no one can wake me; because I am someplace else."

Her expression became serious and she continued without a pause, "My secret is also why I am a freak, a verb, to behave in a wild and irrational way, typically because of the effects of extreme emotion, mental illness (nice word for crazy), or drugs. I don't use drugs and I am not crazy. I remember in detail my adventures in a book; they are not dreams."

She gave him a very determined look and added with emphasis. "I have a good memory and I know what is happening."

Jamison was not one to respond without careful thought. He had watched Lisa carefully as she spoke to him. His first impression was that the girl was telling the truth. Jamison had a gift. He knew the truth; he knew when someone was lying. He attributed this ability to his observation of people, their every movement, especially the eyes. So many people live their lives in self deception.

He smiled at her. "I believe you Lisa, about telling the truth."

He needed to get to know more about Lisa. He asked about her home and important people in her life. Lisa referred to her father as the Dean, and her mother as Mom. She said Ginny lived with them and was also part of the family. Jamison gathered the impression that Lisa's relationship with Ginny was somewhere between a mother and big sister. Ginny had been with the family since Lisa was a baby.

Time was up just as they heard a knock on the door. Jamison decided Lisa was going to be an interesting challenge.

———

When Ginny knocked at the office door, Lisa thought the time with her new psychiatrist had sped by quickly. She liked him immediately and realized she would never have shared her secret with either of the two psychiatrists she had to talk to before, or especially to Doctor Hilton. For some reason she didn't like Doctor Hilton. She climbed out of the comfortable chair and wiggled her toes to bring life back into them and shuffled back into her shoes.

Jamison opened the door to Ginny who introduced herself. "Good afternoon, Doctor Jamison?"

He nodded.

"I am Ginny Piper. I will be the one bringing Lisa to her appointments. Lisa is good at telling me about appointments, but you might wish also to confirm with me." She handed a small business card to him. "Here is my phone number." It read Mrs. Ginny Piper with two numbers, one listed as her cell and the other labeled as the Longford residence. "

Lisa walked over to them, and picked up her backpack. "This is Ginny, she is the one I told you about, my father's cousin who came to help take care of me when I was young, sort of like a nanny, but now takes care of all the family."

Lisa left Doctor Jamison's office feeling happy and relieved. She thought to herself as they walked towards the elevator that she and Jamison had become friends in that hour. Somehow it felt like a weight had been lifted by telling him her great secret. She decided she could tell him anything because they were friends. Then again it might be because he assured her, as her doctor, whatever she said would be confidential. She decided to think of him as Jamison and not Doctor Jamison, except to his face he would be Doctor Jamison or Doctor. Maybe next visit she would ask if she could call him Jamison.

Ginny remained silent until the elevator door swished close, "What a hunk."

"What?"

"Your psychiatrist is so good looking."

Lisa hadn't thought of his looks except that he had piercing bluish grayish eyes that seemed to see right into her brain or perhaps her soul. Maybe that was why she spilled her guts to him. She shrugged. "He must be close to my dad's age Ginny, too old for me and too young for you."

Ginny responded with one of her deep rich laughs. "He reminds me of George Clooney, except for the dark brooding eyes. But your Doctor Jamison's blues are very nice."

Other people got on the elevator and she said no more. Lisa thought about it and looked at Ginny. She decided Ginny looked more like fifty than sixty. She had long dark wavy hair, always wore makeup, a little more than women her age Lisa thought, and always wore wonderful huge earrings. Today she was wearing jack-o-lantern earrings. She smiled to herself, if Jamison wasn't married then maybe... She guessed he probably was.

Lisa and Ginny walked out of the elevator and across the marble tile floor of the large lobby of the office building. Outside Ginny broke their silence. "I had to park four blocks away Lisa. Next time meet me out here." She pointed to the loading zone sign in front of the building.

"Okay."

"How was it to get hypnotized?"

"We didn't get to that today. He wants to see my parents first, maybe next week."

"You too?"

"No, not for that. We will meet on Wednesday afternoons for the next few weeks. Will that work for you Ginny?"

"I will look at our schedule, we can change things if we need to."

They passed a coffee shop on the way to the car and Lisa took Ginny's arm. "Coffee?" She smiled and added, "Please?"

For Ginny coffee was good anytime for any occasion. "Sure, let's celebrate your first hypnotism."

"Okay, even if I didn't." They walked in and found a vacant table.

Lisa walked to the order counter and ordered for both of them. She turned to Ginny, "Money." After paying for their coffees she sat across from Ginny and watched her put Lisa's upcoming appointments into the family calendar on her cellphone. That way they got put on the family's linked calendars; ones at the University for her dad, the dean of the English Department, and for her mom a history professor, with their family calendar at home on the computer in the kitchen. Ginny usually added all the appointments for family events and for Lisa and herself. Their calendars linked to each of their cellphones so that the four of them could know where each of them was to be on any given day and time, months in advance.

Ginny had the updates done by the time their coffees were ready.

"The Dean can't make it next week, but maybe your mom can." She looked at her phone. "Nope, but I will try to reschedule with him for some other time." Once Ginny began referring to Lisa's father as the Dean, her mom and then Lisa also began referring to him as the Dean.

Lisa shrugged her shoulders then took a sip of her coffee and winced, "Too hot." She walked to the counter and asked for some ice and returned to cool her coffee. "What is the plan for this afternoon? May we go to the Grimm's Book Store?"

Ginny looked at her watch and nodded her head in the affirmative.

Lisa told Ginny as much as she could about the visit with her new psychiatrist; she did not include anything about her secret. Her secret she had shared for the first time since she was very young. Back then her family ignored her stories as her imagination. Somehow she was sure Jamison believed her.

She explained, "The doctor will create post-hypnotic suggestions that might prevent my episodes. He said these might work if they are caused by self-hypnotism in the reading process. Hypnotherapy is used as treatment for a lot of things."

Ginny shook her head in doubt. "You read a lot honey without having a sleep episode. But he's the doctor."

They picked up Lisa's book order at Grimm's, picked up dinner at the deli next door, and went home for a relaxing evening; Lisa in the library with a book and Ginny in her room with a basketball game.

That evening Jamison was surprised to receive a call from his uncle Glen in Ireland at eight, since it was three in the morning

there. "Hello Branden. We knew you were expecting our call."
Then his uncle shouted to his brother without moving the
phone, "Ryan I got the laddie, pick up."

Jamison moved the phone away from his ear, then he
heard a click and then the voice of his uncle Ryan, who
apparently was on the other phone in their kitchen. "I am here
Laddie, I got it Glen."

He did not wish to sound anxious, even though he was.
"Why have you called?"

Glen answered, "We needed to know about the lass."

"What?"

"You told us you would be talking to the lassie with the
sleep problem."

A week ago Jamison told his two uncles in Ireland about
Lisa. He told them he would decide whether to take her case
after he talked with her. His uncle Glen, a professor and
researcher in the area of paranormal psychology, wrote several
books including one about sleep and dreams. His uncle Ryan,
a semi-retired priest, shared some of his brother's interest in
the paranormal.

"I did talk to her today. I am still not sure if her falling
into this sleep is caused by self-hypnosis. Even if not, I may be
able to help her with hypnotherapy."

He heard mutterings of 'ah ha' from one of the uncles.

Jamison was well acquainted with their take on extra
sensory perception, dreams and other areas of paranormal
psychology. He respected their views even though they were
the opposite of his. However now he was interested in their

thoughts, and even more so after his meeting with Lisa and getting her opinion of her sleep episodes. "Both of you will be interested that the girl is honestly convinced she cannot be wakened from one of her sleep episodes because she is not asleep. She said that she is in the book she is reading."

Uncle Ryan spoke up, "Interesting, we knew there had to be a reason."

Glen on the other line asked, "Does she remember these experiences?"

Jamison thought the word he used interesting. "You mean does she remember the dreams?"

Glen said with a slight irritation in his voice, "Does she remember the experiences or dreams?"

"It is late, why this interest in my case with the child? I know you like to know what I am working on, but at — hell it must be three there."

"This is an unusual case, naturally we are interested. That is if her experiences are more than normal ordinary night dreams."

Jamison respected the both of them so he continued telling them about Lisa. "She is convinced she is somewhere else and claims her recollection is more than the bits and pieces she remembers from regular night dreams. She claims she can remember them vividly because they really happened. Although I only had one meeting with her, I believe she honestly thinks she was wherever the book took her. My theory is the dreams somehow become false memories."

"What does her family and doctors think of what she says?"

He let out a large sigh. "A problem; she considers the idea belief of going into the story a secret. She said no one believed her years ago when she told them, and says now it is to be a great secret, between herself and me."

Glen then said, "We thought there was something like that Branden. We can talk again when you know more. We both think you should take her case. She might be in great danger if she continues with such serious episodes thinking like she does."

Jamison shook his head at that comment.

Ryan asked, "Can you share the content of her dream experiences with us?"

Jamison was thoughtful, then replied, "You know my theories and that I have no training or experience in dream interpretation. Yes, I could use your interpretation of her dreams."

"We thought you would be needing our help Branden, that is why we called."

"I can't share any of her medical information with you, only the content of her dreams for analysis. I will take her case. I believe hypnotherapy will help her gain control so she does not have the episodes. I will create a separate case file for her as a research subject relating only to the content of her dreams. I will get Lisa and her parents' consent for this separation." He added, "I will need to pay you as consultants so I can send the dream content to you."

"We don't need the money."

"I know, but consultants need to be paid to be legal."

In spite of the late hour the uncles talked a few more minutes about their lives and what had happened that week in the village.

Jamison was not sure what he had committed to with his uncles. His idea of danger for Lisa only related to her inability to understand and have control over her own subconscious mind. He was not a follower of Freudian methods. His understanding of the subconscious mind was as a physical part of the human brain. His interest in hypnosis was what he thought as a physical access to the subconscious.

——

It was almost a month before Lisa's parents were able to meet with him. He was not surprised at the physical looks of the couple. He imagined he could have picked them out in a crowd based on the description given him by Lisa. She told him her father dressed casual chic, but she didn't think that was a term used for men. Then she insulted him by saying, "Just like you Jamison." She said there was nothing casual about the way her mom dressed, that for her, everything was beautiful and impeccable. Lisa's mother, Florence Longford, was a beautiful woman. Jamison thought her looks would have been appropriate in a fashion magazine rather than as a university professor, not that he had seen many such magazines since separation from his wife. He saw where Lisa got her delightful smile.

The couple sat close together on one of the small couches. He joined them in the one opposite. The Longfords' provided him with a brief synopsis of their respective backgrounds. Richard began, "For the last five years I have been the Dean of the English department at the University, in addition to lecturing and writing. Florence teaches several history classes at the University. She is also working on an additional doctoral degree from a university in Rome."

Florence then spoke up, "I have been away from home the last few years, up to three months at a time. We do have Ginny. She is a dear and is a registered nurse. She came to us to help with Lisa when her husband passed away. Lisa was almost two then." Florence continued, "Even though we think of Ginny as part of our family, we continue to pay her to be with Lisa and to manage the household, since I am away so often and the Dean has extensive obligations at the University."

Jamison often had to curtail clients, even those who were not patients, from the extensive confessional they seemed obligated to dump on him. Their conversation about their home life confirmed the description Lisa had given him. His two uncles in Ireland said people tend to begin confessions as soon as they learned their professions; one uncle being a priest, the other a psychology professor. Jamison did not wish to continue the role of guilt exterminator so interrupted and asked more directed questions about Lisa.

"Could you please tell me more about Lisa's reading and her imagination?"

Florence responded, "Imagination. I think she must have one since her reading is quite varied. The Dean," she turned and looked at her husband, "encouraged Lisa with all the classics almost as soon as she could read."

Jamison remembered that Lisa also used that name for her father. He looked from one to the other, "The Dean?"

Florence laughed gently. "It was a nickname that stuck when he was made dean of the English Department. Ginny started using it and it seems that I also gradually began referring to him like that. He doesn't mind."

Richard nodded in agreement and responded about his wife's indication of Lisa's reading. "Lisa is a good reader. When she was ten I gave her my list from the University, of the one-hundred books a student should read before college. She keeps the list in the library and checks off books on the list as she reads them. We are book people. As a family we often discuss what we are reading, that is when we have time together."

Jamison noticed Florence was looking at her husband with admiration. He thought to himself that was an unusual situation for a therapist to encounter, two people who liked each other. He changed the topic, "What do you think of Lisa's friends?"

The couple looked at each other and seemed to be musing on that question. Richard Longford answered the question, "She doesn't bring any home with her. I am not sure why as she is very social and can easily converse with anyone. I believe she can fit in with any group. We have University people and students at the house often. Lisa is a good conversationalist."

Florence looked at her husband and added, "Fit in? Dear, she doesn't quite dress like her classmates."

"Dress?" Jamison asked as a prompt to find out why Lisa dressed opposite of the impeccably dressed Florence.

She was silent for a moment then added, "The Dean and I believe parents should let children dress as they please. They should concentrate on other more important things for correction and guidance." Her face took on an even more serious demeanor. "I disagreed with this philosophy once Lisa began making her own clothing choices at age nine." She let out a deep sigh. "Ginny lets her do whatever she wants. When Lisa turned nine, I went to Italy for five months when I began my degree, which focuses on the sixth and seventh century Italian history. Now I usually go there several months a year for research."

Richard added, "University faculty and students often complement us about Lisa's abilities to talk to nearly anyone." He stopped and seemed in thought for a moment. "Honestly we haven't noticed her with children her own age. I believe our family is overly involved with the University. Family history and all that..."

Jamison did what he usually did in prompting for more information, with a slight raise of an eyebrow. Richard continued.

"Our family is quite involved with the University. My great uncle, Horace Longford, was president for thirty years. I inherited the family home, which is quite close to the campus. Uncle Horace did not live in the residence on campus designated for the president. In the past, the University seemed to think of his home as the president's house, open to University events even though it was his own residence. The University's present president now lives in the designated residence. We still host various formal and informal events. Also, both Florence and I occasionally meet with our students individually and in groups at our home. Consequently, Lisa knows most of the professors and many students ,and seems to fit it very well, especially for a girl her age."

As the couple walked out the door Jamison decided he liked both Doctor Richard Longford, Dean of the English Department, and Doctor Florence Longford. They did exhibit a deep attraction for each other. That in itself had to be a good influence on the girl.

He typed a few notes from the meeting into Lisa's hypnotherapy case file. Jamison had cut his normal consulting fee in half for the Longfords with the understanding he could use her case and research in medical and psychiatric publications. He also had them sign release and permission to utilize experts in dream analysis since that was an area he was not as familiar with. The understanding was that any results would be confidential for his use and for helping Lisa gain a better understand herself. He mused, still all and all, the child would be an interesting case. He remembered the Rudyard Kipling's story of a child raised by wolves and wondered how it would be for a child raised in a university surrounded by books. He remembered Lisa's talk about Ginny, and he had met her. Perhaps she was a stabilizing influence in the child's life.

He then went into his private study where he did his actual work of research and writing. He unlocked a file cabinet and pulled out a folder with notes on Lisa Longford as his research subject, not his patient. Because he intended to keep her secret confidential, he would maintain two separate files. The one file for Lisa the hypnotherapy patient, was out in his office and available upon request from her medical care team. This inner office file was his private research and not part of her treatment file.

He made himself a cappuccino with his espresso machine and relaxed in one of the two large red leather chairs matching the one in the outer office. He thought from now on the chairs would remind him of Lisa who loved the soft red leather of the huge chair in his outer office. From the three meetings he had with her he was amazed that she seemed one of the most well-adjusted people he knew, with what seemed an honest outlook on life.

He knew the girl was telling the truth. He recognized the truth. He felt sure her sleep disorder was a physical abnormality that sent these dreams directly to the memory part of her brain. There was extensive research on the subject of false memories. No wonder she believed she could go inside a book; it was what she honestly remembered. Jamison was a seeker of truth. He wanted to know what was going on in the brain of Lisa Longford.

Chapter 2

"Properly speaking, the unconscious is the real psychic; its inner nature is just as unknown to us as the reality of the external world, and it is just as imperfectly reported to us through the data of consciousness as is the external world through the indications of our sensory organs." [SIGMUND FREUD, *The Interpretation of Dreams*]

SCHOOL WAS OUT and summer was about to begin. Lisa put on plaid cotton shorts and a large baggy tee shirt, pulled a brush through her hair and fastened it back with a rubber band. She looked at her reflection in a mirror and saw two skinny legs hanging out of the shorts. She shrugged her shoulders and poked her toes into her flip-flops as she called down to Ginny, "I'm coming Ginny." She grabbed her backpack and tossed in the book she had been reading and the two little pieces of paper that listed all the books she had read since her last session with Doctor Jamison. She tore down the stairs and into the kitchen.

She came to an abrupt halt when she saw her mother was at the table with a cup of coffee and magazine, "Morning Mom, morning Ginny."

Her mother looked at her with a smile. "Good morning dear. I am driving you to your appointment this morning. Are you ready?"

Lisa nodded her head.

"You are going like that?"

Lisa shrugged, "It's only Jamison."

She sat down and looked at the warm cinnamon roll on her plate next to a bowl of fruit. She started to get up again to pour herself a cup of coffee, glanced at her mother, then sat back down. Ginny let her drink coffee, her parents didn't. As she started in on her breakfast, she asked her mother about her plans for the day, even though she knew what they were since Ginny kept the family's coordinated calendar up-to-date.

"I am going to Flavia's, then to Mister Blake's. Ginny will pick you up after your appointment. I thought we could have a little time together in the drive to town."

"How long does a manicure and haircut take mom?"

"Flavia includes a massage dear; and look at me, Mister Blake needs to deal with the roots." She pointed to her scalp. She rose from the table. "I will be down for you in ten minutes dear," and left the kitchen.

Lisa shrugged. She couldn't see dark roots in her mother's pale blond hair, probably because she saw Mister Blake so often. Lisa started in on the cinnamon roll with the comment, "Oh Ginny, yummy." When she finished, she picked up her dishes and turned to Ginny. "I am going to miss Mom when she goes to Italy next week."

"It is only three weeks this time dear. As soon as she is back, we will all be on our road trip." Ginny seemed to be thinking and added, "We will all miss her, but she is almost finished with her studies."

Lisa loaded the dishwasher and said with resignation, "I know and not everyone can call their mother doctor, doctor."

Ginny chuckled and changed the subject. "Meet me at B and N instead of Doctor Jamison's office?"

Lisa nodded her head in the affirmative just as her mother reappeared. She looked like she had just come from a hair salon, not like she was on her way to one. Lisa thought she always looked like that. Lisa smiled at her mother. "You look beautiful Mom, you don't need Flavia or Mister Blake."

Her mother gave her a soft laugh. "They are why you think I look beautiful."

Lisa hollered as they headed out the back door. "See you later Ginny."

They walked into the cool morning air, and Lisa punched in the garage door code, watching it slowly open to reveal one white Mercedes and a large silver SUV.

Her mother commented on the missing Cooper. "It looks like your father decided to drive today." They got in the Mercedes and she carefully backed it out of the garage muttering as she usually did, "This garage is really too small for three cars. It is a shame the Dean cannot have it enlarged due to the stipulation in the will. The outside of Longford estate cannot be altered."

Lisa smiled because once they were out of the garage and the door closed her mother generally sat there and admired the hundred-year-old carriage house, with its discrete electronic door opener. She knew her mother loved the old house, really loved it. She enjoyed the twenty-minute trip to town with her mother. They always had things to talk about besides the weather.

"Going to Rome seems a greater inconvenience every year. Sorry Lisa but I am nearly finished. Then we all will go there for a vacation. It is a beautiful country."

"And you speak Italian, that is good. Could we also go to Ireland to see Jamison's castle?"

"I don't know why not." She turned to Lisa and sighed, "And while I am gone, Ginny is to take you shopping for summer clothes and something nice for our road trip."

Lisa didn't let her mother see her scowl at that idea. She did not want to go shopping for clothes.

"I didn't have much vacation input this year dear, the Dean did most of the planning. I do hope Ginny got some relaxation into the schedule. The last itinerary I saw included ten book shops. I told him people in the South don't read as much as the East Coast. He said all the better for finding old and rare books. He is excited about it all." She turned to her daughter. "I am thankful for you Lisa, that you love what we love. At least you do understand that we are book people, that you also are a book person. Some people say that book people are freaks, like they say computer people are nerds. Maybe we are dear."

Lisa was surprised at the serious speech from her mother about books. She guessed her family had always known what they were, just didn't talk about it or give it a label. She had never heard either of them suggest book people were freaks. Sure, her dad was really into the rare books. When they found new bookshops, he maintained relationships with the owners by purchasing at least two or three books a year even if they were not what he especially wanted. It paid off when he got first offer on unique first editions or other rare books. Lisa also loved the bookshops, even though she didn't care about the age of the books she bought.

She was startled when her mother got her attention, "Are you okay dear? We really are not freaks; I don't know where I got that word. We just aren't like other people in some ways."

"I'm okay Mom about being a freak. I was just thinking about our trip. Will you be home for dinner tonight?"

"Yes, and so will the Dean. Ginny said she has something special planned."

They arrived in front of the office building where Doctor Jamison's office was located. Her mother leaned over and kissed her cheek. "See you tonight dear." Lisa got out of the car and rubbed her hand over her cheek to remove the lipstick. She walked into the marbled lobby of the large office building. She nodded at the receptionist or guard person at the information desk in the lobby, walked to the elevator and selected the ninth floor.

Jamison stared out the window waiting for Lisa. He turned around when she glided into the office, gave him a perky grin and headed to the large red chair. He returned the smile. Lisa looked the same as she had nine months ago, still with the look of an unkempt gangly preteen. She tossed her backpack on the nearby ottoman, kicked her sandals off, and curled up into the chair with her feet tucked under her. "Good morning, Jamison."

He returned her greeting, "Good morning Lisa," as he pulled his desk chair toward the large red one. She dropped referring to him as Doctor Jamison shortly after they began meeting. He didn't mind. It was better for her to feel relaxed for the treatment to be useful.

"Is there anything important I should know?" He put an emphasis on the word important because Lisa would tell him details about her life as though they were great friends, not doctor and patient.

"You already know I only had one adventure at school since I last saw you. The other two were at home. Aren't you glad I showed you how to save my text messages to your computer?" She smiled and went on, "Our house was in an uproar the last two weeks with University year-end parties, two at our house, a dinner at the president's, and one I didn't get invited to at Professor Mooney's. Ginny didn't get invited to that one either."

"Shall we talk about your dreams?"

"My adventures! Jamison, we shall quarrel about that word the rest of our lives I am sure." She stood and wandered over to the window as she continued talking. "My good shoes from Christmas don't fit now, so mother was embarrassed at my appearance; but I did wear a dress. Now Ginny and I have to buy clothes. That is why I like my clothes large enough that I don't have to shop again." She returned and again curled up in the large red chair. "I don't think clothes are important, but my mother does and so does Ginny. Do you think I will change when I am as old as they are?"

"That will be a while Lisa." Jamison waited patiently for an opportunity to get Lisa back to the purpose of their meeting. "Are you ready to talk about your..." this time he used their agreed upon word, "experiences?"

"Mother will be gone three weeks to Italy. As soon as she is back we take our road trip. I do wish you could come with us Jamison. It will be three weeks and we get together every other week, so what am I to do then?"

"Lisa when you are on your trip, I will be in Ireland with my family."

"Your uncles who live in the castle?" She pointed to a photograph on the nearby wall. "Oh Jamison—I think I should rather go to Ireland than Georgia."

He was about to tell her maybe someday, but stopped himself. Lisa would hold him to it the rest of her life, of that he was sure. He also knew better than to patronize her and explain she would have a great time with her family. Instead he led her back to the present. "Are you ready to talk about your experiences?"

He walked to his desk and pulled out a small tape recorder. Several months ago Lisa also offered to show him how to record their sessions on the computer. He did not want an electronic record of her dreams. Dreams were not his specialty.

He sent the tapes to his dream expert, his uncle who was a professor in Ireland. He also sent along the list of Lisa's reading, since that obviously would relate to the dreams, and notes of any significant events in her life. His uncle would return the tapes with his interpretation of her dreams. So far the dream analysis was unproductive.

She grinned at him, "Sure, since you asked."

"I only had the three adventures, and only the one at school." She frowned slightly, "I was there, and as you know, once in a story I don't have control as to when I come back. Ginny said I was only gone half an hour for the first one." Jamison cringed inwardly. Lisa simply would not say she had been asleep half an hour.

She continued, "The second one at school was also a short one. This was in the school library at noon and I didn't even miss a class. The third time was yesterday after dinner. Ginny guessed it was about two hours. Sometimes she keeps pretty good tabs on me."

Lisa pulled two small pieces of paper, about four inches square, from her backpack. "The list of books I read since we last met," she smiled, "The lists are on my word for a day calendar." She looked down at the small slip of paper in her hand. "The first word is: savior, a noun, a person who saves someone or something from danger; rescuer, liberator, deliverer, emancipator; champion, knight in shining armor, friend in need, good Samaritan." She handed him the paper with the book list on the back. "That is you Jamison, my knight in shining armor. The books I went into are circled."

She then read the second paper from the calendar. "Nemesis, a noun, the inescapable agent of someone's or something's downfall; a downfall caused by an inescapable agent." She looked at him more soberly and added, "Or maybe Jamison, someday you will be my nemesis instead." Then she handed him that small calendar sheet with the list of books on the back.

He took the lists and put them aside. "Are you ready to tell me about your experiences?"

Lisa began, "My first adventure was walking through a wood of trees. I thought they were beeches and elms. They were spaced apart so the sun reached the ground, which was covered with grass and wildflowers. I wasn't there very long before I came back." She told him the name of the book even though she had already told him at the time it happened. When she woke from a sleep episode, she always sent him a text message with a picture of the open page.

"My second adventure did not take a long time as I remember. I was in a strange room of bricks that had a reddish plaster over them. Although they were covered with the plaster, I could still see that they were bricks, smooth but the cracks showed. This room had a small bed, almost more like a cot. The blanket on it was very colorful with patterns that went across, but not really stripped looking. The book I was reading, *Death Comes to the Archbishop*, takes place in New Mexico. I walked out of the small room into a larger one, again the walls were this reddish plaster. In this room there were two beautiful paintings, very European. Some of the furniture was in a dark cherry wood. Today we would consider them fine antiques. Even though we live in an old antique house, at least my mom and dad don't go for the old furniture stuff. The floor was a tile in greens and blues. I think they would be considered nice looking even in our time. I looked around at the furniture and at some beautiful silver candle holders. I wondered about the small room and I started to go back in to look at it more closely; and then I was home again so didn't get the chance to go back to that room. That was all."

"My third adventure was walking through a mansion. In one room some men were at a billiard table. The room was dark as the draperies were pulled, and the wallpaper was a dark maroon. I always appreciate electricity whenever I am in houses lit only with candles or lanterns. I wasn't sure if any of the men were main characters or not since they weren't talking much. I heard voices down a hall, so I left and found the ladies in a magnificent room. I didn't remember this scene in the story, but again most of the time I am in the unwritten or deleted scenes from the book. At least that is what I thought. The ladies were discussing their children and what clever things they had done or what naughty ones. Two of the younger ladies smiled and poured themselves more tea and looked bored. I wandered around the room and even sat on an unoccupied ottoman for a while. The wallpaper in this room was in blues with country scenes of shepherds and shepherdess sitting under trees surrounded by flowers. I have seen wallpaper like that before. I think it is a classic. I was bored with their silly talk and thankfully was home again. I had no control over coming home or I would have been back much sooner. Ginny said she thought I had been gone, ahem, asleep nearly two hours. That is a long time."

Jamison turned the recorder off. He generally did not ask too many questions until she finished talking since they might influence her memory recall. Lisa was getting better at relating details, not only from the dreams, but also from her real life. She said having to recount the adventures to Jamison also made her more observant of what was going on around her at home and at school. He often wished more people would be less self-absorbed and pay attention to details in their lives. He thought there would be fewer needs for those in his profession if they could or would. He thought most people could find happiness if they simply listened and paid attention to others and honestly sought truth in themselves.

They ended the session with the hypnotherapy.

Jamison returned to his desk after Lisa left and made a few notes about her home and school activities and details about the hypnotherapy session for her file. He kept these in electronic format so they could be available if requested from her medical team. He noted they were clearly making good progress since Lisa was a very easy subject for hypnosis. He even began making notes for an article he would write about the use of hypnotherapy for some situations with sleep disorders. She only had three incidents in the last three weeks, a record. Now that they were finding some success, he thought it would be safe to decrease their meetings. For the first time since medical school his work interfered with his personal life.

He cut his usual summer trip to Ireland to only a month, which coincided with Lisa's family vacation.

Jamison took the recorder and book lists to his study to complete his notes for Lisa's other file. He and Lisa had an understanding, one she even asked to have in writing and signed by him, that her adventures or dreams were confidential. She understood the recordings were evaluated by someone else. He told her the dream analysis was being done by his uncle in Ireland, a psychiatrist and a professor trained in dream interpretation. She asked about the uncles nearly every session after that.

He put the calendar pages with her reading list into her research file. He smiled to himself, knight and nemesis, no one could be both. He reviewed some of the notes in her file. He was encouraged. It took six months for them to agree on the definition of words. Jamison was impressed that Lisa knew the power of the meaning of a word, because with that knowledge came reality even though they disagreed on words about what was happening during her sleep episodes. Lisa used the word adventure instead of dream. Jamison did not like the word adventure, since adventures meant exploration of the unknown. Adventures were dangerous.

Jamison was a scientist; he was only interested in reality and truth. He still didn't know how to convince Lisa that her sleep episode dreams somehow went directly to the memory part of her brain as false memories, as if they really happened. And his hypothesis was that for some reason her subconscious put a lock on this deep REM sleep that prevented her waking.

He eventually compromised on the post hypnotic suggestions he used. Lisa claimed his suggesting she wake up was useless, since she was not asleep. He finally compromised and used words suggesting she not go into the book or story. After all, it was her subconscious they wanted to access. She even insisted, since she had been invited in by the book, he need to add she should not go into the story at this time. They devised a beeping signal for the suggestions so that Lisa could access it by pressing a button on her watch if she was aware a sleep episode was about to occur. The beeping signal would trigger her to wake (according to Jamison), or trigger her to not go into the story (according to Lisa).

The hypnotherapy had been successful so far. If Lisa could recognize what was happening, then she could have control over her sleep episodes. In the last three months she only experienced three sleep episodes in a week, compared to sometimes six a week over the previous three months. She was also beginning to recognize when a sleep episode was about to occur some of the time. With post hypnotic suggestions to her subconscious, she had finally been able to prevent some episodes.

He knew she needed to face reality no matter how vivid the memory seemed or how much detail she remembered. He had her read a couple of books and several articles about scientific research relating to false memories; she still seemed unconvinced. He thought when she realized the truth, she could have control over the sleep episodes and have a normal life. When she had control over her life, perhaps he would have indeed been her knight. He shook himself, the girl was getting to him. As he closed her file and locked it in the cabinet, he muttered to himself, "Always use the right words Jamison, remember you are her doctor."

Chapter 3

"Our truest life is when we are in dreams awake." [H<small>ENRY</small> D<small>AVID</small> T<small>HOREAU</small>]

S<small>UMMER WAS OVER</small>, and Lisa had her first meeting with Jamison in six weeks. He had been in Ireland; she had been home except for the family's annual summer road trip. She finished dressing and pulled her hair back into a ponytail with the usual rubber band. She looked out the window at Ginny who was talking to the landscaper. She smiled to herself. She was sure something was going on, but not willing to tease Ginny about it. Why else would Ginny have refreshed her lipstick and changed into a skirt before heading out back to talk to him. Lisa almost felt guilty for having to call her in to drive her to her appointment with Jamison. She took a last look out the window and muttered to herself, "I wonder how someone knows if they are in love and more important how to know if the other person loves them back? Maybe I should ask Ginny?" She decided now was not the time. They did seem rather intent in conversation that had to be about something more than carrots.

She took another look at herself in the mirror before leaving her room. As usual she was wearing her summer baggy plaid cotton shorts and an oversized T-shirt. She was now fourteen and would start high school in two weeks. She realized she had grown the last few months and now was far from the skinny girl she used to be. She took a last look as she shoved her toes into her flip flops. "Love," she muttered to herself, "who could love a freak?" She knew her parents and Ginny loved her, but they didn't know her secret. Only Jamison knew her heart and soul. She considered Jamison as her soulmate. He knew who and what she was and still... She stopped at the word she was about say out loud. The word flirted in her mind; did Jamison love her in some way?

Lisa abandoned her reverie, ran downstairs, and out to the yard to get Ginny. Harrison Landscape Service's owner, Walter Harrison, better known as just Walt, recently began personally providing services for the Longford estate. Lisa waved, "Good morning, Mister Harrison. Things are looking great and we all love the fresh vegetables you and Ginny grew this year."

Walt was about Ginny's age with graying hair and was close to Ginny's height. Although stout, he had the look of a strong man, and handsome with dark tan from his hours working outside during the summer. Lisa liked him even though they hadn't had many conversations; she liked him because Ginny did.

"I am pleased you enjoyed them, but most of the credit goes to Ginny here." He turned and smiled at Ginny.

Lisa was sure she was right about a possible romance because his smile to Ginny seemed to have a personal aspect to it. Lisa then said why she was there. "We need to go Ginny, my appointment."

Ginny's response, "Be right there dear," seemed a hint for Lisa to head for the car while Ginny finished talking with Walt. Ginny went inside, locked up and met Lisa at the garage.

Lisa was sitting in the driver's seat of the SUV, a cream-colored BMW. She opened the door for Ginny. "One more year and I can drive you Ginny," she said in a wistful voice as she climbed over into the passenger seat. She then became pensive as she looked down at the bracelet on her wrist. She would not get a driver's permit or license as long as she had to wear this stigma certifying her as a freak. Her medical team would require Doctor Jamison's clearance to say she was now a normal girl and the sleep episodes were a thing of the past. She let out a huge sigh.

Ginny glanced at her. "Things okay dear?"

"Yes and no. I was thinking about my next birthday and if I would be able to have you here teaching me to drive, like a normal girl." She waved her wrist with the bracelet into Ginny's face.

Ginny ever the optimist smiled. "You bet. Look at the change in the last two years baby. Don't worry about it." When they arrived Ginny asked, "When should I pick you up?"

"We might need more time since it has been six weeks since our last meeting. Make it two hours. Let's meet at the Coffee House."

"I will get my errands done, but remember we have the University Barbecue at five and the Dean and your mom are expecting us to be there." She smiled and added, "The Dean said Doctor Jamison had been invited since he would be doing some lectures at the University this year."

"I think I knew that. Do you think he will fit in? I mean like with all the University people?"

"Lisa, Doctor Jamison is a reputable psychiatrist and researcher, leader in his field. That is why they want him. They want to see some of his articles associated with the University instead of Harvard. I heard the Dean say the president complimented him on getting Doctor Jamison to agree to becoming an adjunct professor with the University."

Although they chatted a little more, it seemed they both were preoccupied in their own thoughts. Lisa saw a soft smile on Ginny's face and she guessed maybe she was thinking about Walt. Lisa wondered how it would be to see Jamison in her world, well her parents' world of University people. For the last two years she and Jamison had their own world in his office. Still the idea of being at a social affair with Jamison intrigued her and she wondered how he acted around other people.

Ginny pulled into the loading zone to let Lisa out. She called out the window, "Two hours, Coffee House."

Lisa waved and headed for Jamison's office building.

Lisa walked into Jamison's office and gave him a brief hug. "I have missed you Jamison. It has been six weeks and I was afraid you might not even know me after such a long time."

He held her at an arms-length and looked at her. "It is good to see you Lisa." He was glad the hug was a brief one, because in the brief moment Lisa felt more like a woman than the skinny twelve year old he began treating two years ago, even though her clothes and look was the same.

She removed her sandals and climbed into the large red leather chair. "First you must tell me about Ireland and the uncles, then I will tell you how I have been."

He indulged her romantic interest in Ireland and the uncles and their little village. Today he humored her and shared a little more about his visit with the uncles. "Father Ryan put an advertisement in several travel journals offering tours of our home. His idea was to get money to restore the half of it that is falling apart."

"I thought you had tons of money Jamison, since you own a castle."

"Castles are expensive, the taxes are high, and it is falling apart. The advertisement resulted in trippers, ahem, tourists, coming through almost every other day. I had to lead the tour when he couldn't be there. After three times he found a way to be there since I refused to tell the legends and tales he did for the trippers."

"I would so love to take the tour and be a tripper. Did he make a lot of money?"

Jamison laughed, "He did, but mostly from the sale of whiskey and bangers."

"Bangers?"

"Sausages."

"You promised me pictures this time."

He went to his desk, picked up the envelope with the pictures he had printed, and handed it to her. He knew she would not forget a promise.

She flipped through the photos. "Who is this pretty woman standing with your uncles?

"Her name is Colleen."

"Is she a relative?"

"A friend."

"Oh, since she is in the pictures with your uncles, and the one with you and the uncles I thought she was family."

He did not respond and reached out an open hand to retrieve the pictures. He noticed Lisa's face had taken on a somber look when she asked about Colleen. Although he and Lisa had informal chats they were about books and ideas; not about his personal life. He knew he would need to talk to her again about keeping their relationship on a doctor and patient basis. His uncles and Colleen had even commented on Lisa's text messages, though brief, were about things other than if she had a sleep episode. This instant was not the time for that discussion.

"Are you ready to tell me about your..." he paused, "your experiences."

They began the session. Jamison retrieved the recorder and got it started while Lisa pulled out her notes. She had five episodes in the last six weeks. As always, she had sent him a text message whenever she had a sleep episode. Although she sometimes took notes, even so, her recollection from several weeks were sketchy at best. Lisa told him what she remembered about the episodes.

"Looks like we finished early Lisa."

"That is your fault for being gone so long Jamison. I can't remember so many things, and you said I wasn't to write them out, just notes."

"You know that is because once you write them down, they become solid, and you forget other little things that may be important."

Lisa's voice had a slight whine, "Then you need to be here for me. I thought you cared about me Jamison since we are soulmates."

Inwardly he winced at the word soulmates. She once rattled off the definition for him, that it had many implied meanings, many of which she thought applied to their relationship. When he was in Ireland, she often added little comments when she texted him that she had a sleep episode. Little comments about him deserting her, and being gone so long. "Now Lisa you know better. You know I do care and have for two years now. Remember we are a team and need to keep working together."

She said it again, "We are soulmates Jamison, not just a team."

"I am your doctor." He hesitated and added, "And we are friends Lisa."

She sighed as though in resignation, "I know. It is just that I missed you. I can share everything with you."

"You mean your dreams?"

"No — well yes my adventures, but we can talk about school and my family; and about books and ideas and philosophy." She slowed down and looked somewhat somber. "I know I can talk about almost everything to Ginny and my family." She swallowed hard. "But you are my soulmate Jamison."

He knew he had extended their relationship beyond that of a therapist, acting more as a guide or teacher by allowing a friendship to include deeper subjects such as ideas and philosophy. He sometimes wondered if it was more than her extensive reading that had created such an old and wise soul in such a young girl. The terms seemed contradictory, old and wise soul and young girl. On the outside she was young and not fully aware of her culture outside of her books, her family, and the University. Jamison feared that sometimes maybe she didn't want to get better. Perhaps he needed to be firmer with her. Then again, maybe she only needed to grow up to become a normal girl, if that could be a possibility for someone with her imagination.

Since they had time, he went through the hypnotism session, which should trigger Lisa's awareness of the real world and bring her out of her subconscious dreams of being part of a story in another world. He decided to resume meetings back to twice a month since her progress had stalled a little. Although the hypnotherapy was working, it was also a sign Lisa was still not in control herself. They scheduled her next appointment and talked a few minutes about the University event that evening. Lisa left and Jamison went to his study to copy the tape to send to his uncles, and make his notes for her hypnotherapy file for her care team as well as those for his own research file regarding her dreams.

———

Lisa ran to catch up with her family on their way to the University for the annual barbecue. Her mother, looking lovely and elegant in a cream-colored pantsuit, turned and looked at her somewhat shabby teenage daughter approaching still in her baggy shorts, oversized tee shirt, and flip flops. "Lisa dear, run home and change."

"I thought this was a picnic?" She often got comments from her mother on her choice of clothes. She added, "Everyone is used to me Mom."

Her father in his kind but authoritative voice said, "Lisa, do as your mother asked. The University has even invited the mayor and other important community members. We want to fit in with the community dear."

Lisa took a second look at her father who was wearing a tweed jacket, but no tie. Ginny was wearing a colorful sundress, red sandals and large red earrings. Lisa decided Ginny knew how to be her unique self and still fit in with the University crowd. She looked at herself. "Sorry Dad, I will be back in a few minutes."

Ginny asked. "Do you want me to come with you?"

"No, I will be back in a minute."

She headed back up the block, tore into the house, re-placed the large tee shirt with another large tee shirt, but this one had the University emblem and name on both sides. She exchanged the old flip flops for her new Birkenstocks.

By the time she got back to the University, which was only four blocks away, she saw that her family members were already socializing with the crowd that had gathered on the grounds. Everything looked festive with colorful awnings and brightly colored cloths on the tables spread under the trees. Only at the University would a barbecue picnic take on the form of a formal dinner party. Caterers were preparing the meats at several large smoker grills. The appetizers, side dishes, and deserts were under the colorful awnings. A local pub had been contracted to provide bar services.

Lisa looked around. She guessed there were over a hundred guests at the affair. She knew the deans and most of the tenured faculty since her father frequently entertained. As a dean the additional housing allowance was for the purpose of opening his home to the University for social occasions. Florence Longford, as a tenured professor, also entertained frequently because she enjoyed doing so.

Lisa began to mingle and talk to people. She always enjoyed social meetings with University people since they were easy to talk to, quite unlike her junior high classmates. University people talked about books and theater and music, not about television and rock stars and movies. She finally spotted Jamison, who was as she expected, dressed in the formal casual as most of the University people. He looked different here under the trees, a soft wind blowing in his hair. Out here with other people, she suddenly saw him differently. Ginny was right that first day when she said that he was incredibly good looking. He was incredibly good looking; and he was her Jamison.

She filled her plate and sat at one of the tables next to a very pretty young woman who she found out was a new adjunct professor named Donna. Lisa kept an eye on Jamison while carrying on a casual conversation with Donna. She watched him walk toward the bar with a very pretty young woman holding onto his arm. Her conversation companion noticed Lisa's gaze and asked her if she knew the man with Professor Rebecca Taylor.

"Yes, he is Doctor Jamison. My father said he would be adjunct in the school of psychology."

"Very handsome man. Do you know if he is married?"

She looked at the pretty young woman by her who seemed to assume since she was the dean's daughter, she would know everyone. She suddenly didn't feel like responding, but did so. "I understand that he is divorced."

Donna stood, "I am going to get a beverage, Lisa was it? May I bring you something?"

Lisa gave her a large grin and responded, "Thank you, I would like a white wine."

Donna's face showed a slight frown as she gave Lisa a long look, then a smile. "I am not sure I should do that since your father is the dean of the English department, and will be my boss. What do you think?"

Lisa continued the tease. "Bring the wine and I will put in a good word for you."

Donna burst out in a delightful laugh. Lisa joined her then pointed to her can of Coke on the table. "I'm fine, but thanks for the offer Donna."

She watched as Donna joined Jamison and the Rebecca person. He was smiling and talking with two of the prettiest young women there. Lisa felt a gray cloud move over her heart. He was her Jamison, why was he smiling and laughing with those two? She thought she would wander over and join them. Donna was wearing a white sundress that made her tan look rich and elegant. The Rebecca was much more casual with white shorts and a blue knit shirt that revealed cleavage almost as much as did Ginny's usual shirts and blouses. They both had short hair and wore makeup. They looked almost as elegant as her mother, but younger and sexier. She didn't move.

A little later Jamison walked over to where she was sitting by herself. He talked with her a few minutes and was charming and kind as always. She knew he realized she was not her usual talkative self and excused himself after a few minutes. She watched him stop and talk with both her father and mother. He did have good manners. She did not wonder what they talked about, it had to be her, what else.

She did not feel like joining the chatter among her parents and Ginny as they walked home. Much of the talk was gossip and news about the next academic year. She often wondered why and how Ginny, who was so very different from her parents, seemed to fit in with the University people. Maybe because Ginny was intelligent and a good listener.

Her mother turned back to look at her. "You haven't had much to say. Did you enjoy the evening dear?" She didn't wait for an answer. "It was nice to see your Doctor Jamison there. He seemed to fit right in."

Her father added, "With his credentials he will be a great asset to the University for the Psychology Department. Dean Norlan prides himself on getting him, but did give me a little credit."

They then went into more gossip and left Lisa to her own thoughts as they approached the house. All she could think about was the very pretty young women hanging on to her Jamison. She did not like those thoughts. She was just a kid too young to drink wine. They were ladies, sexy ladies.

———

That night after the University barbecue Jamison could not sleep. He gave up and headed for the kitchen to make a cup of coffee. Instead he poured a shot of Jameson whiskey and turned on his computer. He scanned through pictures he had taken in Ireland, ones he had shared with Lisa that morning. She clearly had reacted to the ones that included Colleen. He was troubled; he knew he had to deal with her patient/psychiatrist infatuation. His uncles suggested he turn Lisa's treatment to someone else since she was making progress. And there was the rub, he knew his affection for the girl might be an issue. Perhaps they were right. He had to admit he did miss Lisa in the six weeks he had been in Ireland. She sent him a brief text message a couple times a week, in addition to the required text messages if she had a sleep episode. Colleen even called him on that.

Lisa had been happy to see him that morning, although she complained about being apart six weeks. Then, she ignored him at the barbecue, even after several minutes attempted conversation. He poured out another shot as the turned off the computer. He knew he would need to create more distance with Lisa as the realization of how far her patient/therapist infatuation had gone. All the signs were there. Although Lisa was not lonely, how could she be with her parents and Ginny hovering over her. But she seemed to lack friends, so of course she latched onto someone who listened to her and cared about her; her psychiatrist.

He paced the floor and poured himself another drink. He did not wish to look at his own feelings toward Lisa. He knew he had developed an affection for the child over the last two years. She had an old soul, an ageless quality about her. Perhaps the depth in the girl resulted from her life in books, and her social life she was primarily interaction with university professors and students. She had no peer context, no wonder she still felt like she was what she termed a freak.

Both of his uncles suggested he turn Lisa's case to someone else, especially since the track they were on was proving to be successful. He respected his uncles. He spent every summer of his life since early childhood with them in Ireland. The exception was the four years of his rocky marriage.

His uncle, Glenn Jamison, the professor of paranormal psychology, provided the dream interpretations for Lisa's case, and he shared everything with his brother, Father Ryan Jamison. The Jamison family had been a family of monks and mystics. He had been raised on the strange stories of the castle his family had occupied over four hundred years. What Jamison considered scientific observation as to why he knew when people were telling the truth, his uncles claimed was one of the family's mystical gifts.

They also suggested he should turn Lisa's case to someone else because of the family's special gifts, his special gifts. They suggested that Lisa was almost other worldly and could be a risk to someone like Jamison who they claimed was a mystic in the family tradition. Uncle Glenn said that was why Lisa referred to their relationship as soulmates. Somehow, she also felt the connection.

He knew the signs were there of patient infatuation with her therapist; that was nothing really unusual. Since she was just a child, he didn't agree with the uncles that there was any risk. Although he admitted to himself that he had affectionate feelings toward Lisa, they were clearly fatherly feelings. He admitted it was not acceptable professionally to allow a friendship between patient and therapist. He also knew Lisa would be devastated if he turned her case over to someone else. He finished the drink and made a decision. If Lisa continued progressing in treatment as she had been, she would no longer need him or hypnotherapy in perhaps as little as six months. He was in control of their relationship.

Chapter 4

"We are such stuff as dreams are made of, and our little life is rounded with a sleep." [WILLIAM SHAKESPEARE, *The Tempest*]

THE NEXT MORNING Lisa walked into the kitchen where her mother was drinking coffee and chatting with Ginny. "Morning Ginny, morning Mom." She sat down by her mother. "School starts next week. Mom, can we go shopping for school clothes, some like other girls wear?"

Her mother looked up startled, dropped the cup of hot coffee, which splattered down the table and onto her white skirt, then crashed to the floor. She ignored her hot wet stained skirt and stared at Lisa. "Of course, sweetie. What brought this on?"

Lisa looked down at her flip flops, baggy shorts and tee shirt. "I guess high school girls probably dress differently?" She mused to herself. She didn't really guess; she knew she wasn't like other girls. They were normal, she was a freak. What she wore really didn't matter, they ignored her and she ignored them.

That morning when she was brushing her teeth she stared into the mirror. She realized she was beginning to look a little like her beautiful mother. Her brown hair glowed with rich highlights from the summer, her face was pretty and if she wore makeup would probably have a closer resemblance to her mother. As she was dressing, she realized the spindly legs and flat chest had filled out. She decided her body was okay. She took a second look, smiled and thought maybe better than okay. It was as good as the sexy young women at the University barbecue.

Her mother had to say her name twice before she really heard her. "Are you free today Lisa?" Then before getting an answer she instead turned to Ginny who was wiping up the floor. "Will you be a dear and see if you can get Lisa in with me at Flavia's and Mister Blake's this morning?" Florence then hurried out of the kitchen.

Ginny called after her retreating figure. "Bring the skirt right back so I can get the stain out." She looked at Lisa. "What's with you girl?"

Lisa winked at Ginny and pulled up her shirt. "Remember how we had to get me new bras, see. I'm growing."

Ginny broke into a loud laugh. Lisa joined, then asked, "Breakfast?"

Ginny pointed to the stove, "Oatmeal."

Lisa dished up a bowlful and poured herself a cup of coffee. She was fourteen and coffee was now allowed. She ate while Ginny made the phone calls. She grinned to herself. Her father, the Dean, could make things happen at the University.

Her mother could make things happen with Flavia and Mister Blake. Yes, they could work Florence's daughter in, no problem.

Her mother was back with the damaged skirt. She was now wearing a denim skirt, which necessitated a different shirt and different sandals. "Ready dear?"

Lisa ran upstairs to get her backpack.

Ginny said, "Florence, they both can fit Lisa in at the same time as your appointments."

"Thanks so much Ginny; and thanks for trying to get the stain out. I don't know what made me so clumsy." She absently poured herself another cup of coffee and sat back at the table. "Is the Dean planning on being home for dinner? He was late last night and we didn't talk."

Ginny looked at the calendar on the kitchen computer and replied, "Nothing scheduled, except the golf today. He ate early this morning and left by seven."

Lisa was back down with her ancient green backpack slung over her shoulder. Her mother shook her head. Lisa understood and opened it to retrieved her cell phone and credit card, which she stuffed into the large pocket in her shorts. She deposited the bag on the floor. They were off.

"This is what I want," Lisa said to the beautician, Carol, who had handed her a stack of hair style books to look through.

Carol looked at the picture, then at Lisa. "Are you sure you want it short? Most girls your age wear their hair long. Yours is very healthy, we could give it a trim, maybe give you bangs."

Lisa was sure. "This is it."

Carol looked at the photo. "That is Ashley Green as Alice from the Twilight movie." She looked from the picture and back up to Lisa. "With this cut you will really look like her, you have the same smile."

Lisa pointed to another photo and added, "But I want highlights like this one. Can you do that?"

Carol looked at both pictures, then gave Lisa a great smile. "We can do it. But you realize you are gonna look too damn sexy for your own good."

They were in the middle of the highlights when her mother, who was finished, walked over to see the transformation of her daughter. She agreed with Lisa's choice, then asked Carol if she had time, could she work on Lisa's makeup, said she would be back in an hour, and left. The makeup session involved plucking of eyebrows, application of eye makeup, lipstick and other cosmetics with the purpose of making her look natural. In the past, both Ginny and her mother made several failed attempts to introduce makeup to Lisa. Now she liked this new look. Her mother's look was what she considered sophisticated, Ginny's look was flamboyant almost what she thought a barmaid might look like, if she had ever seen one.

When she was done, she sent a couple of selfies to Ginny, who responded, "No way!"

Lisa and her mother were in and out of each other's dressing rooms as they tried on clothes at three different shops. Lisa thought she hadn't seen her mother act so young as they giggled and laughed together. They each selected skinny jeans with bling down the legs. They stood together for a picture to send Ginny, hip-to-hip, with silly looking grins. Before they left that shop, they decided to wear their jeans and new tee shirts out. Shoes were next with Lisa two pairs of boots and her mother one. Lisa always knew her mother loved clothes, but hadn't realized that it was such a deep passionate love. They ended up with two pairs of sandals for Lisa and some exotic red high heels for her mother because they were irresistible. Lisa said she would try some heels and ended up with the brown version of the irresistible red heels. Shopping was done, but only because they were both exhausted and hungry.

While her mother was paying for the latest purchases Lisa called Ginny. "Mom wants to know if you and the Dean can meet us at Pizza Pizza at seven?" She waited a few minutes until she got a response. "We will see you there."

Lisa knew she would get a reaction of her transformation from both her dad and Ginny; she hadn't expected such a reaction about her mother's new look. Her father said he loved Lisa's look even though it made her look seventeen. He seemed to be staring at his wife. Lisa took a second look in her quest for being more observant. Her mother did look younger. Her hair and makeup were the same as always. It was the softer more casual look with the skinny jeans, something Lisa knew she would never have bought if Lisa hadn't insisted. She realized her mother never wore tee shirts. This one, again purchased in the excitement of shopping with her fourteen-year-old daughter, fit well and showed enough cleavage without looking overtly sexy. Careful observation was that her mother did look sexy tonight. Lisa smiled to herself with the strange idea that her father might think of her mother as sexy.

After dinner he asked Ginny to take Lisa home and he would drive his wife. He even forgot to pay and Ginny had to pay the bill. Her parents didn't get home until after one, something about stopping for a drink.

Since her high school merged three schools into one, Lisa had been hoping there would be a lot of kids who didn't know she was a freak. After a few days Lisa decided clothes do make the woman, well at least the teenage girl. The first week of school she quickly felt the difference in how her former classmates treated her. She was sure many of them didn't even know who she was with a change from a frumpy girl with hair tied back with a rubber band, to the one in a short skirt, long boots, and a fitted sweater, not the baggy size large she usually wore.

Lisa didn't have a sleep incident until the second week of school. She was reading in the library and felt herself doing what Doctor Jamison called falling asleep and what she called going into the story. She had time to push the button on her timer before her head dropped into her book.

Lisa came to with a start and found a girl from her Biology class sitting by her.

"Hey— are you okay? Should I get help?"

It happened again. At least this time she was aware and was back in a couple of minutes instead of hours.

"No thanks Jane, I'm okay." Lisa didn't know what else to do so gave Jane the explanation that gave her the label of freak since the second grade. "I have this sleep disorder and sort of pass out sometimes when I am reading. If I don't come to there is a number here to call." She showed her the bracelet with the epilepsy symbol and her doctor's phone number. "I don't have epilepsy, but since there is no diagnosis except as a 'sleep disorder' this gets to my doctor before someone panics and calls nine-one-one."

Jane looked at her with what Lisa thought she would call kindness. "What does it feel like? Do you have any pain?"

"No, I am in what the doctor's call a deep dream sleep cycle." She showed her the special watch and pressed the beep button that gave off a low series of beeps. "I sometimes feel it coming on and press this timer, which after thirty-seconds will beep and I wake. Otherwise, it will be an hour or more before I can be roused by any means."

"How does that work?"

"I am hypnotized to wake on the beep. My doctor has to do this every few weeks."

"Wow, how does it feel to be hypnotized?"

"No feeling."

"Are you frightened?"

"No, I guess not."

"How long have you had this sleep thing?"

"Since I was a baby I guess."

They talked until the class bell rang and they headed to Biology together.

She was surprised she told Jane so much about her freakiness, but it wasn't too difficult since she seemed to really care. Lisa thought maybe she now had a friend, someone who cared about her besides Jamison, and of course her family.

———

Doctor Jamison was looking forward to seeing Lisa. The plan was to meet in two-week intervals. Lisa sent a selfie to him two weeks ago, then earlier this week a message, "At school had adventure - woke self - all is well." He mumbled to himself as he scrolled through his text messages to the selfie Lisa sent him; a picture of a beautiful teenage girl who did not look fourteen. He was amazed at the transformation of the adolescent he began working with two years ago, even from two weeks ago.

He thought to himself, "Lisa, Lisa what now girl?" He thought perhaps making such a change could be a turning point from her need for the experiences she considered adventures into books; thereby speed up her ability to recognize the dreams and put an end to them and the sleep episodes. He turned from his musing as Lisa walked into his office. She indeed looked like the picture she sent. Her hair was now short with soft curls and highlights making it nearly blond. He noticed she was wearing makeup, very subtle. She was wearing boots, a short skirt and jacket. She was in fact a vision of loveliness. He gave her a large smile of approbation. "The new you is quite lovely Lisa."

He did notice she had the same old green shabby back-pack, which she dropped by the door. She walked to the red chair and he was amused to see her realize she couldn't snuggle in the large chair with her booted feet tucked under her. She sat, then pulled up the nearby ottoman feet while Jamison wheeled his desk chair toward her.

"How do you think you will like your new school?"

She started in at once with excitement, "Oh Jamison. Did you realize that the clothes make the woman, or in my case the high school freshman?" Lisa's face glowed as she told him of her experiences shopping with her mother and the fun they both had with all the clothes she bought and the matching jeans.

"Kids I have been in school with for eight years didn't know me. I almost felt like I was in disguise. James Keen even argued with one of my teachers that I was not Lisa Longford. I hoped having three schools put together would made it easier because so many wouldn't know I am a freak. They didn't know me and smiled at me in the halls. I think some boys even flirted with me like I have seen boys do with pretty girls."

They talked a little about her family and her idea that she thought Ginny had a budding romance going. She seemed pleased with herself and smiled when she told him about her experience with Jane. "I was reading in the library; it is a lovely library for a school. We get one period a day to use as we like, in the library, at home room, or computer lab. I was in the library reading for my American History class. I set my timer because I felt the book was calling me."

"I saw a girl sitting beside me when I was back again. I don't think I even had time to go into the story. The girl is Jane; she is in my biology class. She was very kind asked if I was all right. I think I was surprised because she seemed to honestly care. I told her about my sleep disorder and that I could sometimes prevent it by setting this signal to wake me with post hypnotic suggestions. Jane asked how it worked and whether I had any discomfort. No one has shown such sweet concern for me Jamison, except you Jamison, even though you always disagree with me. I think she may become a friend. That would mean three for me; Ginny, you and now Jane. She invited me to have lunch with her group, that's what she calls her friends. I had lunch with them on Wednesday and today." She ended with one of her lovely smiles.

Jamison returned the smile.

Since Lisa was an easy subject for hypnosis, they finished the hypnotherapy session in twenty minutes. Then he got out his recorder for the two experiences or dreams she had since they last met. Lisa retrieved a few notes from her backpack and they recorded them. Over the last two years recording any experiences had helped Lisa become more observant and provide more details. They also recorded any regular night dreams, the kind Lisa admitted were dreams, to see if there might be any relationships. Lisa left with an appointment to be back in three weeks.

Jamison sat at his desk and made notes in Lisa's file. He noted that Lisa had changed her appearance to conform with her high school peers, and that she may be making friends.

He indicated she was able to wake herself in two of four sleep incidents. Again, she was reporting fewer sleep incidents from prior years. He decided he had enough support documentation to write an article about Lisa's case showing the success with the hypnotherapy. He also decided they could move the therapy sessions further apart by another week, to monthly, since in the latest incident Lisa had been able to wake herself and it had been three weeks since their last session.

He locked the office and took the recorder into his study. He made himself a cappuccino, pulled out Lisa's file and sat in one of the two large red leather chairs. He did most of his work in his study, the office was for seeing the occasional patient and consulting meetings. Lately he had become more noted for his research on how the human brain recognizes and processes reality. He sighed to himself. Why should the truth be such a difficult concept?

He copied the tape and his handwritten notes and packaged them to go to his uncle Glen in Ireland. His uncle had not come up with any theories relating to the dreams, either her episode dreams or normal night dreams.

———

Lisa hurried down to the kitchen for breakfast. Ginny had her bowl of oatmeal and a cup of coffee ready.

"Look'n good Lisa; only I think your mother created a clothes monster in you. Have you had to wear the same thing to school more than once in the last three weeks?"

"It is already October and I needed warmer clothes." She ran her fingers over the sleeves of her red cashmere sweater and grinned, "I'm not a monster Ginny." She gave Ginny a peck on the cheek. "Besides you have often suggested I needed more variety in my clothes."

Ginny shrugged and sat at the table by Lisa. "You have ten minutes dear."

Lisa finished the oatmeal and poured her coffee into a travel mug. "Ready."

Ginny drove her to school, as Lisa got out, she reminded her she had a hair appointment at Mister Blake's after school, and that her parents had an evening function at the University and would be home late.

Grace and Sara, two of Jane's friends, caught up with her on the steps to the main school building. Grace had straight black hair slightly longer than Lisa's. She had beautiful large dark eyes, evidence of Chinese heritage. Sarah was petite with long blond hair. She intrigued Lisa who thought she had a look of a young princess in need of rescuing. The two girls greeted Lisa like old friends and immediately entered into conversation about one class they shared; then asked if she had watched the last evening's episode from one of the popular television shows. Lisa hadn't.

As each parted for their classes, Sara reminded Lisa that their group was going to sit at the other end of the cafeteria for lunch. Lisa headed for her math class. She liked Grace and Sara. She was beginning to think of them also as her friends. She reflected on the idea of our group. Eight years of school and she never had friends, let alone a group. Now in three weeks she was part of a group of friends; it seemed most of them considered her one of them. They were nice, maybe lots of kids were nice, only those who called her freak made her think everyone thought that of her. She realized she had missed a lot of socialization others get before they reach high school, being a freak and all. She had much to learn and quietly listened to the conversation of this new group, as well as to those of other classmates.

Lisa had just gone through the lunch line for a salad and apple when she saw Josh Eviers standing at the end of the cafeteria waving at her. She smiled and waved back and headed in that direction. She thought it seemed almost as if he had been looking for her and done all the arm waving when he knew she had seen him. Josh was good looking, dark hair, average size, and on first string for football. She was told first string was great for a sophomore. As she approached, he pulled out a chair for her next to his. The tables seated ten, but there were twelve today as part of the group; sometimes there were more or less.

She still found it difficult to contribute to most conversations because she simply didn't know what they were talking about. She generally could converse easily with her parents' friends on most subjects. She even knew a little about sports, thanks to Ginny. Ginny loved sports and shared some of her enthusiasm with Lisa. Her lack of topics as well as her sleep disorder was part of why six and seven-year-olds had put the label freak on her. They talked about toys and television characters and movies. When she didn't know the names of these characters or anything about them, they had added stupid to the freak label.

It seemed high schoolers talked about music, actors, movies, television shows; and added to that gossip. Lisa's family were book people. Ginny had a television in her room, but her parents got their news from journals and newspapers, not television. When she was ten, she asked her parents why they didn't have or watch television. They said there wasn't much there she couldn't get from books. She watched a couple of age appropriate programs with Ginny and decided her parents were right. Television was boring. By then at age ten, Lisa had read more books than many adults did in a lifetime. Family vacations were often planned around a city visiting special bookshops and museums. Books had been Lisa's life since she learned to read. She and Ginny made weekly trips to several local bookstores, from all of which Lisa had unlimited credit and no censorship. Books called to her and she responded.

In the middle of lunch Lisa noticed Jane give Josh a strange look and finally said, "Josh."

He turned to Lisa, "Would you like to go to a party with me, ahem, with us, with our group?"

Lisa suddenly felt nervous. Was this great looking football player asking the freak for a date?

Josh seemed to notice her somewhat puzzled look and continued with an obviously a nervous tone, "The group, well some of us in the group, are going to our Youth Night Out on Friday at our church. We have pizza and play games. It is always fun. Jane and Grace and Sarah and David and all of us usually go. Would you like to come?"

She still wasn't sure if this was a date, but it sounded like it or Jane might have given the invitation. "I will need to ask."

In biology class Jane confided to Lisa, "Sorry for the poorly put invitation Lisa. I overheard Josh. Several of us wanted to invite you for Friday." She smiled at her. "I think Josh has a crush on you. He insisted he be the one to ask you. Lunch was nearly over and he hadn't asked so I was about to when he did the invitation. I do hope you can come with us."

Lisa decided to be blunt. "Was he asking for a date?"

Jane looked thoughtful. "When we all talked about asking you, he didn't talk like that. Sorry Lisa, I'm not sure what is in Josh's head."

"I don't think I can go. Ginny reminded me on the first day of school, no dating until I was fifteen. I don't even know why she brought it up."

"Lisa, I honestly don't think you realize what impression you make. Josh and the other guys in our group openly say you are the hottest freshman on campus. And I know it is not just their opinion. Do you call your mom Ginny?"

"No, Ginny is or was my nanny; she is my father's relative. She lives with us and takes care of our family." She had never needed to explain Ginny before and hadn't even thought about her friend's families, whether they had nannies or housekeepers or whatever it was that Ginny was to her family.

As usual Lisa told Ginny most of what happened and thrilled using the word my group. Ginny said she needed to meet some of the group before she had permission to go. Two days later when Ginny picked Lisa up from school she also drove Jane, Grace, and Sarah to Lisa's house for cookies and cocoa. After driving the girls home, she gave Lisa her approval for the Friday event, explaining she also needed parental approval. Lisa knew if Ginny approved so would her parents.

———

Lisa worried about what to wear on Friday. She had only been to a church twice in her life, both for weddings. The idea of pizza and games seemed to call for something informal. Friday at school Jane told her to wear school clothes, because that was what she was wearing. Even so she tried on four different outfits before selecting something a little nicer than school clothes; grey slacks and a turquoise sweater. She had no time to change her mind a fifth time since she heard the doorbell ring.

She wanted to get there before anyone else, but was too late. Her dad and mom and Ginny were all ushering Jane and Josh in. Lisa's father looked out the door, then motioned for the others in the car to come in. Lisa groaned in embarrassment. She didn't know for sure, but this didn't seem like teen etiquette. It was parent etiquette. Josh's father, the driver, herded the other passengers, Rachel and David, into the house. Everyone was introduced to everyone else. Josh's father, Marcus Eviers, knew her father from Kiwanis, so they chatted a few minutes. To make things worse, her mother suggested they all have coffee before leaving. Josh's dad, more savvy about teenage culture saved the day by suggesting they needed to leave, and also for turning down the invitation for coffee after the party.

They ended up with four in the backseat, trying to scrunch together to pull the seat belts over all of them. That didn't work. Now suddenly she was pressed close to Josh with his arm around her. She had never been that close to a boy. Jane and David were even more compressed and ended up with Jane on his lap, sharing their seatbelt. Even with the more space, Josh was still close to Lisa and kept his arm around her. Although the backseat rearrangement only took a few minutes, Lisa's emotions swung from embarrassment to fear to pleasure to fear. She settled on pleasure. She still didn't know much about teenagers, her knowledge of the world was from books, mostly with adults as lovers with motives and plots and dark secrets. She had a dark secret.

Once the four in the backseat said they were all belted in, Mr. Eviers departed. Lisa hoped her parents hadn't seen the seating arrangement, especially since this wasn't a date. David began the conversation with politeness, "Your parents sure are nice and friendly."

Lisa wasn't sure if this was a compliment or not.

David then asked, "Who is Ginny?"

"She lives with us. She used to be my nanny, since my parents both work. Now she cooks and does shopping and I guess lots of things."

Rachel leaned back over the front seat. "And drives you to school and everywhere else."

David didn't stop there, "Yeah, Jane was right you do live in a mansion. Pretty nice."

Again, Lisa lacked reference as to how most people lived. Many of her family's friends lived in homes similar to theirs. But she knew what a mansion really was. She had been in many, all with servant quarters and ball rooms and dining rooms large enough to seat at least fifty or more. She couldn't tell them that.

Mr. Eviers seemed to be a wise man and managed to turn the conversation away from Lisa's lifestyle. The ride was only twenty minutes and it took that long for Lisa to finally relax and feel comfortable in Josh's embrace and hope her face was no longer flushed.

When they got to the church, she was relieved that they were in a basement, not a sanctuary with stained glass windows and statues. The room was decorated with streamers and tables stacked with a variety of board games as well as some group games.

Lisa won many of the trivia game questions that didn't involve popular music, movies or sports. Most of all, Josh was attentive to her, but not in the clingy way she saw with couples at high school. She decided they were all very kind to someone who didn't really speak their language. Like all other classmates they talked about music and television and movies she knew nothing about. She did overhear a girl she didn't know ask Jane if Lisa had been home schooled. Jane whispered back, no, but that Lisa's family was a little strict, like the Brown's. Lisa didn't know what that meant; she guessed the Brown family didn't allow their children to watch television or movies. She decided that night that it was all right to be a freak in that way. She still liked who she was and was not going to begin watching television programs just to have something to talk about. She did wish some of them read books. She knew books.

She was home at ten thirty, half an hour after the curfew she had been given. Her parents were reading in the library. They had no comments on the time being after curfew. They asked about the party and she gave them a five-minuterun down. Now if her group would still include her after tonight of winning so many of the trivia games and nicknaming her IQ, and in spite of her living in what David said was a mansion. After all they didn't know she really was a freak. All some of them knew was that she had a sleep disorder. Mostly she wondered if Josh would still be interested in her.

———

Doctor Jamison sat at his desk completing a report for Lisa's medical team. When he began treating Lisa she was often experiencing four to six sleep incidents a week. In the last three months, Lisa reported only six sleep incidents; only one occurred at school and that was one in which she woke herself. She also woke herself in two of the five incidents that occurred at home. He thought the team would be more pleased than warranted. He equated some of this success to the fact that her list of books she read was half what it had been over last two years. Decreasing her sessions did not seem to have an effect on her ability to wake herself. He completed the report and sent it to the medical team. Perhaps the fewer incidents really was an improvement.

Jamison looked up as Lisa came in with a cup of coffee, and as usual tossed her backpack on the floor.

"Good afternoon Jamison," Lisa gave him her usual bright smile.

"Lisa."

"Love that new drive through, good coffee. As you know I have no adventures to relate." She handed him her reading list for the last three weeks. She went to the red chair, sat her coffee on a nearby table, and pulled off her boots so she could curl up in the chair with her feet under her.

Lisa had few restraints in sharing the details of her life. Sometimes Jamison would remind her he didn't need to know that level of detail. Her response was that since he was her friend, he did need to know. He reminded her he was her doctor. She would laugh and agree he was her doctor-friend, with an emphasis on the word friend, and go on.

"Jamison, I went to Sunday church with my friends last week. Before it was only youth nights. The church is already decorated for Christmas, so very lovely. Ginny drove me, but Josh was waiting for us and sat with us. I think I now have a boyfriend. What do you think of that Jamison?"

Jamison tried to maintain his concerned doctor face. He remembered one day when Lisa once told him she was tired of the 'concerned doctor face,' and that he needed to smile more.

Lisa gave a slight frown. "I think maybe he is my boy-friend. He came over to do homework together, and formally met Mom and the Dean, although they did meet him a few weeks ago on our date. The one I told you wasn't supposed to really be a date. Anyway Jamison, Mom invited him for dinner. I am sure my parents think he is my boyfriend. Ginny says so." She suddenly changed the conversation. "Jamison, do you go to church?"

He was surprised and took a moment to respond. "I used to."

"I think I like it; but I don't understand the language or music. They used words and talked about things I know noth-ing about. Of course, Ginny read the Christmas story when I was a little girl so I know about baby Jesus. When I asked Josh what Jesus was about, he said I should talk to the pastor."

"Priest?"

"They call him pastor. Then there is the youth pastor who is just called Lars. He is funny, I like him. The pastor per-son, I think his name is Reverend Conway, is the Sunday one. Is priest another word for pastor?"

"In some churches I believe it may be."

She shared more about her friends and some of her classes and plans over the school holiday. Lisa seemed to be the happi-est person Jamison thought he had ever known, even when at age twelve when she declared herself a freak. She was charm-ing and intelligent. He understood why her parents had no clue about her lack of friends the first eight years of school, since she conversed intelligently with her parents' friends from the

University. That afternoon they talked books; a subject Lisa could easily lead him into since his list was equally as long as hers, though his was heavier on the non-fiction side.

The hypnotherapy session took the usual twenty minutes. Before she left, he reminded her they would not meet until the second week of January since he would be in Ireland the next six weeks. As usual she complained about him being away so long. She said his leaving her that long wasn't a good plan, and she would probably have all kinds of adventures when he was away. She also always apologized immediately after such outbursts.

When the session was over Lisa pulled on her boots. She came close and gave him a hug and kiss on the cheek, "Merry Christmas Jamison—- until next year," and walked out of the office.

Jamison thought sometimesit was a little difficult to maintain the doctor patient role with the girl. He remembered back when she told him, "Jamison I decided you are not my knight in shining armor." He felt relieved until she added, "We are soulmates." Before he could stop her she added, "I looked it up. A soulmate is a person with whom one has a feeling of deep or natural affinity and may involve similarity, love, romance, intimacy and trust. Now, now Jamison I know about words and we don't have romance." She giggled, "That is saved for Josh. Love has many meanings from opinions about pizza to feelings of a couple when they say, 'I do.' Surely you feel we have a spark of some kind, and some of those other words like similarity, natural affinity and intimacy and trust. We are soulmates Jamison."

He again gave her his lecture, which he had used a number of times, about their professional relationship and how easy it was for a patient to become infatuated with her psychiatrist. As usual Lisa simply grinned at him with sparkling eyes. Then she added, "I know about words. Infatuation is 'an intense but short-lived passion or admiration for someone.' We have more, you will see Jamison."

Jamison shook his head, but smiled as she left the office. He took the list of books she read in the last three weeks into his study. At the bottom of the page she included the definition of soulmate, underlining the words similarity, natural affinity and intimacy and trust. He completed his notes and added one, that he thought Lisa's possible infatuation would be short-lived due to her growing list of friendships and even admiration for this Josh.

Chapter 5

"I believe in everything until it's disproved. So I believe in fairies, the myths, dragons. It all exists, even if it's in your mind. Who's to say that dreams and nightmares aren't as real as the here and now?" [JOHN LENNON]

LISA FINISHED DRESSING after twice changing her mind of what to wear. Josh was coming to study with her for their final for their English literature class. She thought about their relationship and realized they really had not been alone even though they sat close and held hands at church, never at school. Grace said they needed to kiss before she could really consider him her boyfriend. She wasn't sure exactly what that meant. She thought of the kiss she had given Jamison that afternoon and guessed it was a friendship kiss; because a kiss on the cheek was not really a kiss. She often exchanged those kinds with her family. She finally settled on a bright blue silk shirt that looked casual enough to go with jeans.

She heard the doorbell and raced downstairs to let Josh in before Ginny got there. Ginny beat her. Before Lisa opened the door, Ginny reminded Lisa of the house rules with boys. "Be in the library or the kitchen. Coffee is on and I made cookies. Gotta go before the game starts," and she was off.

"Hi Lisa."

"Come in. Sorry for the delay, got the boys in the house lecture."

"Lot of boys?" He asked with a grin and wink.

"Na, it's just Ginny's way."

Lisa took Josh's coat and led him to the library. She had been to Jane's house in a newer part of town. It had a formal type living room like theirs, but also another similar room furnished with sofas and large chairs she called the family room. Jane said the family used it mostly except for formal occasions. Lisa thought their library served that purpose in her house. Besides three walls of books and two desks, the library had two small sofas with a low table between and two large recliners. A fireplace was at one end with two tall windows on each side. Her family, when together, were often here or the kitchen.

Josh looked around and muttered, "Nice."

Lisa picked up her book from the table and sat on one of the small sofas.

Josh dropped his backpack on the floor and sat by her. "Are we really going to study?"

"Josh!"

He scowled and pulled his book out of his bag. "Dad will pick me up at nine. I can't wait to get my license so I can drive. Three weeks and I am sixteen." He added grinning, "I drove tonight."

Josh sat close to Lisa as they went over the study questions. Lisa was glad she qualified for an advanced literature class even though she was only a freshman, because it provided one more reason to see Josh, and now he wanted to study with her. They finished and Lisa suggested they go to the kitchen for the cookies and coffee Ginny had ready. Josh stood before Lisa, reached for her hand, and pulled her up into his arms. She felt confused and didn't know what to do. She liked the feel of his strong arms around her, but didn't know what the boyfriend protocol included.

He kissed her gently on the lips then pulled her away from him. "I'm sorry Lisa." He stuttered, "I didn't mean to, well I did. I should have asked you first." He stared at the floor then looked up at her with a sheepish grin. "I'm ready for one of Ginny's cookies."

Somehow his embarrassment endeared him to her. She gave him one of her winning smiles. The kind she didn't know was part of her reputation of being hot.

At school the next morning Lisa waited for Grace and Jane who generally sat with her in the library for their free study period.

Grace plopped her books on the table. "Heard you and Josh were together last night."

Lisa felt her face getting warm. "We studied English. Where did you hear that anyway?"

"Josh, I got the impression he was bragging."

"What?"

Jane added, "So, are you a couple now? You have to tell your best friends. Do you like him?"

"I don't know. Of course, I like him. No, we are not a couple. I don't even know what that means. And why would Josh be telling you that?"

"It is okay Lisa, he only told me and Jane because he knows we three are best friends."

The girls got a few shushes from the librarian, so went to whispers as they spread out their work on the table. Grace went on, "Best friends tell."

"Tell what?"

"Did Josh kiss you?"

Before Lisa could answer, the librarian came to their table and shushed them again. Lisa opened a book and stared at it. Her blush must have answered Grace's question because she saw both Grace and Jane give each other knowing smiles.

Lisa stared at her book without reading. She never had girlfriends before and didn't know what kinds of things best friends shared. She did know she would be sharing the details about Josh's kiss with Jamison. Lisa decided to tell them 'yes he kissed me.' Secrets, Lisa thought, maybe secrets bring people together and telling was part of being best friends.

She looked across the table at Grace and when she caught her eye she mouthed the word, yes. Grace grinned back at her. Lisa mused, now she and Grace and Jane had added a secret to bind their friendship, maybe.

She stared out the window wondering. If secrets create bonds between people, then she and Jamison had a strong bond. She contemplated the idea that she and Jamison were friends. Then she pulled out the word soulmates and knew that was the real word, not friends.

She noticed Grace staring at her and thought maybe she was thinking Lisa's smile had been about Josh; she couldn't know it had been for Jamison, not Josh. She wondered if she would need to tell Josh her secret for him to love her. She didn't know if that was what she wanted from him. Right now having friends was so new to her, and especially having this good looking guy like her made her feel; made her feel less like a freak. She was not ready for a word as heavy as love. She remembered a casual philosophical conversation she and Jamison had once over a cup of coffee, not as doctor patient, but as friends. He said one had to be careful of the spoken word. Once it became sound it became hard like a rock; then you had to do something with it. Love was such a word if used to define a relationship.

The Christmas holidays were usually hectic at the Longford house. They generally hosted one formal dinner and one formal cocktail party to cover those not invited to the dinner; and a couple of informal gatherings, all for the benefit of the University. The Dean was expected to entertain the professors in his department, his colleagues, and occasionally students.

The University expected both formal and informal entertaining from the deans, that's why they got a substantial housing allowance, so their homes would be open to the University.

Richard Longford inherited the large formal home from his great uncle, who had served as president of the University for nearly twenty-years. The dining room seated twenty, but on occasion could seat more for a formal dinner. He also inherited a trust to maintain the Longford home in addition to a sizable income trust for his lifetime. Uncle Longford had also provided a sizable trust for Lisa who was just two years old when he passed.

Although the Dean and Florence spent many hours in the planning the entertainment; it was Ginny who put the plans into results managing all the arrangements with caterers and florist. The Longfords included Ginny and Lisa on the guest list for every event in their home, including the cocktail party. Consequently, they were also frequently included on guest lists of the other University deans and professors. As long as she could remember, Lisa enjoyed mingling and talking with the University people and her parents' friends. Until this year these were her only real social contacts.

This was the first time Lisa didn't mind clothes shopping for the Christmas events with her mom. Early in November they took an entire day shopping for holiday dresses. Florence adored everything Lisa tried on and declared her beautiful daughter needed them all, and would have bought Lisa everything she tried on. Lisa ended up with only three. Lisa exerted her new role as shopping partner with her mom and nixed several of her mother's selections for herself. Lisa selected dresses her mother said were not appropriate for a professor in her position. However, she happily succumbed to Lisa's taste. When they finally left the last shop, she told Lisa she didn't know what the Dean would say about some of her choices. Lisa thought she knew.

Lisa was allowed a party of her own for her friends. She now even had new friends not part of the group. She and Ginny went over the food selections for the caterer for Lisa's party. She was nervous with her first party. "Oh Ginny, do you think many will come?"

"Social events are obligations at the University so your parents seldom get declines. You invited twenty. Honey, I don't know what teenage etiquette is for accepting invitations. We need to order food enough expecting that all will accept."

Lisa sat thinking and added, "Ginny, the boys eat a lot. When we have pizza or sandwiches at Youth they all eat twice, no five times as much as I do. Should we order more food?"

"Maybe we could add another fruit tray?" Ginny looked back at the caterer's menu on the computer screen. "I have an idea Lisa. I will call them and let them know who our guests are and let them make suggestions as to what and how much teenagers eat." She looked back at Lisa, "And you and I can make cookies and other treats to supplement whatever the caterer doesn't do."

"Oh Ginny, that would be fun. I would like Josh to know what a great cook I am."

Ginny raised her eyebrows with a questioning look; then they both laughed at Lisa's comment.

Lisa's party was a success, in that all who were invited came to her house. Her parents greeted her guests, then disappeared. Later Jane whispered to Lisa, "You and Ginny must have taken days to put all this food together."

Lisa looked confused. "We only baked the cookies; it didn't take all that long." She looked around the room at her group and the other classmates she had invited. All seemed to be enjoying the food and each other.

"Your mom didn't do it, did she?"

Then Lisa understood. "No, the caterer did all the food, except the cookies." She and the group had been invited to a dinner at Jane's house where Lisa thought the table and food were wonderful and assumed it was catered also. "Jane, the wonderful dinner at your house last week. Didn't you have a catering service?"

Jane gave Lisa a hug. "You are a such a dear." She walked off with David who said he needed her.

Lisa and Ginny sat in the kitchen after clearing up the party remains in the living room after everyone thanked her for the party and wished her a Merry Christmas. Ginny had stayed around and moved platters of food from the kitchen to the living room during the party so Lisa could mingle with her guests.

"Ginny, I think it went well. Thank you for all your help."

"Josh was attentive, a good trait in a boyfriend." She grinned at Lisa, "And you seem better at talking to kids."

"No, it is just that we were playing some games and stuff. I still don't know what they are talking about with music and movies."

"You are learning dear. Keep trying. It is working for me. I am reading garden magazines so I can talk to Walt about something besides soccer and football."

———

That spring, when her family didn't have plans on a weekend, Lisa began going to church on Sundays with her group. Josh's father picked her up several times, then Ginny agreed to drive since it was out of the way for him. After a few weeks Ginny began staying for the service and told Lisa she liked her church better than hers. Lisa was surprised since she didn't know Ginny had a church. She asked Ginny about it. Ginny, who seldom mentioned her late husband told her, yes they had attended a church regularly before he died. When Lisa asked why she didn't go any longer, she was evasive—almost in tears and muttered something about, 'he doesn't care,' then would say no more. Lisa knew then was not a time to talk about whatever changed Ginny about church.

Lisa didn't understand the music for the youth nights she attended, or for the Sunday services. She was attending church to be with her friends. But lately she began paying attention to these new ideas as she read the words of the Apostles' Creed along with the congregation on Sundays. Ginny's vague explanation helped her see where Christmas and Easter fit in for Christians. She wanted to know more. When she asked Josh to explain it to her, he said she should talk to Charlie, meaning the Reverend Clarence Conway. She decided to do that.

Lisa was delighted when she left Charlie's office; she had a new label, a Christian. For some reason having this new identity felt exciting. Ginny picked her up on time, and when she climbed into the car she immediately told her, "I am now a Christian!"

She looked at Lisa strangely. "Of course you are Lisa, what else would you be?"

"No Ginny, what I mean is now I understand about Christmas. I understand that God became human; and I know about Easter, that Jesus died for the world." She silently thought about it and softly added, "For me."

Ginny didn't say anything on the drive home. Lisa was so intrigued with the thought of what she now knew about Jesus she didn't pay attention to Ginny's silence. When they got home, she was excited to share what she had just learned with her mom and dad. They were each in their respective studies, so she waited for dinner time when they generally talked about things. Ginny made a wonderful chicken casserole and salad and fruit and fresh baked bread, and a pie. Lisa helped her finish with the table setting then called her parents for dinner.

"Lisa, I heard you singing in the kitchen; did you have a good day?" Her mother asked as she placed a kiss on her forehead.

Lisa hadn't realized she was singing.

Her dad just grinned at her as he opened a bottle of wine and poured some for her mother, Ginny and himself. As usual Lisa asked, "Where's mine?"

As usual he gave her a big smile and shook his head.

Most kids at school talked about drinking, she wasn't sure if it was talk or if they really did drink as much as some said they did. She was almost fifteen and sometimes wondered what the magic age of twenty-one had to do with it?

Her dad gave her the opening to share her news when he repeated her mom's comment. "You look happy today sweetie," as he sat down. "Something exciting happen?"

She looked over at Ginny who looked disturbed as she dished up casserole on her plate and passed it on. Lisa only took a small portion. She was into salads right now as she didn't want to look like so many overweight high school girls. Also she knew there was a pie in the kitchen and wanted to save the room for the good stuff. She began with "Yes, I had a great meeting with Charlie."

Her mom gave her a questioned look.

"Charlie is the pastor of my church."

Her dad turned toward her, "Your church?"

Lisa ignored them and went on, "I asked him to explain about Easter. He told me the story from the Bible about Christmas and Jesus being God's son and how he taught and healed people and how he died cruelly on the cross, and then rose from the dead, and will come again." She caught her breath then added, "Now I am a Christian."

They both stared at her like she had grown two heads. She watched them blink back the looks she got as a child when she had done something embarrassing. She didn't know what she expected from them; but some acknowledgment since she felt good inside at having the label as Christian.

Ginny said, "We are all Christians Lisa."

Then her parents looked at her like she had two heads.

"Oh," Lisa tried to think of how to explain. All she could come up with was, "Now I understand what it means to be a Christian." She felt it was hopeless, and turned and smiled at them all.

The rest of the dinner conversation was about the weather and their plans for Spring Break. Lisa helped Ginny clean off the table. The talkative Ginny was unusually quiet.

Lisa headed for her room and homework. She wanted to know more about being a Christian. Charlie suggested she begin by reading the Gospels. She decided to start that night. Although they had a very large library, she could not find a Bible on any of the shelves. Her dad loved old books and had a large collection of rare books in his newly remodeled study in the basement—- some in special environmental glass cases.

Lisa was determined to find a Bible. After her futile search in the library, she knocked on her parents bedroom door. "Mom, Dad, do we have a Bible anywhere?"

Her father came to the door. "What do you want with a Bible?"

"I wanted to see one."

"I have two copies Lisa; one dated 1735 and an older one

1687. They are in older English and very fragile. We can look at them on Saturday if you wish to see them dear."

Then he began to explain their history and how he had come by them until Lisa kissed him on the cheek and said, "Good night. Certainly I would love to look at them on Saturday."

He gave her a hug and closed the bedroom door.

The next day after school Lisa asked Ginny to take her to the bookstore to buy a Bible. She found out that there were many translations, so bought five different ones. She was excited when she got home and planned on starting in at the beginning. Then she remembered Charlie said the Bible was really many books all put together, so it didn't matter where she started, but if she wanted to know more about Jesus she should start with the Gospel of John before reading the other three Gospels.

Jamison was lecturing out of town for a week. She sent him a text. "No adventures. Guess what, I am now a Christian."

Chapter 6

"We have forgotten the age-old fact that God speaks chiefly through dreams and visions." [C. G. JUNG]

SUMMER WAS NEARLY over. Jamison had been in Ireland the last six weeks with his usual summer visit with his uncles. He was expecting Lisa, as he had copies of the two professional publications featuring their articles about the success of his hypnotherapy with a patient's sleep disorder— their success. He had not included particulars of the disorder, but described the process and documented the success, as the occurrence of patient's events decreased over the three years of treatment with the ability to control the events. In writing the articles he allowed Lisa to add her input and review the articles before he submitted them. She wanted to include her name. He insisted case studies required anonymity.

He was already receiving speaking invitations related to his research and treatment methods. Over the last three years he declined many such invitations. He admitted to himself he thought he needed to be available for Lisa. Now she would no longer need him. He knew that was good, and still ... Perhaps she was right when she told him they had some kind of bond. He would not admit to anything as abstract as the idea of soulmates.

He reviewed his notes. Lisa only reported four sleep incidents over the last six weeks. For two she had control and was able to wake herself within minutes. He thought he had helped her in other ways besides the ability to have control over her sleep disorder. He knew part of having control over one's life involved being observant. Lisa had learned to become aware of what was going on around her, of listening to what other people said, actually said. She was learning to be aware of her own actions. Although he considered this growing up; he thought it was something some people never did at any age.

She once told him she felt like a foreign exchange student struggling with the language and culture in high school. Prior to high school she didn't care if her classmates thought she was stupid and a freak. Now she cared. Jamison had confidence that Lisa would not change for the sake of fitting in. Only a few months ago she told him she realized she had seen herself as smarter than other kids because of the way she was treated around the University people, as the Dean's precocious daughter. Jamison was proud of her when she told him, "I wasn't smarter, just read different things; and in a few years they will all be reading the same books I do, well some of them will. Then I will be normal, the same as them. But I can't go backwards, and I don't want to. My family are book people."

He was startled when the door opened. He closed the file just as Lisa came in the office, and gave him a hug, "It has been a long time Jamison." She went to the large red chair, kicked off her sandals, and cuddled into the soft leather.

He handed her the two publications.

"Thank you. For me to keep?"

He nodded.

"I have copies, but I know the Dean will like to have these. I didn't have time to share mine yet."

He smiled as he went to his desk and pulled out his chair and wheeled it toward Lisa. She looked like a different girl compared to a year ago. In his articles he did mention maturity as part of the reason for success of Lisa's treatment; he did not mention the significant change in her appearance from a unkempt adolescent to a very lovely teenage girl. Today he thought she looked more like a woman than a fifteen-year-old girl. She had a rich summer tan that contrasted with the blond highlights in her hair. Although he prided himself in his ability to be observant, he could never come up with words to describe women's clothing, other than the impression they made on him. He knew the names of some garments, like skirts, and suits, and dresses, and shirts (they call blouses), and slacks, and denim ones called jeans. He also knew the names of many colors; but any woman would tell him he had the wrong one if he intimated he knew the shade she was wearing. All he could think was that Lisa was wearing a dress with a bright floral print that said summer.

They talked about his time in Ireland with his uncles. As usual, Lisa was interested in the village and what she called the castle his uncles lived in. She often told him she wanted to visit the uncles in Ireland. This time she even inquired about Colleen; was she still in the village? Then Lisa gave him the details of her weeks, although as usual she had kept him updated with text messages. This summer, fewer than other times he had been out of the country.

"Friends do keep one busy. Jamison, this is the first summer not dedicated to our family road trip and my reading. Of course, we did take the road trip. Jane, Grace, Sarah and I are now great friends. We met several times a week; since Sarah's family has a pool, we were generally at her house." She paused as though to catch her breath and continued, "The Dean is back from Italy, but Mom will be there six more weeks working on her degree. Ginny doesn't fuss at what I do so much now, my going out with friends and all. I think because she trusts me, and then there is Walt. I think I told you she took a vacation away from the family in July to meet Walt's family in Oregon." She giggled, "I think it is love Jamison."

"I'm not complaining about being busy with friends, Jamison. Like you advised, I am learning from them and— and, enjoying it. But I did catch up on some of my reading." She dug through her beaded purse and pulled out a list. She handed him her list of books she read over the last six weeks. "See!"

Jamison took the list. Once the four of them, Lisa, his two uncles, and himself had done an analysis of the books that led to an episode and those that did not. They could find no correlation that might predict an episode by the kind of book or part she was reading at the time. The sleep episodes appeared to be random even though she was always reading when one occurred. She never had a sleep episode without a book. Sometimes he wondered how often in the past she had simply not had a book in her hand.

Lisa gave him an overview of the two episodes that had resulted in her having a dream. They ended the meeting with the usual hypnotherapy session to help her avoid going into a deep sleep with her episodes. Jamison scheduled a meeting in four weeks, he suggested six, but allowed Lisa to have her way. When she left, he took her list to his study to include in her other file. The short list included three novels, history of Amelia Earhart, and Matthew, Mark, and John. He recognized those as books of the Gospels in the Bible.

School was starting in a few days. Although her summer had been busy with two family road trips and friends, she did get through all four of the Gospels. Charlie suggested she begin her reading in the Gospel of John. She picked one of the five versions of the Bible that she thought was easier to understand. She liked it that what Jesus said was printed in red. It seemed some of the things Jesus said made good sense and was common knowledge, then other things were rather radical. He told a lot of very short stories. Book people love stories.

She met with Charlie a couple of times to make sense of some of the things she was reading. Charlie said some of the difficulties were that the Bible was written over two thousand years ago and in a very different culture. She really hadn't thought of that, but realized actions of some characters in books written only two hundred years ago wouldn't make sense to our culture now. He also explained many beliefs of the church were based on looking at the Bible as a whole and included the Old Testament books, the Gospel stories along with letters of the Apostles. He likened it to science, which takes many individual facts all together to create a scientific theory. His explanations satisfied Lisa.

Lisa read some of the Apostle Paul's writings, and was now back to reading in the Gospels. She wanted to know more about Jesus. She stretched out on the small sofa in their library, one of the cooler rooms in the house. She wondered what it would have been like to see Jesus in his culture and time. She turned to a story in John about Jesus miraculously feeding thousands of people. She liked the story; it had a lot of things going on as she remembered from when she read the story several times in the past in three of the Gospel accounts. She opened John's account of the story and she was there face to face with Jesus.

She came to with a start and sat up spilling her Bible to the floor. She looked up and Ginny was standing over her. Lisa was shaking and burst into tears. Ginny sat beside her and took her in her arms. "Bad dream dear?"

Lisa wiped the tears away and muttered, "Yes, I guess, I think so. I don't know."

"Dreams can sometimes be like that. They fade away so fast all you have left are the emotions they might have caused."

"How long was I gone?"

"You mean asleep. I brought you the cocoa and the cookies just before the basketball game, about seven. You were awake then." Ginny looked at the large grandfather clock by the window. It was nearly nine. "The game was over, so I came to chase you off to bed. I saw you were," her voice lowered to a whisper, "perhaps having an episode. I shook you. Needless to say, I pushed your alarm thing, and you woke. The therapy seems to be working with that part."

The tears began again. "I'm frightened Ginny."

"Do you want to talk about it dear?"

She shook her head as she sniffled into her sleeve. "I need Jamison."

Ginny handed Lisa a tissue and retrieved her Bible from the floor.

Lisa found Jamison's name under favorites. After several rings she heard the familiar voice telling her to leave a message.

Ginny picked up the cup of cold cocoa. "Want a refill?"

Lisa nodded, a few tears still trickling down her cheek.

Ginny retreated. "I will be back in a second."

Ginny was her dearest friend, and always a comfort. She wished she could have shared it all with Ginny, told her where she had been and who she had just seen. But she still didn't want Ginny to know she was a freak. Once Jamison told her she should share the content of her dreams with her family. She refused on the basis they were not dreams, and she knew they would not believe the truth.

Half a minute later Jamison returned her call.

"Jamison, I need to see you now!"

She heard concern in his voice. "What is going on Lisa?"

"I had an adventure different from any before in my life. I am frightened Jamison."

There was silence for what seemed minutes to Lisa. "Lisa I am in New York and will not be home until tomorrow evening. Can it wait until the next morning? Do you wish to talk tonight?"

She tried to calm herself and speak without bursting into tears again.

Jamison spoke first, "You sound distressed. I will call a prescription in for you to help you sleep tonight. Tell Ginny you had a very distressing dream and that I have ordered something to help you. It will be ready at the drug store on Liberty, that is close to you."

Lisa thanked him through sobs and said she would.

Ginny was at the door again, and came in when she heard a sob from Lisa. She wrapped her arms around her.

"Called Jamison. He ordered something at drug store on Liberty."

"I don't want to leave you alone. Get a sweater and come with me."

In the car Ginny asked if she wanted to talk about it. Lisa shook her head, no. When home Ginny got Lisa into bed. She read the directions on the prescription and doled out two pills, telling her it was a mild sedative. Although she kissed her goodnight, she returned to check on Lisa every two hours.

Lisa didn't wake until noon. She stumbled downstairs to the kitchen. When she didn't find Ginny, she went back up and knocked on the door to her rooms. Ginny turned off her television and let Lisa in. "Hungry dear?" She went on, "Doctor Jamison called earlier to ask how you were doing. I told him still sleeping, and he said that was good. Jane also called to remind you the group had a hike at noon, and you were bringing cookies. I told her you were ill and couldn't make it."

Lisa sighed and relaxed back in Ginny's colorful floral recliner. Ginny threw an equally colorful throw over her. "I will bring you coffee and a muffin," and left.

Sometimes Lisa wished she could confide in Ginny and her parents. They hadn't listened when she was young and tried to share her adventures. Now she was afraid. She wasn't sure what she feared, but decided numerous times it would not be a good idea to tell them. They knew she had a sleep disorder, she thought perhaps she didn't want them to know she was a freak. She knew they would side with Jamison, that it was all a dream. Jamison didn't entirely agree with her about not telling her secret. Later that afternoon Ginny took messages from Jane, Grace and Josh who called to check on how she was feeling. That evening Jamison called when he arrived back in town. She told him she could wait until morning to see him.

Jamison had only just arrived and was unlocking the office when Lisa appeared with a coffee in each hand. She waited for

him to set his briefcase on his desk and handed one to him'
"Cappuccinos, one for each of us." She went to the red chair,
kicked off her shoes and curled up with her coffee.

He thanked her and wheeled his chair beside her, then
went back and brought the tape recorder they used when she
related her dreams. He took a sip of his coffee and waited for
her to start. Tears began to trickle down her cheeks. He handed
her the tissue box and waited. She whispered. "I saw Jesus."

He didn't know what he expected, but this was not it. He
remembered the text message last spring, 'No incidents. Guess
what, I am now a Christian.' He knew the details about how
she was attending church with her friends, and she included
the Bible on most of her reading lists. He waited.

She wiped her eyes. "I was very close, maybe three feet
from him, we were outside. I was in a Gospel story Jamison.
The first thing I saw was him. Because he was sitting on a large
rock and I was standing it seemed that our heads were at the
same level. He looked at me. Never have I gone into a story
where anyone ever saw me. He did! His look Jamison was
like he really saw me; saw inside me and knew me — a look
that said I was okay — I was accepted. Then he spoke to me
Jamison. He said, 'Welcome Lisa.'" More tears came and she
reached for the tissue box, grabbed some and blew her nose.
"I wasn't frightened then, only later. As you know I have never
had any fears in my book adventures since when I am there, I
somehow know the characters can't see me."

Lisa took several sips of her coffee and Jamison drank
some of his. He glanced at the recorder as he sometimes did to

be sure it was working. He knew now was not a time to be asking questions. She continued, "I looked around and saw hundreds, or perhaps literally thousands of Arabic looking people, mostly sitting in sort of separate groups. Arabic because of how they were dressed, but of course, they would have been Jews. Many were sitting on blankets, which I later realized were their head coverings or outer garments. The women in the crowd did not remove their head coverings. Some made use of large stones in the area and were using those as seats. I obviously was not visible as no one pointed or stared at me in my shorts and tee shirt. I didn't know what to do since this was a new kind of adventure. I turned back toward him and he said to me, 'You may wish to look around, then please do return.'

"We were on a slope. I walked down about ten feet closer to where people were. Two young boys were running near me and one bumped into me. I fell and hit my knee on a nearby rock. The boy looked startled and shook his head, then ran after his fellow. This was not like my other adventures when someone moved to where I was, then we were suddenly apart, like opposing magnetic fields, which happened in my other adventures. I didn't think about that until I was home again." She pointed to her knee, "See I have a bruise."

"From the sun it looked like late afternoon, maybe three or four. I saw some people stand and pick up their cloaks from the ground and mill about like they were leaving. People in one of the groups nearest me were putting something in a small basket on a large rock near me as they began moving out. I moved closer and saw they were putting pieces of bread and fish into the basket. It was then I realized this was feeding of five thousand, one of Jesus miracles I had read several times, and the story I was reading before I found myself there. I moved closer to where Jesus was sitting and looked up at him; he nodded his head, which I thought was that what I wanted to do was okay. I think he could sense my question without my asking. I walked over and reached into the basket and pulled out a piece of bread and small chunk of the fish. Jamison I actually ate the bread and the fish in this adventure. The bread was like pita bread only not quite as thin. It was soft and seemed fresh but tasted a little bland. Maybe it lacked salt. The fish on the other hand was quite salty. It seemed to be a smoked fish with a strong fishy taste, somewhat like fish jerky that I once tried.

"I stood there and watched as people were all moving away in large groups. Some men picked up the small baskets and began dumping the contents into several larger ones. I heard thunder and realized the sky had darkened with some clouds and the wind picked up. The crowd seemed to know what that meant and many began leaving. I had been in adventures with storms before and even heard thunder, but never felt wind. Again I didn't think of that until I was home again. The men who seemed to be in charge, and I guessed were Jesus disciples, gave the larger baskets of bread and fish to various groups of men as they began leaving the area. I looked around and realized Jesus was no longer there.

"Again Jamison, I didn't know what to do so decided to follow one of the larger groups of people, one that had a number of children. Then suddenly I was at home in the library with Ginny looking down at me."

Jamison turned the recorder off just as Lisa broke into tears again. He was surprised because she was normally not an emotional person. He silently waited for her to compose herself.

"He spoke to me Jamison. I ate the bread and the fish; I felt the cold wind. I was really there." She gave a gulp. "I was really there."

He reached down and helped her out of the chair. "It sounds like you experienced a much more vivid dream this time Lisa."

"No, Jamison, not only was this adventure real, but even more real than my other times in a book; not a dream."

He was very concerned. "We should meet tomorrow if you can, so we can have a regular therapy session, we don't have time for it now."

After Lisa left, he took the recorder to his study and made himself a coffee. The one Lisa brought him was cold since he was listening and not drinking. He pulled her file and made notes. He didn't ask questions as he occasionally did after she related a dream since she was in an emotional state. She had the Bible on most of her lists of reading. He thought perhaps that was one of the reasons for this change. He had other concerns over the intensity of her continued assertion that her experience was real and not a dream. He thought somehow she was beginning to agree with his diagnosis of her dreams as false memories, certainly not now.

Jamison made notes for Lisa's other file. He made a copy of the tape and got it ready to mail. He decided a phone call would be needed to prepare his uncles for this tape. He needed to put his thoughts together before he called. He closed the office, headed for the post office, then home.

He was home by two. He listened to his copy of the tape of Lisa's dream twice while sipping a Jameson whiskey. He shook himself and realized he needed a clear head. He changed his clothes and ran his usual five miles. Running in the hottest part of the day after drinking was not a good idea. At home he sank into a large chair and stared at the ceiling until his breath and senses returned. Lisa said she was frightened, which was why she called him, rather than the usual text message saying she had experienced one of her sleep episodes. He thought, now he was — what was he? He grabbed onto the word 'concerned.' Concerned enough to make a call to his uncles in the middle of the night.

He cooled off with a shower and felt he was ready for the call. He walked by the Jameson and put it back out of sight muttering to himself. There is a logical explanation Jamison, and besides you don't drink during the day or alone. He made a sandwich then dialed the number for his uncles in Ireland. His uncle Father Ryan Jamison answered on the third ring.

"Branden me boy."

"Uncle Ryan, I hope I did not wake you."

"No fear of that, Glen and I finished off a game of chess and a pint. We thought you might be calling." His uncle, whichever one answered the phone, invariably said that to him.

"Is it well with ye Laddie?"

"I am well, thank you. I need Uncle Glen also Father." Sometimes he referred to his uncle Father Ryan as Father as well as calling him Uncle Ryan. He heard shuffling and clicking sounds as his other uncle picked up on the other line.

"I am here Branden," came the voice of his Uncle Glen. "Is it well with ye?"

Jamison reassured them both, "Thank you, I am well. I am sending you a tape from Lisa. It should be there in a couple of days as I expedited it. Although I sent notes, something needs to be explained in person." Jamison sighed and wished he were there instead of thousands of miles away.

"Tell us what happened."

"Father, this dream of hers was that she went into a Gospel story, the one of Jesus feeding five thousand or maybe the four thousand. She said she actually saw Jesus. She said this was different from any she had in the past because in this dream he saw her and spoke to her. She said she could feel the wind and heat and that she tasted and ate food."

Father Ryan spoke, "People have been known to have vivid visions of the Christ. You said she had a religious experience and was going to a church often."

"There is more. As Lisa began relating her dream to me I realized I had already heard about it, like déjà vu, rather remembering. Maybe because she has been reading the Bible, so my mind went to stories of Jesus in it." All was silent for perhaps a minute, then uncle Father Ryan asked, "You still there Laddie?"

"When she finished, I actually believed her, that she had been there and was not dreaming this time. She made it all seem real." He shook his head in disgust even though he knew his uncles couldn't see the expression.

A long silence and his Uncle Glen spoke up. "Ye be wanting logic or answers Branden?"

"Listen to the tape." He took a deep breath. "She was frightened. She clearly feels this one is different. Maybe you are right, maybe I am being influenced by her emotions and putting pieces together that don't really fit."

"Branden take care. Truth is not always logic as we and thee have often discussed."

Jamison didn't really think he would get an answer from his uncles, he simply needed to confide in someone — to say the words out loud so he could understand them better. But how to find words for feelings? When he was a practicing psychiatrist he never asked a patient, "How do you feel about that?" It was always, "And what did you do, or what did you want to do?" If they responded that they threw something or wanted to throw something he knew they felt anger.

"Did you hear me Laddie?" came a voice.

Jamison came to and gave what he hoped was the right response. "I will take care. Please call me when you have heard Lisa's dream."

His uncles were much like him and generally took time to think before speaking. Even though both of his uncles were well-educated men, they still had a tendency to lean toward the family's ancient past of mysticism that almost verged on superstition. He leaned to logic and science as protection from his family's past. The uncles still lived in the four-hundred-year-old ancestral house that resemble a castle surrounded by myths and legends. Legends he had grown up with.

He would work on Lisa's therapy in the morning, and increase her sessions. They had made such good progress, now to go backwards was unsettling. He hoped this incident might be an anomaly, and Lisa would gain control over her sleep episodes, her dreams, and her life. But now, what about him?

———

Several days later Jamison's uncles called him. It was two in the morning. He asked them to wait a minute while he cleared his head. He had paper and pen by his bed as habit as a doctor and as a psychiatrist. Also because his uncles had little concept of time, let alone of time differences on another continent.

"Did we wake ye Laddie?" asked Uncle Glen.

"You did."

"Then ye can talk now," said the Uncle Father Ryan.

Jamison smiled to himself and moved from the edge of the bed to a small desk. He turned on the lamp and sat with his pen and tablet ready. "I can talk now."

"We listened to the lassie's story."

"Could be a vision. More people than you might think have had visions of the Lord," Father Ryan said.

Uncle Glen added, "Or a significant dream, I am thinking dream."

"We Jamisons have been known to have visions, Branden."

"It is the lassie we are talking about Ryan," argued Uncle Glen.

Jamison cut in, "Why did you think as she said this one was different, other than having a religious subject matter?"

"Aye Branden, that is another thing."

He wished they would get to the point, but waited.

Uncle Glen spoke, "Several things. She has had fewer of her dreams. Perhaps her subconscious wants her attention, to go back to these incidents for some reason."

"Or it could be a vision," interrupted Father Ryan.

Uncle Glen continued, "Emotions are the key here Branden. The girl may be emotionally connected to her reading of the Gospel story she dreamed about. Her emotions may have created the added reality to the dream."

Jamison already had those ideas.

Before he could say anything, Father Ryan added, "Her mind may have created a more vivid dream, if it was a dream and not a vision, because she is reading the Gospel stories as real, not as stories from someone's imagination.

Jamison winced inwardly at that idea. He worked with Lisa three years so she could recognize reality and the truth.

Uncle Glen spoke up, "Now about yourself. We both agree Lisa has a strong mind. The two of you have shared a close intimacy by her sharing details of her life and all her dreams, these from her sleep episodes, and the ones from her night dreams. On her part we know she thinks of you as her soulmate, the word you said she sometimes uses. We both think you had a wee peak at her dream as a shared dream, maybe why you felt the déjà vu. Such a thing can happen between two people, the sharing of a dream. And Laddie, we Jamisons have been mystics, we have a past even before history, before the building of the castle, of seeing and knowing what others do not. We warned you to give her treatment to someone else."

"I should not have told you of my déjà vu experience when she told me about her dream, but I guess you know I am keeping all honest if you are to help her. I am disappointed, she has been progressing to the point I was ready to close her case, but now with this setback."

"We know."

Another long silence before one of the uncles spoke again. "We fear for her safety."

"What do you mean?"

Father Ryan responded, "There are some true things the things, which you do not acknowledge in your reality Branden."

Suddenly the uncles dropped the subject of Lisa and went on to talk about people in the village, about their goats, and that the dog had a thorn in his paw. He felt he might have drifted off and missed the last part of the call.

His uncles did not provide any new information for him. He did appreciate their wisdom, and advice, even if he did not take it. After all he decided to be a scientist and seeker of truth. Naturally, Father Ryan would see it as a vision. Jamison as a psychiatrist was not sure there was a difference between a vision and a dream. He had to admit the uncles were also seeking truth, only in what reality? He didn't know about Lisa, but he was beginning to think he might need to make some changes in his life.

It was late before he was able to sleep, then not well as his dreams included Lisa surrounded by bearded men in what he considered Biblical clothing. When he woke, he knew the dreams related to his conversation with his uncles and his concern of her Gospel story dreams. Jamison's new found difficulty was separating what he knew from what he felt.

———

The next week as Lisa walked out of the elevator toward Jamison's office, she rehearsed in her mind what she would tell him. The memory of her second adventure yesterday was clear. Only she knew Jamison would be disappointed that she had not said no, had not prevented it; as she knew she could have done. She wasn't as frightened this time as she had been last week. Instead of simply sending the usual text when she experienced a sleep episode, she called him as she had done a few weeks earlier.

Jamison met her at the door, and after the normal pleas-
antries brought the tape recorder to the table next to the large
red chair and started it. This time Lisa was able to share the
memories of her experience without the emotion and tears.
She began. "I was on a small hill overlooking what I guessed
would be the Sea of Galilee since that was in the story I was
reading. Anyway, it was a large lake. I saw what looked like
little farms and orchards scattered around, and not far below
me buildings grouped together. I guessed it was a small village.
I walked down the hill toward the village. I saw a man walking toward me. When he got closer, I hoped it would be Jesus
again, and it was. He saw me, waved and when he got closer
spoke to me, 'Welcome Lisa.'

"Before I could respond, a group of people came down a
different path and three of them walked up to Jesus. One
bumped into me but acted like he hadn't seen me. He looked
around and shrugged his shoulders as I moved out of the way.
The larger man moved close to Jesus and asked him if he was
coming. The others with him acted like they hadn't seen me,
like in my other adventures where I am like invisible.

"The larger man and Jesus broke from the group and
headed towards a path with stone steps leading to a few buildings. I followed. I saw something like a tarp spread from the
entrance of one of the buildings to a nearby tree creating a
shade of sorts. The other thing Jamison was the heat. I felt a
hot wind blowing and the sun was high, like at noontime. I
never before physically felt the weather in my adventures even
though I could see if the sky was clear or cloudy.

"When they approached the dwelling, he led Jesus to a wood bench under the awning. Jesus said, 'Thank you Simon.' The Simon person went inside. Jesus turned to me and said, 'Again, welcome Lisa. Have you come to meet the boys, eh?' He did Jamison. He said the boys instead of my disciples. He obviously knew the story we were in about calling the first disciples. Later I remembered Simon was another name for Peter. Simon came out of the house and headed back down a road or large path toward the lake. He hollered. 'Be back with my brother and the others if I can convince them.' Simon, or rather Peter, was about the same height as Jesus, but of a stocky build. His hair was a medium brown, with some reddish tints. He didn't have a head covering. All the men I saw had beards. Simon has a round face and strong smile lines around his eyes.

"A woman came out of the house with a large ceramic jar. She had a head covering that hid all but her eyes. I couldn't guess her age from what I could see. Her clothing was loose and the fabric was a creamy color in a soft weave. I noticed a woven decorative pattern at the hem of the gown. She walked over to Jesus and he held out his hands as she poured water over them. He thanked her. She left the jar on a small table nearby. He rose and picked it up and turned to me. I seemed to intuitively know what to do so I held out my hands and he poured water over them. I rubbed them together. The cool water felt good. I was still in awe Jamison, because I actually felt the water.

"A minute later she reappeared with a basket and handed it to Jesus. I moved closer and saw it contained something that looked like a trail mix with nuts and maybe dates and roasted grains. Jesus took a handful, and when she turned back to the house, he handed it to me and took another for himself. It was tasty but no salt. I think the dried fruit pieces were dates. Jamison I actually tasted food again like my last adventure.

"A dog came running up the path straight to us. It walked over to me and sniffed my feet and legs and looked up at me. I was nervous because I don't especially like dogs. Following the dog were four men accompanying Simon. Jesus stood and hugged two of the new comers. The dog then walked to Jesus and sniffed his feet. One of the four, a young-looking man called him back. 'Down Gideon.' The dog returned to where I stood, looked up at me and sat down at my feet. I reached down and patted his head; he licked my hand then lay down at my feet. I was quite sure the dog could not only see me, but it responded to my pats on its head.

"I looked back up at what was going on. Jesus said, 'Greetings again Andrew,' as he clasped him by the arm in a friendly gesture. He asked about Philip and Nate. Andrew told him they were not in town as they were home on business, but would be back before Sabbath. Andrew reached for the jug of water and poured some over his hands. The others stopped their conversation while Andrew did the same water pouring for all of them. Once the hands were clean, they all began in on the basket of trail mix.

"The woman came from the house with a larger basket with grapes. An older woman, her gray head uncovered brought out a basket filled with some kind of baked goods, cakes or cookies or bread. I saw Andrew reach in for two. He glanced to see that neither of the women were watching and tossed one to the dog Gideon while he quickly devoured the other.

"One of the men was older with a very gray almost white beard. I must mention they all had a rather rank fishy smell about their clothing. I listened as carefully as I could from my distance and found out that the older man was Zebedee, and the other two were James and John. James was above average height. He and John had more of an olive complexion (looked very Arabic to me) than the others. He had an air of being better groomed than the others, perhaps he had changed his clothing earlier. He also had a serious demeanor about him. John looked young with a light beard. I wasn't sure if he kept it that way or if that was just how much it was. His eyes were very blue. Because of his dark complexion, they seemed even more so. His hair was shorter than most and very curly. He sat nearly opposite of me and stared in my direction. Even more than that I swear he made eye contact, but didn't acknowledge having done so. You know how you can feel if someone is staring at you.

"The older woman came out with cups and a large jar with what appeared to be wine. The men all shifted places and continued to eat and drink. John turned the wine down, but seemed hungry as he kept going back to the trail mix bowl. I moved to get closer so I could hear what they were saying. I had to stay far enough away that no one bumped into me after it happened a couple of times. I thought it would be easier if this adventure was like all my others where people couldn't physically touch me. A girl, maybe ten years-old, ran up to the group. She went to James and said something softly to him. He said something to Simon about a boat and suddenly all were up, abandoned the food, and headed down the path toward the lake.

"Before the exodus I had heard much of the conversation and none of it was a call for them to follow him. It was all about fishing and the weather and boats and the economy. I followed the group down to what seemed like the wharfs, such as they were. Some of these boats were rather large, some were smaller and pulled up onto shore. The group seemed to be in rather festive mood with laughing and thumping each other on the shoulder. I think that is still a man thing.

"Gideon circled back and forth between Andrew, the young girl, and myself. I was at the back of the group so she kept calling to him to catch up with her. Again, I felt John had an awareness of my being there because he turned two or three times to look where I was following. I swear he was looking at me.

"We got to where several larger boats were moored, men were climbing in and out of them. From the conversation I learned that one was a new boat for Zebedee and Simon fleet; thus the commotion as it had just sailed over to their moorage.

"Then I was sitting in our library and it was already dark out, and I called you."

Jamison and Lisa sat in silence; the only sound was the faint hum of the recorder. Jamison, as usual wanted to be careful with his words. He finally spoke, "Again this time did you feel you might be going into an episode?"

Lisa frowned at him, "I guess I knew you would want to know that." She had what he thought was a sheepish or guilty look when she replied. "It was more than that Jamison. I wanted to go into that story and was thinking hard and wishing that I could go there again and see Jesus."

The room was silent again with only the faint sound of traffic in the street below and the hum of the elevator. Jamison turned the recorder off.

Lisa finally broke the awkward silence. "It was a wonderful experience Jamison. I feel great peace when by him. The group he was with looked like ruffians, but since he was there I felt," she paused as though looking for the right word, "happy, I felt happy after it was over and I was home; not frightened like the first time. Even though people could touch me, I didn't feel like I could get hurt."

More silence. Finally, Jamison asked, "Why do you think, not feel Lisa, but think the two experiences about Jesus were different from your prior sleep episodes?" He watched her face turn into a slight scowl. He knew words were as important to her as to him. At least he had not used the word 'dream.'

"Maybe because they were real. What I mean is that reading the Gospels is about something that really happened. I don't know Jamison. Biographies and history are written by people who think they knew the person they are writing about. Even autobiographies are written by an author who wants readers to see their life from their personal point of view. Jamison, I think the fact that so much detail is left out is what makes the Gospel stories more real. Readers can't misinterpret words if they are not there. All that is there is what actually happened."

Jamison realized Lisa was groping, and rather wildly, for an explanation. He did not fault her for that and decided not to belabor the issue, at least not now. His greatest concern was that hypnotherapy would not be very useful if Lisa was deliberately choosing to experience a sleep episode, which seemed to be the case lately. What she needed now was to be brought to reason. He found that people with religious experiences usually were not susceptible to arguments of reason.

He ended the session and asked Lisa to come back next week for her regular hypnotherapy session. Her smile seemed pensive as she left him with a hug and whispered, "It is real Jamison."

He made notes for her regular file. He even noted that he thought there might have been a setback in her treatment since Lisa told him she did not try to avoid the sleep incident and even wanted it. He had to be honest in his reports for her care team. As usual there was no mention about the content of dreams during any of her reported episodes. He then took the tape into his study and made a copy to send to the uncles and to make notes for her case in his research files. His uncle Father Ryan Jamison would love this one. No, both of them would probably have equal interest. Perhaps their concern of danger for Lisa was that instead of trying to prevent these episodes, she wanted them.

Jamison made himself a cup of regular coffee and sat in one of the large red leather chairs to think. Lisa had not wavered from her ideas that her life had changed since she became a Christian and believed in Jesus. He was raised Catholic and also believed, but had not been to Mass in years. He sipped his coffee and wondered why he quit going. He wondered if somewhere along the way he had turned from his faith. As he searched his soul he thought not. He still held to his faith, only had pushed it away as though faith had nothing to do with his present life, with reality, even though it existed. The word paradox came into his mind.

Chapter 7

"He had the face of one who walks in his sleep, and for a wild moment the idea came to me that perhaps he was not normal, not altogether sane. There were people who had trances, I had surely heard of them, and they followed strange laws of which we could know nothing, they obeyed the tangled orders of their own sub-conscious minds. Perhaps he was one of them, and here we were within six feet of death." [DAPHNE DU MAURIER, *Rebecca*]

LISA WOKE WITH a fuzzy head, then began to feel severe pain in her left leg, then felt the pain all over her body. She looked around and realized she was in a hospital emergency room, which brought back childhood memories of often waking in such a room, back when her family first noticed her sleep episodes and took her to the hospital. She turned and saw her father sitting next to her bed. She muttered, "What happened Daddy?"

He jumped out of the chair and stood by her and kissed her cheek.

"She's awake Florence."

Lisa turned and saw her mother at the end of the bed.

Florence's eyes lit up and a smile replaced her serious demeanor as she looked at her daughter. "You're awake dear." Lisa's father moved over so her mother could get closer to the bed and try to hug her daughter through all the medical attachments.

Lisa smiled up at her, but cringed since every movement registered pain. She asked again, "What happened?"

"You fell down a cliff honey."

"I don't remember." She closed her eyes, her head hurt. Then suddenly she did remember exactly what happened. She had been in another place and another time. She couldn't tell them.

Ginny came in and handed two cups of coffee to Lisa's parents. She smiled at the girl in the bed with the dirty and scratched face and arms. Lisa still had remnants of leaves and sticks in her tangled hair. Ginny gave Lisa's parents look of apology and asked, "Jane and Josh are still waiting, could they see her for a quick moment?" Just then Doctor Aubry came into the room. Ginny left and mouthed the word, "Later."

Doctor Aubry had been Lisa's doctor for all of her fifteen years, yet he still had a fresh look like he was an intern just out of medical school. She gave him a feeble grin.

Lisa's father spoke up, "Thank you Doctor Aubry for coming. The in-charge doctor said she was in no immediate danger and since you were already here at the hospital he would monitor and wait for you. Again thanks; you know her special condition."

He responded simply, "Hello Richard, Florence."

They all watched the doctor log into a computer in the room. Her mother moved to the other side of the bed and took Lisa's hand. After a few minutes of reviewing her notes on the screen Doctor Aubry walked over to her bed and gave her his doctor look of sympathy. "Looks like you took quite a fall."

He began poking at her and asking where it hurt. It hurt everywhere, but she quickly understood what he wanted and yelped loudly with any movement of her left leg. He prodded it more gently, "I think it may be broken. We will need an X-ray." He then felt her head and she winced at one spot. He softly chuckled as he added, "And you have a nice goose egg here. A few cuts, but I don't think any of them will require stitches."

When he was done poking, he smiled. "Lisa is going to be fine." Although he was looking at her, he seemed to be talking to her parents. "She will need to go to X-ray, then someone will set her leg if it is broken, as I suspect. I think her shoulder may be dislocated, no breaks, but we need to check that out. A nurse will be in to treat her scrapes and cuts. She obviously has a mild concussion, but all her vitals are good. Still, I would like to keep her here for the night."

Lisa scrunched up her eyes and scowled. Even that hurt. She grumped out, "I want to go home Mom. You just got home two days ago and I then was gone and I missed you so very much."

"Don't worry honey, I will stay here with you."

Doctor Aubry left just as a nurse came in. The nurse began gently washing her face and putting antiseptic on the cuts on her arms and legs. No sooner had she left than another one came in, introduced herself and began unplugging Lisa from all the medical attachments. She said someone would be in soon to take her for X-rays.

Everything was happening too fast and Lisa was frightened. She was grateful for her parents, that they were here by her side. She was grateful for her dear friend Jane, and her boyfriend Josh, that they were here, even though she didn't get to see them. Her mind whirled as she thought that the person she most wanted right now was Jamison. He was the only one she could tell what really happened.

She didn't have time to think. Her father was ejected from the room, while her mother and a nurse helped her into a hospital gown. Her head hurt; every move hurt. She tried not to let out the moans she felt. It seemed like just minutes before she was put in a machine, then a large brace like thing was wrapped around her leg and she was wheeled to another room. Her mother was waiting for her there.

"That was quick honey." She approached, but the nurses asked her to move so they could move Lisa to the bed. The nurse said a doctor would be in to take care of her broken leg once he had seen the X-ray. She insisted Lisa swallow pain medication and left.

They were suddenly alone. "Where is Daddy?"

"He went with Ginny to get some clothes for us. I will spend the night with you here Lisa." She stood by her bed, "Do you want to change the bed to a sitting position?"

"Yes, please."

Her mother began combing her hair with her fingers, pulling out a few twigs and leaves. "Maybe they will let you have a shower when the leg is ready."

"Tell me what happened Mom."

The short story was that she had been on a weekend retreat with her church friends. Ginny was there as girl's counselor. Saturday afternoon Lisa had apparently gone off on a hike by herself, why no one knew. She wandered off the trail and fell down a rather steep slope. They didn't find her for a couple of hours after she had gone missing; and then couldn't wake her. That was the story. Her mother wasn't sure of all the details. She and her father drove straight to the hospital when they got the call. She said Ginny, Josh and Jane had given some details to him, but with all her concerns about Lisa, she hadn't pressed him to tell her yet.

Just as she finished talking a doctor came into the room and put on what he said was a temporary cast. They wanted the swelling to go down before putting on a more permanent one. Lisa was beginning to feel drowsy from the medication. When she woke, she wasn't sure how long sleep had taken her. She looked over and saw her mom asleep in a large chair with a pillow and blanket.

Lisa lay there thinking, "I am a freak." Tears slowly slid down her cheek. She closed her eyes and wondered if Jamison was right; that she could control the adventures. Lately with the most recent ones she really hadn't wanted to. She loved the places she visited when she was in a book; especially now when she could go into a Gospel story and see Jesus.

Lisa's head hurt even with the pain medications she had been given. The hospital seemed too noisy to sleep. However, the noise and the pain were not what kept her awake. Lisa was scared by what happened to her—by what should not have happened. She knew her adventures were real, that she actually went into what she was reading, into another place and another time. She was frightened because that other reality had intruded into this reality. Last week she had an incident she didn't tell Jamison about, a frightening one like this one, which resulted in her fall of a cliff. That was first time she had not been open and honest with him.

———

Because of her dislocated shoulder, Lisa couldn't use crutches so had a wheelchair to get around. Ginny wheeled her in and left her in Doctor Jamison's office. She was anxious since she hadn't been honest with him about one of her incidents about two weeks before the accident. She had always been honest with him, but lately she felt guilty because she was not even trying to cooperate with her treatment. She knew she had to tell him what caused the fall.

"Good morning Lisa, I am glad to see you are able to be up and about."

She smiled, "Hi Jamison."

"Would you like sit in your favorite chair?"

Lisa nodded and he helped her hobble from the wheelchair to the soft red leather chair near the window and prop her leg up on the ottoman. He pulled out his desk chair and rolled it to face her. He got straight to the point. Lisa liked that about their relationship, it had always been honest, well nearly always honest until now. "Tell me about what happened to you Lisa."

She took a deep breath and began, "When I sent you the text last week, no it was the week before last, saying I experienced a sleep episode. I didn't say it was another one from a Gospel story."

He simply nodded his head.

"I knew I would be seeing you this week. Jamison I was scared and didn't know how to explain it. More frightened than from the two before."

"What is frightening Lisa?"

"I am scared Jamison that maybe I'm crazy."

"We have talked about that before. You know I do not think you are what you call 'crazy' because of your episodes."

It was a few minutes before she could go on. As usual he waited patiently. She continued, "I told you how my experiences when I went into one of the Gospel stories were different from when I went into other books. Like when I go into these stories I not only see and hear what is going on around the story, but I experience other senses like smell and the heat, and I can taste food. All my senses are involved."

He nodded like he always did.

"Two weeks ago, I was in our library in my favorite chair when I went into a story. I didn't set my timer that time even though I had time to do so, and knew I could have. In the story I was in a boat during a storm. The storm had wind and waves and the waves splashed over the boat and I got soaked. When I got back home I was sitting on the floor in the library and I was really soaked; I mean physically. My clothes and hair were dripping wet just like what happened in the adventure. I went to my room and dried off and changed my clothes. No one saw me; I think Ginny was in the kitchen, I remember hearing her singing. She does that a lot lately."

Jamison was silent. He noticed Lisa's cheek was damp with tears. They could have no therapy today with her in such an emotional state. He needed to reassure her that she was not losing her mind. "Lisa, what I am thinking is that even the part of waking in the library and finding yourself, what you considered soaked, may well also be part of the dream. You may not have awakened until sometime later."

She shook her head. "No, I don't think so."

He continued, "Lisa, you and I have agreed to be seekers of truth. There are other logical explanations as to what might have happened then."

"Such as?"

"Sleep walking is a possibility."

"That would not say how I got wet."

"Sleep walkers can do very bizarre things, even strange enough for you to have gone upstairs and stood in the shower with your clothes on."

"I didn't do that Jamison! I know I didn't."

He said nothing, then brought up the question he was sure he knew the answer to. "Where were you when you fell down the slope or cliff?"

"I know you mean — was I having an episode; was I in a Gospel story last week?"

He nodded.

"You think I was sleep walking then, don't you?"

"What do you think it was Lisa?"

She began to cry. "Don't know Jamison. My memories, my adventures. I don't know what is real anymore." Between sobs she choked out, "Help me Jamison."

He wanted to walk over to the chair and put his arms around her to comfort her. He did not. Instead he suggested, "Lisa your parents and Ginny need to know."

"Know what?"

"They need to know during your more recent sleep episodes you have dreams that have become more vivid, that you are now at risk of sleepwalking. Sleepwalking is dangerous Lisa."

"What will you tell them?"

"I will say the fall down the cliff was probably an incident of sleepwalking."

"And the storm?"

"You can tell them as much as you are comfortable with."

"You promised to keep my secret Jamison."

"I shall. They need to know Lisa. It is the only way we can protect you."

"Like lock me up?"

Jamison was silent and gave her time to think. He knew Lisa was intelligent and sensible. She would come around.

"We will move our sessions to weekly for right now. You have had control for several months. This is only a setback. You can do this Lisa."

"Do you want to hear about my last two adventures, the dangerous ones?"

"No time for that today. Will tomorrow work?"

"Sure."

"I will set up a meeting with your parents. Think about how much you want them to know. I also need to notify your medical team Lisa. I have no choice."

"What will you tell them?"

"Only that in your last sleep episode you had a vivid dream that resulted in sleepwalking. They already know about your injuries."

She motioned she was ready. He helped her get from the large chair, put his arm around her to help her to the wheelchair. "Friends?" he asked. Before he could stop her she kissed him on the cheek. He guided her to the wheelchair and helped her settle.

"Soulmates, Jamison."

The next day Ginny again brought Lisa to the office in the wheelchair. She generally came after school, but she was not yet back to classes after her accident, so available for a morning appointment. After their normal greetings, he again helped her get to the red chair. He returned and got out the recorder.

She decided to first share the boating incident from three weeks ago. This was her third adventure from reading the Gospels. She began, "This story is about the huge lake called Sea of Galilee. Jamison, unlike the other two times I went into a Gospel story, I sort of had a warning." She stopped and knew she had to tell him everything. "I often wonder when I am reading if this will be a book that invites me, but I don't ever think the idea, 'yes I want to go in this one.' But when I read a Gospel story, I think I do wish to go into the story I am reading, maybe even hoping I could go back and see Jesus again. Naturally, nothing happens with most of those thoughts or wishes."

She sighed and continued, "But this time it did, and I was there. In this story Jesus' friends, or disciples, were going to the other side of the lake to a place called Gadarene. I don't know how to pronounce it. I was standing there looking on not sure what to do. I didn't think there would be a way for me to go because there wouldn't be room for me in one of their fishing boats, and if there was, how to not get bumped into this time. In some book adventures in the past the plot moves on and I go someplace else in the story. I thought maybe I would wander back up and look at the small town. It seemed to be late afternoon, was cloudy and very hot and humid. I saw James in the large boat shouting at men on the shore. John tossed nets into the large boat and others were loading wooden boxes and baskets of food. It looked like a mess with everyone coming and going out of the larger boat. The gist of the talk was that James and John, and some of the others would follow Peter who was getting a smaller boat ready. Those in the new larger boat would do some fishing on the way over the lake. They were all to meet on the far side by morning."

Lisa's voice was raspy. She turned toward Doctor Jamison and pointed toward the water cooler. He got up and poured her a cup of water. She turned back and stared out to the window and continued, "Peter got into one of the smaller boats, then Philip, Nathaniel, and Jesus. I thought it was great that I could recognize them from before. Andrew jumped in and called Gideon to come. I made an instant decision to go, so when Gideon jumped in I followed. They all looked at Gideon. My guess was they wondered how a twenty some pound dog could manage to rock the boat so much when he jumped in. Three individual seats were along each side of the boat, I think for rowing. None full across as in most boats I have been in, I guessed this was so they had plenty of room in the middle for the nets, and hopefully fish.

"I sat in one of the seats near the back of the boat and Gideon clambered onto the seat by me and snuggled close to me almost on my lap. The boat was still rocking while Philip and Nathaniel moved to the front seats at Peter's instruction and Jesus moved toward the back where there was a low shelf type seat piled with nets at the far back. As he passed by he looked down at me and the dog and gave me his welcoming smile but said nothing. I didn't think I had seen him look so exhausted in my two adventures there before. Andrew and Peter were still standing and it looked like they would take the middle seats. At least I hoped so, or I would have to move if one of them wanted to sit where Gideon was since they could not see me. We were about ten feet from shore when Andrew raised the sail and we moved quickly out into the lake. I was looking forward to sailing on the Sea of Galilee. My family went sailing a couple of times with my Uncle Leonard who has a sailboat. I liked it.

"We didn't go far before the wind picked up. Andrew pulled the larger sail down and pulled up a smaller one. Peter tossed the sail back toward where Jesus was and he picked it up, lay down and pulled it over himself. Most of my attention moved to watching the wind and waves increase as the shoreline receded. As things got rougher the boat's motion was not just up and down but moved from side to side. I was concerned for Gideon and so held onto the seat with one hand and onto Gideon with the other. I didn't want him swept overboard, and the story didn't mention anything about a dog in the storm. You know the Gospel stories don't have much detail and wouldn't have said even if a dog went overboard."

She sipped on her water. Doctor Jamison had not asked questions. Sometimes he did at the end to help her remember details. She went on, "After being drenched by a couple of waves we both ended up sitting on the floor, Gideon and me. By then there was at least four or more inches of water in the boat. The boat also seemed lower in the water now, which brought waves even more easily over the edge. Also, it had quickly gotten dark."

"Then things seemed to happen fast. Peter handed oars to Philip and Nathaniel. Philip's oar went overboard and

Nathaniel didn't seem to know what to do with his. Andrew and Peter grabbed more oars and Peter found a bucket and gave it to one of them, I think to bail water out of the boat, which was getting deeper. That also went overboard. Philip knelt on the bottom and clung to the mast. Nathaniel like me, also found something to hang onto so he wouldn't be swept overboard. The water inside grew with each wave that made itself over the side. Once when I lost my grip the boat went sideways and Gideon almost went over. I dived on him and pulled him back as the boat righted itself. When the top part of the mast snapped Peter left his oar and stumbled through the water to the back of the boat where Jesus remained asleep in the sails. I saw him shake him several times as much as he could with the rolling of the boat from side to side.

"Jesus sat up, looked around and said the word 'peace.' That is what I thought he said, but I really didn't hear with the roar of the wind. And the wind stopped. As the boat righted Gideon who was still in my arms looked up at me and licked my chin. Peter looked up at the shattered mast and tattered sails. He and the others crawled up to the benches. Philip put his head in his hands and cried, that's what it looked like. The others turned first to Jesus then to Peter. Andrew grabbed Gideon in his arms and hugged him. Everyone was soaked through, so I didn't know if water dripping over their faces was sea water or tears. Andrew almost bumped into me so I had to move to one of the other seats. Suddenly I was back home, soaked through and dripping."

Doctor Jamison click the recorder off. Lisa then turned to face him.

It seemed like minutes before he spoke. He seldom asked Lisa about her feelings or emotions, but now he did. "Did you feel frightened when the waves were coming over the boat?"

"Maybe, but for some reason I was mostly concerned about Gideon, that he wouldn't go overboard."

"Why do you think you weren't frightened?"

Time slowed, finally she responded. "Jesus was in the boat and in that story, he calmed it all down. I wasn't afraid until I was sitting on the floor by the chair at home in the library soaking wet. That is what scared me, being so very wet."

"Why didn't you tell me this when it happened?"

"Oh, lots of reasons Jamison. I was confused and it happened on Wednesday. I was going on the retreat that Friday, my first ever with my friends, and Ginny was going to chaperone our cabin. I was going to talk to you when we got back from the retreat; and ..."

Jamison added, "And?"

Lisa frowned, "I was scared, and you would ask why I didn't stop the episode and I would have to tell you not only that I didn't want to, but that I think I even started it by wanting to go back there so very much. To see him."

Jamison did not give Lisa what she considered one of his understanding smiles. Instead he looked grave. Again, she felt uncomfortable, like she had created some kind of barrier between them because she had not been forthcoming and honest about the episode; and because she was sure she had permitted it to happen. Still she wanted to continue. She asked him, "Are you ready for the next one?"

He nodded, then looked at his watch. "Let's get some lunch. When is Ginny to be back?"

"In about an hour."

"Call her and ask if two is okay. I will call downstairs and order sandwiches. You still prefer tuna?"

They finished their sandwiches and Jamison put a new tape in the recorder. Lisa began on the story that led to her fall and broken leg.

"I was in our cabin. The girls wanted to go on a little hike and I didn't, so asked if I could stay there. Ginny went to a counselor meeting and I was alone. I sat on my bed with my Bible and read the miracle of the woman who was healed of an issue of blood. I had not seen a healing miracle and again wondered how it would be to see crowds around Jesus. I wanted so see a miracle actually happen.

"Then I found myself on a narrow street in a town, well narrow by our standards; it would have been a one way street with room for one car and not one of the one-ton SUVs common here. Looking down the street I saw a lake. I guessed it was the Sea of Galilee, but not where I was before since this place was much larger than what I considered a village, such as where I had been before. I was part of a crowd slowly moving up hill in the other direction into the town. Since no one could see me I had to step into a doorway to keep from getting smashed by the crowd.

"As in the other visits, Jesus was there. The disciples I recognized were close to him, and it seemed they were trying to prevent people from getting too close to him. I saw a well-dressed younger man near him and thought he might Jirus since Peter and James had allowed him such close contact. The story I was reading was about this Jirus person. Even though he was a distance away, Jesus glanced toward me, made eye contact, and smiled. Perhaps this moment, his smile, is what keeps me wanting to continue going into the Gospel stories."

She sighed, "Sorry Jamison." The room was quiet except for the soft whirl of the tape in the recorder. Lisa continued, "A minute later I looked down as a wet slobbery nose sniffed at my feet and then a warm tongue licked my ankle. It was Gideon. I think he liked my little nook so he also would not get trampled, and he likes me. Andrew was not too far behind Gideon. He scooped him up, tied a rope around his neck and carried him the other way back to the lake and I guessed to the boat. I read that people of that time did not have dogs as pets, at least the common people did not. Being restrained in the boat was probably the safest thing for Gideon. I was glad that Andrew cared."

"I followed a little way behind the crowd, unfortunately so did five Roman soldiers. I hadn't seen any of these in my three visits before. Their presence was probably for the same reason law enforcement appears here whenever there is a large crowd that could turn into a mob. I was able to get on the edge of the group around Jesus and thought perhaps I saw the woman in the story who was going to be healed. She is also in this same story as Jirus. The crowd was mostly men, but I caught sight of a woman who was completely covered, even her face was veiled. The crowd stopped and I saw Jesus turn to her.

"Then I felt a nose again at my feet. I looked down to see Gideon back with a rope trailing behind him. It looked like he had chewed himself free. That was fast. Three soldiers came towards where Gideon was sitting at my feet. People moved aside to give the soldiers room, but Gideon stayed at my feet. One of the other soldiers shouted to the one that was grabbing for Gideon. 'Not him, he is too scrawny, he won't do in a fight.' The other one hollered back. 'He will be good bait, draw blood and get them all going.'

"I immediately knew they intended to grab Gideon for dog fights. I ran down an alley and Gideon followed me, as did the two soldiers. We were ahead only because our move had startled them. I saw light at the end of the alley which ended in a small courtyard garden fenced by a rock wall about three feet high with a wooden gate. I picked Gideon up, he was heavier than I remembered, and pushed him over, then climbed over just as the soldiers got to the gate. I turned to see them look somewhat surprised that the dog had gotten over the wall like he did. That slowed them, but only slightly. The other side of the courtyard also had a stone wall the same height as at the entrance. I again picked Gideon up and helped him over the wall and followed.

There was only a narrow ledge of land and then the ground sloped steeply down at least twenty or more feet toward the lake. The soldiers were now looking over the wall. I guessed they were wondering if it was worth it to chase the dog down such a steep slope. They sat on the wall and watched us; not us, watched Gideon since they could not see me. They began calling to him and held out some kind of food or meat to entice him back. Their efforts may have worked, but I grabbed the loose end of his rope when he turned toward them.

"I looked over the slope and wondered if I could get down by grabbing onto some of the bushes on the slope. Even if I could, would they hold me? I wondered how was I to hold Gideon in one arm and onto rocks and bushes with the other. It is interesting Jamison how fast your mind can go when you are in trouble. When I saw one of the soldiers turn and put his legs over the wall, I knew I had to try it. I wrapped the end of his rope around my arm and moved to a large bush, grabbed it and felt for a foothold with my feet. I found one that felt solid and even while hanging onto Gideon. He was heavier than I expected. I did not look back up to see what the soldiers were doing, but guessed the chase was off because I heard commanding voices and commotion in the courtyard above.

"Gideon and I slowly made it down the first few feet, then we both tumbled down the remaining. All I remember is that I hoped Gideon would not get hurt in the fall. My head hurt and I had a great pain in my leg. I was dizzy and could not stand up and must have passed out. I came to in the blazing heat and felt a wonderful relief when I felt a wet tongue lick my face. I don't know how long I lay there but the next time I came to I saw two men approach. Gideon ran to them and I was conscious enough to recognize Andrew. I watched them walk toward the lake. I wanted to be home. I closed my eyes and waited. I even wondered if this time I would come back home. I was terribly frightened then. The next thing I remember is being in the hospital."

Doctor Jamison turned off his recorder. He tried to put what Lisa called his 'understanding doctor's face' on instead of the one he felt of deep concern.

"I don't like the look on your face Jamison. I am sorry I didn't stop myself from going into the story. I know I should have," she sighed, "could have."

He was thoughtful before he responded. "I am concerned about that. However, I am more concerned because, like I told you earlier, I believe you may be sleepwalking, which can be very dangerous as we now have evidence."

Lisa stared down at the floor.

"I did notify your care team Lisa about that as a possibility. What I reported was that you had a sleep episode that possibly involved sleepwalking. They are as concerned as I am. We have a meeting set up for Friday for all of us to meet, including your parents and Ginny so we all can find a way to keep you safe and still keep on living a normal life?"

Lisa burst out, "I am a freak and I am not normal." He had heard all that many times. The tears reappeared, "Am I crazy?"

"You are not crazy Lisa. But we need to work together Lisa, all of us."

Jamison made copies of the two tapes to send to his uncles for dream interpretation. He needed to make a call so that they would know about her new condition of sleepwalking in addition to the vividness of these new dreams. He already notified them of her fall and injury, since they would have wanted to know. They had almost as intimate relationship with Lisa as he did, since they listened to and analyzed her dreams. He made the call.

"Laddie we knew you were about to call. It be about the lass?"

"Yes, Uncle Glen; Two tapes are on the way. Is Father Ryan there?"

"No, he is about."

"I sent notes with the tapes. Both of her dreams were again from Gospel stories." Jamison didn't want to say it as he knew they would both say they told him so. However, he did. "Uncle Glen, she experienced sleep walking in these last two dreams. In the first she was in a boat in a storm."

"Yes, Uncle, it was with Jesus. When the dream was over she said she was soaking wet. My first theory is that the dream continued and she dreamed she woke and found herself soaking wet. The other theory is sleepwalking, that she stood in the shower with her clothes on and got wet; perhaps to add reality to a dream that seemed real."

"Did anyone see her in this condition?"

"She said not."

"The other dream she was fleeing Roman soldiers and fell down a cliff; again sleepwalking. The actual fall I already told you about two weeks ago."

"We thought no one could see her in her dreams?"

"She thought they were after the dog, the same dog she dreamed about in the storm. In both of these instances she may have felt danger, though she told me she did not. And in both she was attempting to rescue this dog."

"The dog in her other dreams?"

"Yes."

"How is she now?"

"Her leg is in a cast, she has had no more sleep episodes in the weeks since those occurred."

"Sleepwalking sometimes may verge on the paranormal Branden."

He chuckled. "I knew you would say that Uncle Glen."

"Our minds can take us to strange places."

Then both uncles spoke together as one, "This is serious, she is in real danger."

He nodded in agreement, even though they couldn't see the nod. "We can talk after you get the tapes."

Chapter 8

"Truth is stranger than fiction, but it is because Fiction is obliged to stick to possibilities; Truth isn't." [MARK TWAIN, *Following the Equator: A Journey Around the World*]

LISA WAS NERVOUS for her first day back at school. She knew everyone would ask, 'How did you break your leg?' Then she would have to say, 'Fell off a cliff.' They would say, 'How did you do that?' She would say, 'Sleep walking because I am a freak!' Of course, she would not say that, just felt like it. Her actual response was, "I accidentally got off the trail and fell."

Ginny picked her up from school early for the meeting with her parents, and the medical team, and Jamison. She could now use crutches and get around better than the wheelchair, but she thought the wheelchair had been fun. When they got there she found it was only her parents, Doctor Aubry, and obviously Jamison, for the meeting. Ginny led her to where her parents and Jamison were already seated on the small sofas. She sat next to Jamison and Ginny sat by her mother and father.

Jamison began the meeting as he turned to Lisa. "Lisa you know all of us, including yourself, have concerns about what happened last month with your accident. You realize we need to find a plan to protect you."

Lisa did not react, just nodded her head. She felt she knew her parents would not let them lock her up. She had that much confidence in their love. But didn't know what the protection plan would be. She felt scared.

He continued, "Your parents and I and several consultants have an idea that we would like to try. You are fifteen and don't need someone watching you all the time."

She let out a soft sigh of relief but didn't say anything.

"Our concern is that sometimes you are not aware of the beginning of an incident and don't set your timer. The timer has been working very well so far."

She finally responded with a nod.

"The plan is to get you a service dog, one trained to keep you out of danger and wake you if you didn't have opportunity to set your timer."

Lisa opened her mouth to say something. Jamison slightly raised his hand, which was a signal he sometimes used to keep her outburst under control. Lisa felt like shouting at him, 'what, make me even more of a freak than I am?' She didn't.

He went on. "The dog will be well trained. Lisa, you and I will work together to teach it a certain bark that will wake you, just as the beep from your timer does. Only you will not need to set it. The dog will recognize if you fall asleep, and know to give the bark signal for you."

145

Lisa scowled. Then Jamison added, "The dog will not go to school with you, but will be with you other times."

Lisa's father spoke up, "We did tell Doctor Jamison that you didn't especially like dogs, but he thought perhaps you are older now and it might work."

Lisa realized that again Doctor Jamison knew more than her parents, he knew about Gideon. She sat quietly and didn't make any objections. She decided after a few weeks she could tell them the dog was a bad idea and to come up with another one.

There was more discussion about the training needed. Her parents agreed that a dog would not be a problem in their household, and thanked Doctor Jamison for working with all of them. Lisa was going to let Jamison have it as soon as they were alone together. No one had included her in the dog planning. Then her parents had the affront to say they already had a meeting scheduled with an organization that trained service and companion dogs. These were generally fostered with families so they would be used to family life. The plan was to meet the first dog candidate on Saturday with the understanding if they didn't get along, they could try another dog.

———

Saturday morning was a bright sunny day for November, two days before Thanksgiving. Lisa hobbled to the car on her crutches. She was healing quickly and would be free of them next week and have something called a walking cast, and begin physical therapy. Her shoulder was fine now. Her parents let Josh come with them, so they picked him up on the way.

A Mister Wallace answered the door and introduced them to his wife and son, George, who had trained the dog. George explained about the program and told them the dog was two years old, very obedient, loving and intelligent. After about half an hour of conversation, he went to another room to bring the dog out.

Lisa was in shock as soon as she saw the dog, who immediately walked to her, sat at her feet, and looked up at her. George must have noticed the shocked look on her face. "This is a Canaan dog, it is a very old breed from Israel, very smart and a loving dog."

Lisa smiled and patted the dog on the head. He looked exactly like Gideon from her experiences in Gospel stories, only a little larger.

George added, "His name is Gideon."

When Gideon looked at her in what she considered his big tender doggie eyes, she knew he had her heart and soul in that moment.

George said, "I think he honestly likes you Lisa, he went straight to you with four new people here in the room. He generally goes first to my dad."

Lisa wasn't sure if Doctor Jamison had not somehow mentioned she might like a Canaan dog. She knew he would not have revealed her experiences. And Gideon might be a normal name for a Canaan dog, maybe.

They would get Gideon the second week of December when George was out of school and could work with the family to integrate him into their lifestyle. George was attending the State College, about a two-hour drive. He said he could work with the family to learn the commands Gideon knew so he would have consistency in obeying his new family. He said Gideon could heel without a leash, but as a service dog should always wear it outside of their home. At home he didn't need the service vest or leash.

When Gideon arrived at their home, he quickly became Lisa's best friend. Needless to say, she still liked Josh and Jane and others. Gideon slept on her bed, which her mom didn't approve. Ginny liked him.

Lisa had another week of school before her Christmas break. Ginny told her that Gideon seemed restless whenever Lisa was out of the house. Because she was still in a cast, George came over every evening and on Saturday's and Sunday's to walk him even though both of her parents and Ginny said they would love to do that.

Her parents suggested that George was attached to Gideon and wanted to keep in contact. She thought she understood that and tried to make him feel welcome. Then again she thought George was very good looking, and very nice, even though he was nearly five years older than she.

The holidays were usually busy for the Longford family. The Dean gave two formal parties, a formal dinner and then a formal cocktail party for all those not invited to the dinner party. Ginny and Florence had everything planned months in advance with the caterers and the florist. They catered with a local bar to manage the drinks for the formal cocktail affair. They expected both Ginny and Lisa to assist them as hostess, and leave serving the food and drinks to the catering staff. Most of the guests were from the University, but also included some non-university friends of her parents. Lisa knew Jamison had been invited, but declined as he would again be in Ireland for six weeks during the holiday season.

Lisa was proud of the new family member, Gideon. She was also in a quandary since George insisted on stopping by to walk Gideon twice a day. She couldn't walk with them yet, but realized she greatly enjoyed George's visits with her. However, Josh, who also had more time for her during the holidays seemed out of sorts when George was around.

Several days before the evening cocktail affair her father joined Lisa and George's chat after Gideon's walk. Lisa noticed her father always seemed to spend a few minutes talking with George if he was around. Once he even told her he rather liked George. She thought that was a strange comment, especially since he never had such a compliment for Josh.

That Wednesday, as George was getting ready to leave, her father asked him, "We are having a little party on Friday, would like it if you could join us."

George replied, "Thank you Mr. Longford, I am free and would like that."

Lisa's father smiled, shook his hand and headed for his study.

Lisa knew she had to say something to him, but what? "George, I would love to have you come." Then what, she summoned the courage. "It is kind of formal. Men will be in suits, well at least slacks and jackets. Kind of the way the University culture is."

George grinned at her, "Great, I have a suit I haven't worn since my cousin's wedding."

Lisa didn't want George to feel out of place, but didn't want to discourage him either. After all her father liked him and had invited him. She knew he wasn't quite twenty-one. She was about to mention that it was mostly drinking and obviously rather good food, decided George probably could guess that when she had mentioned University culture. After all he was going to the State University. She didn't say anything.

George stooped and patted Gideon, even allowing a dog kiss on his chin. "I will see you tomorrow Lisa. Oh, what time is the party on Friday?"

"It starts at seven." She watched him walk to his car just as Josh drove up. Josh had gotten his license several weeks ago, and even got a car to go with it.

Josh waved at George and gave Lisa a quick kiss as he went in the house with her. She knew George had seen it and wondered why that made her uncomfortable. When the door was closed, he pulled her into his arms and gave her a longer more intimate kiss. Lisa sighed to herself and pushed the uncomfortable thoughts out of her mind. Josh was her guy and she... She stopped the thoughts, now wasn't the time to be thinking about their relationship.

They went into the Library and sat on the smaller sofa. Josh began with kind solicitations about her healing leg. "How are you doing Lisa? Still get the cast off next week?"

"Yep, I can't wait. Well, I think I get it off. They will do an X-ray and if all is good, then it goes."

Josh pulled her a little closer to him and kissed her neck. Gideon lay at her feet. He talked a little about some of their friends, and what they all were doing. Several of them were going skiing and sorry she couldn't come with them. Then he brought up the subject he had last week. The one she couldn't answer. Jamison told her before he left for Ireland, to use her mind as well as her heart; and to think about what 'commitment' Josh wanted.

Josh again proffered the little box with the heart necklace he had used when he asked Lisa for a commitment, to be his girl. She told him then she needed to think about it. Lisa looked at his pleading eyes; they were almost as effective as Gideon's. She took the box in her hand. "Josh, when you say commitment. What does that mean?"

He looked serious and hesitated, "I think it means you won't be going out with others, just me." He gave her a shy smile. "It means that I won't be going out with other girls, only you."

Lisa silently cursed Jamison for telling her to use her head as well as her heart. Her heart said yes to Josh. Her head wanted to pursue the idea of commitment, to talk about it. She knew it did not necessarily involve the word 'love.' That was a word that was as serious and heavy as a rock, and also as light as air in a balloon. Love could lead to the 'I do' forever type vows, or could describe a feeling for ice cream. And 'like' didn't really need a commitment. Her hesitation seemed to make Josh uncomfortable. Last week Lisa thought it would have been nice if Josh had simply given her the gift without strings, strings of commitment. Commitment had to do with the future, to sharing. Lisa was not ready to share her secret with Josh.

"Sorry Josh, I don't want to go out with anyone but you. You must know that. To me the word 'commitment' means something more serious than I am ready for. To me it is getting close to serious intent that I don't think you or I are ready to make." She desperately hoped he would not use the vague word 'love' on her.

He surprised her with, "Maybe you are right Lisa. Still will you accept the necklace as a gift with no strings attached?"

Lisa smiled, then pushed Josh onto the sofa and kissed him long and hard and he responded passionately. Their passionate embraces and kissing was interrupted by Gideon's whine and barking.

Lisa crawled off Josh and tried to straighten her sweater and smooth her hair. Just then she heard, then saw Ginny at the door with a tray. Lisa felt like she looked guilty, but didn't realize she had another look, one of pleasure.

Ginny had a plate of cookies and two cups of coffee on a tray. She sat it down and said, "What is with Gideon? Is he okay?"

Lisa shrugged.

Ginny left with a curious smile. "Enjoy the cookies and coffee."

Josh and Lisa looked at each other, then laughed at Ginny's retreating back. Lisa gave Josh another kiss and whispered, "That was a close one." She wondered how people could feel like she did, and hoped Josh did, and not use that heavy word 'love.' She felt like she should apologize.

"Sorry Josh, it was my fault for attacking you. I think the guy always gets the blame."

He laughed, "Not like I wasn't big enough to fight off a cripple like you. Sorry, did I hurt your leg?"

She shook her head. He picked up the little box and opened it and his eyes asked and she nodded her head. He took the little heart on the chain and fastened it around her and kissed the back of her neck.

Lisa wanted to get back to the kissing and snuggling, but somehow knew she should not. When Jamison told her to depend on her mind, not emotions; she wondered what he knew about the emotions created with the touches and kisses. Would she feel the same with the kisses of someone other than Josh? George suddenly came to her mind and she quickly shoved the thought out.

Ginny came back with a dog biscuit for Gideon, before either of them could have gone back to what they had been doing. Lisa felt awkward. She stood. "Look Ginny, the early Christmas present Josh gave me." She held the heart out for Ginny's inspection.

They ate the cookies and drank the coffee with somewhat embarrassed glances between them. Somehow both knew something had happened that drew them closer to each other. However, Lisa knew it was not commitment.

———

Jamison was quite pleased that Lisa had no incidents the six weeks he had been in Ireland. He had expected as much. When she was occupied and reading less, she tended to have fewer sleep episodes. Today they would resume her hypnotherapy sessions and begin training her service dog. His only concern was that the dog would have been with the family over a month now and it would be difficult to replace it for another if the training was not successful. Lisa and the dog's trainer George talked with him a couple of weeks ago by phone, and reported that he was already doing well at giving a special or different warning bark, as service dogs learned to do. They agreed that the next step would be to teach it the idea of danger if she appeared to be asleep with her head down on a book or table.

He heard a knock on the office door and realized he had forgotten to unlock it. He opened the door for Lisa and a medium sized dog.

"Good afternoon Jamison, please meet Gideon." She made the appropriate signals and Gideon sat at her feet and raised a paw toward Jamison.

He felt awkward but as expected reached down and took the dog's paw. He recognized the unique breed. The dog was a Canaan dog. He looked up at Lisa. The cast was gone and instead she had on a large black boot type thing. "You are looking very well, and are walking again."

"Yep, this..." she pointed to the boot, "is a walking boot. It can be removed, so no cast at night. But I need to wear it for a few more weeks. She hobbled to the large red chair with the dog following close at her heels. She unfastened the boot thing and put her feet up on the ottoman. The dog set next to the chair.

Jamison pulled his usual chair up to them. They started with the usual small talk. He wanted to know about how she had selected the dog, but thought he knew why the name Gideon. Lisa wanted to know about his time in Ireland and had much to tell him about getting rid of the cast and the holidays and that Ginny was now dating the owner of the landscape service that did their yard. He was glad they scheduled a long session.

"Now Lisa, I do want to know about how the training of Gideon is doing, but first tell me how you selected this particular dog."

"We got Gideon from the Medical Service Dog Referral Agency. It was all so very simple. As you know, Doctor Aubry contacted them and put in the request based on what he referred to as the consultation agreement. Two days later the agency called us and said we were extremely lucky as a dog that fit the request was available now. We got him Friday after Thanksgiving, and you left that weekend. The trainer, George, suggested we keep his name, Gideon, as it would be easier; but we could change it if we liked as he is a very smart dog." She grinned at him as she finished, and reached down and patted Gideon's head.

"I know you and George talked about what George is to do with the training. Do you like George?"

"Yes, he sounded like he understood what we needed. You were very fortunate. It often takes many months to match a dog with a patient." He hesitated a little, but had to ask the question. "Did you have any input in selecting this particular dog breed?"

Lisa laughed, "I knew that would be a shock to you Jamison. I should have told you a month ago that he was a Canaan dog, and that his name was already Gideon. You just wouldn't believe what a shock it was to me to see this dog that looked like the Gideon in my adventures, Andrew's Gideon. And then even more when George told me his name. Sorry Jamison it was too much of coincidence, and I could have told you, but I wanted you to get to experience the same shock I did — a little anyway."

Jamison was not used to dogs. The only dogs he knew were from the village in Ireland. There were a few of these that lived from house to house and were welcomed and fed and found a bed wherever they ended up that day.

"We will need more frequent sessions. One hypnotherapy session for the dog's bark as a signal, and a separate one for our usual beeper signal."

Lisa interrupted. "His name is Gideon not 'the dog.'"

Jamison shook his head, "Yes, all right, Gideon."

Gideon looked up at Jamison when he heard his name spoken.

"I understand George is back at school. I will check with him to get a demonstration of the training he has already done for you on a Saturday that he might be in town."

"He is in town most weekends. His school is only a two-hour drive, so he says it is quite easy. He spent a lot of time over the holidays with us." She looked down at Gideon. "Since I couldn't do it, he walked Gideon every day."

"Who is doing that now?"

"Mostly Ginny, and now sometimes me; he can do his business in the yard since it has a good fence. But he needs his exercise to be happy. I think George is attached to Gideon; that is why he wishes to spend time with him."

Jamison noticed Lisa slightly blushed when she mentioned George. Unless something was wrong with George he could not help but be attracted to the beautiful Lisa. He asked, "Do you think George may be wishing to spend time with you?"

Lisa looked down at the dog. "I don't know. Gideon is such a dear. I don't think I could stand to part from him and I have only had him a little over a month. But Josh might think that. We almost quarreled over it. Well, I almost did. Then things got better between us."

Lisa seemed to look embarrassed. "Jamison, Josh and I have kissed. Nice kisses. But just before Christmas we almost had a quarrel, and then he was so sweet and we made up and were much more intimate in what we were doing and Ginny came in." She stopped because Jamison's normal 'I'm listening' face grew solemn. "Oh, we weren't doing that, not sex. But Jamison I think I wanted to right then at that moment."

She looked down at her hands. "I think Ginny can read minds. Now she watches Josh and me more closely, and I know it was her back then, who put the idea into my parents' head to remind me I couldn't really date, meaning be alone with a boy, until I was older. I think some high school girls do it. But I won't, so don't worry about me Jamison."

He knew someday they would need the sex talk and had expected it much sooner. Lisa was a beautiful girl nearly sixteen, who could probably pass as twenty. He tried to prevent it by talking about love and passion and other emotional things compared to thought and reason in some of their occasional philosophical discussions. He had no doubts about how a seventeen-year-old boy would or could respond to her. But he also knew Lisa well, she was strong and knew herself and respected herself. Those qualities would help her in most situations.

Lisa went on, "I think our relationship changed after that, um, almost experience. We are closer now." She looked at him, then smiled, "We didn't do it Jamison."

They talked about other things for a few more minutes while Lisa put the awkward boot back on and prepared to leave. Ginny arrived and collected her two charges, Lisa and Gideon.

Jamison prepared his notes for her two files. In the hypnotherapy file he noted she had no sleep incidents for three months. He also noted her reading had decreased and that her social life had increased, without many details. He knew they would interpret it that she was better. Maybe she was and maybe growing up and becoming a normal teenager was the cure for the sleep disorder. Now she would only have the issues of any other teenage girl — boys and sex.

The next Saturday Jamison met George at Lisa's house to observe Gideon's training.

George explained, "We train protective dogs like Gideon to bark or perform certain actions if their owner is in distress or trouble. Gideon was designated, even before coming to Lisa, to bark if he saw his person slumped in a helpless position. That is a common thing we do for medical companion dogs. Dogs are more observant and can sense something is wrong with someone they know well, even better when trained. Lisa and I only needed a few sessions to get Gideon to bark when he saw her sleeping, not just slumped over."

Lisa seemed excited to show off Gideon to him. She added, "We even are working with him so he doesn't bark when I go to sleep in bed at night."

Jamison asked, "You expect him to sleep in your room at night?"

Lisa gave him one of her large sparkling smiles. "Of course, he will be in my room." He heard a whisper, "On my bed."

George added. "We are still working on that one. I think Gideon is smart enough to know the difference."

Jamison asked, "Will he do this, his response, if other people are around?"

George responded, "We want our dogs to be that closely related to their owners and trainers. Often people are not observant, or might not say anything if they see, say an elderly person slumped. They might think they had simply fallen asleep and not express concern. They would if the dog was concerned and barking. We train the dog especially to perform when the situation is not normal, even when many other people are around. Most dogs are pretty smart, and Gideon is especially so."

Jamison was again impressed with George's dedication and thought it might be that dedication and not Lisa that kept him frequenting the Longfords. George told him that he had been training dogs since he was a kid, and began volunteering with the medical dogs since he was a fourteen. He once told him a well-trained dog could do its 'stuff' alone, without its trainer putting it through its moves. Trainers for dog shows had it easy as they were always present, giving the clues.

Lisa and Gideon went into the library for a few minutes before George and Jamison were to come in, hopefully at Gideon's barking. They heard three sharp barks, silence, three more, silence, then three more barks. They came in and found Lisa slumped over a book on the desk. After a moment Gideon barked again, and she sat up and praised and loved on him and gave him a treat.

They went over the exercise several more times and Gideon responded as he had been trained every time. All of this seemed to be new for Jamison, until he realized he had been training Lisa's subconscious to respond to a stimulus, just as George had been training Gideon. His next concern was over stimulation. "Does Gideon bark very often?"

"No!" Lisa and George responded in unison.

"Why?" George asked.

"We want Lisa to wake." He looked at her slight frown but knew now was not the time to change language. "The signal needs to be unique. My concern was if he barked often, the signal might not work."

George had a huge grin on his face. "Gideon has his own language of barks. I taught him one to say he wanted fed; in the event I might be late at it. That bark is very different from one for safety, which all guard or companion dogs learn if they sense danger. Then to make sure, we trained him to use the S.O.S. bark sequence of three short ones with spacing. Like I said Gideon is an especially clever dog."

Jamison noticed George had frequently used the term 'we' for Gideon's training, but did not ask if it was we the institute or we George and Lisa.

Jamison procured one of the best recording devices to ensure he had Gideon's right tone, as George called it. George and Lisa were to make the recordings a number of times so he would have an accurate one to use in Lisa's hypnotherapy as the signal to wake up when she heard it. He often shared any new ideas or breakthroughs in his specialized field of hypnotherapy, but he was not going to suggest a dog bark as one of these, at least not now.

Since it had taken months, almost a year for his efforts to work for Lisa with her wrist signal, he wondered how long it would take to get Gideon to wake her. He had tried to put verbal commands such as 'wake up' and hand claps into her hypnotherapy. Instead he limited the signal to the beeping on her watch, which anyone who knew her could use by pushing the button to signal Lisa to wake. She had told Jane about it. Once Jane was with her and when she realized what was happening was able to get her awake in a few minutes.

Chapter 9

"With regard to sleep and waking, we must consider what they are: whether they are peculiar to soul or to body, or common to both; and if common, to what part of soul or body they appertain: further, from what cause it arises that they are attributes of animals, and whether all animals share in them both, or some partake of the one only, others of the other only, or some partake of neither and some of both." [ARISTOTLE, *On Sleep and Sleeplessness*]

IT WAS THE first of February and Jamison decided the Gideon training was going well. For the last three weeks Jamison worked with Lisa to wake, or as she insisted, to come back when she heard Gideon's bark. Gideon as usual was with her during all of their sessions. He had clearly puzzled look when he heard the recording of his bark. He did nothing. He was praised every time, even though the sound was from the recording and not directly from him. Lisa told Jamison she had been testing him at home several times a week by feigning sleep over a book. She proudly stated that Gideon always responded with the bark intended to bring her back out of the book.

Lisa was there for her session for setting her wrist timer when and if she felt she might be starting an incident. They did the normal catch up, but this was taking less time with weekly meetings rather than the three-week gap from before.

She handed him her reading list from the prior week.

He commented as he quickly scanned it, "List is a bit longer."

"I think we, Gideon and me, and the family, are settling into a routine, which gives me more reading time. And school has been a bit lighter this term." He looked more closely at list. The word Bible was included but no details. He wanted details, especially of what she was reading in the Bible. "No reading of Gospels?"

"I am reading them. Right now I am very interested in the parables, those are stories Jesus told as a way of teaching people. Have you read the parables?"

He answered, "Yes." He began reading the Bible since Lisa's first dream in the Gospel stories.

"They aren't stories of something that really happened, they are illustrations Jesus made to get a message across. That's what I think."

They talked a little about a few of the parables she was intrigued with. He was surprised at her understanding, especially since some of them were rather radical for both then and now.

Lisa gulped and said, "Jamison I want to tell Josh my secret about what is really happening with me. I wanted to talk to you about it before I did that."

"I thought he knew about your sleep disorder."

"I mean the truth, that I am really there in the story. I want him to know I was there and saw Jesus."

He was surprised, "What if he doesn't look at your experiences like you do? That could have an effect on your relationship."

"Our relationship is what I want to have affected. If Josh cares about me, he will believe me. Not everyone is like you Doctor Jamison, some people accept things on faith and don't need scientific proof."

"You did not answer my question."

"I have been thinking about it a lot. I want Josh and me to be honest together, so we can be close."

"Lisa, I didn't say not to tell him, although I think it is not advisable. Remember, you don't share your dreams with your mother and father or Ginny. You are close with all of them."

"I told them when I was young, they didn't believe me then. If I told them now, they would know I'm a freak kid. They would think I was crazy." She sighed, "Then they would want to know what you think, and they would believe you and not me—they would agree with you that my dreams get distracted and go into the part of my brain where memories go and that I remember things that didn't really happen. But isn't that being crazy. People who think they are Queen Elizabeth or George Washington or whatever?"

"You are not crazy Lisa. I get paid to diagnose if someone is. You know who you are and understand truth and reality. Most people do experience false memories at some time. That is a reality. I loaned you that book."

She interrupted him. "I know the one about memory and experiments in creating false memories." She shook her head. "So, tell him?"

"You probably already know his response. I don't think you will be surprised by how he takes it." He paused and looked at her. "And I am fairly certain you will be disappointed."

"Relationships need trust Jamison; like we have, you and me. Trust even if we don't agree on stuff."

She reached down and patted Gideon. "And trust, like Gideon and I have."

———

Lisa decided to tell Josh her secret the next day. She wanted an open and trusting relationship with Josh. If nothing else, Jamison had taught her trust was important for relationships. She thought Josh would need to know her secret and trust her if they were to build a close and intimate relationship. Jamison said it was a mistake to tell, no he used the words "not advisable" to tell Josh about going into books. She had not shared her secret with her parents and Ginny because she knew they would be on Jamison's side. That was why she never told them. She shared everything with Jamison, all of her heart and feelings and opinions; and still he cared about her. Cared very much.

Although she saw Josh often enough at church and at school, they didn't have much alone time. Last week she invited him to dinner so she could tell him, if Jamison approved. She was going to, even though Jamison implied she should not. That was one of Jamison's faults, that he wouldn't tell her what to do but made her to decide and be responsible.

The family had an early dinner since the Dean had to go to a meeting. Ginny left to watch a football game with Walt. A few minutes later Florence left after a call from a student who asked for help with their study group. Lisa and Josh were left alone in the library.

They curled up on the sofa in the library with Gideon at their feet. Lisa found that Gideon was getting more protective every day and often tried to sit between her and Josh. He began the conversation after she had delayed with small talk and school gossip. "You said you had something special to talk to me about Lisa. Was it about the commitment idea?"

"No, I thought we had a good understanding about that."

Josh smiled and put his arm around her and gave her a long kiss.

She didn't know where to begin. Maybe it was a bad idea. Maybe she should relax into Josh's strong arms, let him hold and kiss her as he was starting to do. She thought it might be wonderful to feel as good as the time when he was touching her breasts and kissing and holding her just before Christmas. She had been embarrassed when Jane explained in detail what they meant in their slang of getting to first base or third base in the sexual realm. Lisa was even brave enough to share that experience with her. Jane said that was a second base, going toward third and that Lisa better look out and not let Josh get to home plate. Jane shared her own experience and told Lisa it wasn't fair to let a boy get past first base because they didn't have much control. She was silently thankful for Jamison and Jane. She responded to Josh's kissing and kept it at first base. She was not concerned about Josh lacking control, but about herself and the way he made her feel.

She gently moved away. "Josh I need to tell you something important about myself." She relaxed when he let her go and moved slightly apart. She thought he was wonderful in his respect for her. She was now sure he would understand her and believe her. She stared into his golden-brown eyes and began, "Josh, please keep what I am telling you between ourselves."

He nodded.

"You know I see a psychiatrist regularly."

"Yes, for the hypnosis to help you wake up from your sleep episodes."

"Right, I see Doctor Jamison for hypnotherapy, the hypnosis session. We talk about everything. He knows more about me than anyone, even my parents."

"So he knows about me and stuff?"

She laughed, "What stuff?" She was not going to tell him that Jamison did know about the intimacy Ginny broke up that day in the library. Or that she told him, like not every time, but did tell him they kissed whenever they had a chance, and that the kisses were quite wonderful, in her opinion. She thought Jamison seemed uncomfortable when she did, maybe because they were soulmates, even though he would never acknowledge it. She didn't want Josh to be a soulmate; she didn't think one could have more than one soulmate.

Lisa went on, "The only time I need this is that sometimes when I am reading a book people can't wake me." She held up her wrist to show him her medical bracelet with the epilepsy symbol. "Doctor Jamison and I have been written up in several psychiatric and medical journals for his work with me with hypnosis that allows me to set this." She held up her other wrist with her watch and timer on it. "I never have this experience except when I have a book in front of me and have been reading."

"Okay, but you explained this to Jane and me and others; like at the beginning of school."

This was going to be hard but she wanted Josh to know, to care about her, to trust her. "Josh, sometimes when I am reading I actually go into the book, into the story I am reading. That is why people can't wake me, because I am there and not here."

Lisa immediately saw a look in Josh's eyes that she interpreted as doubt or puzzlement. "What does that mean Lisa?"

"I go someplace; maybe to another dimension. I walk around and listen to the talk of minor characters, and some characters not even in the written story. I love going into stories with large mansions that I can wander through and I listen to the servants talk about the characters in the book."

She thought Josh was sort of trying. "What kinds of books?"

Judith DeVilliers

"Mostly novels, sometimes a history book if interesting; but more recently I have been there in the Gospels, in the stories in the Gospels."

He frowned, then gave a slight smile and his eyes lit up as if he suddenly understood.

"You have these dreams and can't wake up, right?"

"Not dreams, the experiences are real Josh."

He shook his head. "Come on Lisa, are you trying to make a joke?"

"It is real Josh."

Although he moved again only slightly, Lisa felt it as the beginning of a separation. She did not like the feeling.

"What does this doctor, who you tell everything, think about this?"

She didn't want to tell him Jamison's viewpoint, but did. "He claims that my brain takes the dream and channels it to the memory part of my brain so that the dream is a false memory. He says people can occasionally have false memories of something that never happened to them. For me the dreams are the same as real memories."

She felt Josh's body relax. "Oh, and that is why you think that it actually happened."

Lisa felt trapped. Jamison's trap had been set, his logical trap that she wasn't crazy; just had this brain disorder.

Josh put his arm around her for a hug. She pulled away. "You don't believe me."

"What?"

"Josh I was there. I have gone into Gospel stories and

170

seen Jesus and Peter and Andrew. I have tasted their food and been in a boat on the Sea of Galilee."

Lisa thought his smile of understanding was simply too much. She shook his arm off, stood up, and repeated. "You don't believe I was really there."

Lisa saw the bewildering look again when he responded. "I understand that you do, you believe."

"I saw Jesus and, and..." She spluttered.

Josh stood. "Lisa, I don't know what to think. What do you want me to think?"

"Believe I was there."

"Like in a vision?"

She shook her head and slumped back on the sofa feeling tears pushing their way up. She turned her head. She didn't want to cry in front of Josh.

"I better go Lisa. Can we talk about this later?"

She stood and let him put his arm around her waist and walk with her to the door. He kissed her on the forehead. "I want to. I do believe you Lisa." He walked out into the night.

Lisa stood at the open door. She knew he believed Jamison not her. The tears trickled down. Gideon snuggled next to her leg and looked up. She looked down and him and felt sure the dog had love in his eyes. Gideon knew about love and trust.

Lisa was relieved that Josh acted like nothing had changed between them at school the rest of the week. Except she thought he showed a little more affection, little things like holding her hand and putting his arm around her shoulder a couple of times when they were walking together. It felt odd to her. But she decided that was all in her head due to the distance she felt because she thought he didn't trust her to be telling the truth. Finally on Friday Lisa confronted him.

"Josh, about what we talked about Tuesday?"

He shuffled his feet and took both her hands. "Thanks for sharing with me. I know it was probably hard."

"Do you want to know more about my experiences?"

"Sure, Sunday afternoon? May I come over?"

Lisa nodded and they walked to the street where Ginny and Gideon were waiting for them. Sometimes she also drove Josh home even though it was out of the way. Today he had a Year-Book planning meeting and had to run. He gave her a cheek peck.

Ginny grinned at her as she got in beside her. "Kisses now, eh?"

Lisa was surprised. She thought for sure Ginny had seen them together back then before Christmas. She wasn't going to bring it up. Instead she said. "That wasn't a kiss. That's what I call a kiss that almost misses the target. The kind aunts and uncles give."

"Looked like one to me girl."

Lisa wrinkled her nose up at her. "Do you know if we have plans for Sunday?"

"Football for me, and you dear?"

"Josh wants to come over Sunday afternoon."

"Homework?"

"No, we kind of had a little misunderstanding Tuesday. We are okay now, but need to talk."

"Do you want to ask him to dinner again? We should all be home Sunday."

"No, not really."

Ginny gave her a concerned look, then added. "Remember your parents have a funeral out of town Saturday and will be gone most of the day. You and Gideon will be on your own when I go to my garden club in the morning."

"What does a garden club talk about in February?"

"Gardens." Ginny laughed, "We share seed catalogs, not real ones like in the old days, but websites for our favorite nurseries and seed and plant distributors. In the winter only six or seven of us show up, come spring we have twenty or more at our meetings."

Lisa knew one of the six or seven was Walt, but knew better than to mention him to Ginny who seemed to protest too much when any relationship was hinted at. She was sure love was the reason.

Lisa sighed to herself and looked in the back seat at Gideon who had his big brown doggie eyes on her. She reached back and he licked her hand. She knew Gideon loved her and knew he certainly would believe her if she could talk to him.

Ginny changed the subject from the garden club. "How was school? Get through the Biology?"

"It was okay. I like Biology, but don't know why we have to memorize so much stuff. We can look it up if we need to know the plant classes. I don't know why memorizing lists just to take a test to show you have a good memory is education?"

Ginny just shrugged her shoulders. "Lisa did you remember George is coming Saturday afternoon?"

"I did forget. I guess my mind was on Josh."

Ginny suggested, "So training memory might not be such a bad idea."

Lisa gave her a look and gently thumped her on the shoulder. She appreciated that Ginny never asked questions about things. Probably because she knew Lisa would tell her sooner or later. This time Ginny had comments. "I think Gideon is already trained. He woke you up when you fell asleep over your Biology homework a couple of days ago."

Lisa didn't comment.

Ginny went on, "George's school is two hours away; but he stops by almost every weekend. I'm not so sure that George comes to train Gideon."

Lisa looked back at Gideon. "I think he is attached to Gideon; he is such a loving dog. I am sure he misses him. Sometimes I feel guilty for taking him. But not enough to give him up."

Ginny chuckled, "I think Josh is a little jealous."

"Why would you think that? Of course not; after all he knows why George comes by."

Ginny turned and looked at her, "Maybe, maybe."

The George discussion resulted in them making it home without any discussion about the slight misunderstanding with Josh. Lisa shared almost everything with Ginny, since she was a baby, everything except her great secret. Lisa remembered once Jamison suggested she tell her family that she had these vivid dreams when experiencing one of her sleep episodes. She told him she couldn't do that because it was not the truth, not reality. Truth and reality was something they talked about often, even though disagreeing.

———

That Saturday morning Lisa found her family making breakfast. Her father was monitoring the sausages in one skillet and eggs in another; her mom was in charge of the waffle iron; and Ginny was filling the table with bottles of syrup, jars of jam and compotes, apple sauce, and several small bowls of fresh fruit. Ginny greeted her, "Just in time dear, would you please put plates on the table and pour coffee?"

"Good morning to you too."

The three turned to her, then back to what they were doing.

Lisa knew she should say sorry, she didn't. "When do you leave Mom?"

Her mother brought a plate stacked high with at least six or seven waffles. "About ten I think. Right Richard?"

He placed a bowl of sausages and platter of scrambled eggs on the table, and sat down. "That should work. Thanks Ginny, for the wonderful breakfast."

Ginny laughed.

Lisa poured each a cup of coffee and sat with them. Gideon was on his bed in the corner. He was never given table food, but that didn't prevent his nose from twitching at the aroma of the sausages.

Her parents talked about why they felt obligated to attend the funeral of someone they didn't know all that well, a University thing. They expected the roads would be clear and were thankful snow was not expected until the middle of the week.

Lisa wasn't feeling hungry but knew she would be questioned if she didn't make an attempt at the bounty before her. She surprised herself with a second waffle topped with sliced strawberries. Her family did not say grace at meals, except Thanksgiving and other special occasions. She thought today thanks should go to the farmers in Mexico who grew the strawberries, and the truck drivers who drove them across the country to their supermarket, and Ginny for slicing them. Oh, and to thank God for all.

Before they all finished Ginny reached in one of the drawers and pulled out a stack of envelopes, "Valentines!" she cheered. The family tradition was they all had to wait until the morning of the fourteenth to open any suspected valentine card. The four of them generally did a great job of selecting the right card for each other. This year Ginny had one extra card, one from Walt. Gideon only got two cards, one from Lisa and one from her father; the others apologized for forgetting him.

Lisa had cleanup duty since everyone else had a destination for the day. Before her parents left, they came into the kitchen, she thought looking rather elegant for a funeral. Her mom told her she had a gift for her in the library, kissed her good bye, and said they would be home before dark. Lisa grinned to herself; things weren't too bad and maybe she was over reacting with the Josh thing. Her mom never forgot the Valentine's gift. She knew it would be clothes of some kind, what else would her mother buy her.

As soon as they walked out the door, Ginny was back in the kitchen, also looking rather nice for a garden club meeting. She came back to retrieve a plate filled with a variety of heart shaped cookies she made the day before for the meeting. She told Lisa she would not be back until two or three since Walt was taking her to lunch after the meeting. Lisa sighed; everyone had a date but her.

Lisa finished the kitchen clean up and headed for the library. She tossed half a sausage to Gideon as he followed her out of the kitchen to the library. There she found a box with a pink bow; the gift from her mother. She knew it would contain clothes as her mother's gifts always did. She got books from her father, and jewelry from Ginny. She held up pink denim jeans complete with bling; and a white sweater. She grinned, her mom was getting better at the clothes shopping, especially since they went together more often now. At least this time she told her where her gift was hiding; she used to make Lisa search the house for the special mushy type gift. Lisa liked this one.

She was back down to the library a couple of hours later in the new outfit. Even if she didn't have somewhere to go, she could look great. She curled up on the sofa and let Gideon climb up beside her. She had the impression he had a guilty look on his face since he wasn't allowed if anyone was home. But he loved her and came up beside her because she asked him. She picked up her Bible to read. Gideon's head rested on her lap. She turned to Matthew and read a little. She thought it would be great if she could go to a story when she wanted instead of when it just happened to her. She read about Jesus going into the synagogue and healing a man with a withered hand. She read that one three times, wishing she could be there; and she was.

An hour later she found herself at home on the sofa in the library. Gideon had just jumped down to the floor and was whining. He bolted from the room. Lisa ran after him and watched him race up the stairs and back again in a few minutes. It seemed to her he had searched the house in a whirl; then came panting and stared up at her. She didn't blame him. He had been there in the story with her.

She pulled out her phone and sent Jamison a text. 'New adventure in Gospel story. Gideon went with me.' Even though it was Saturday, she was sure Jamison would respond. He did. This was the first one she had since her accident back in October. Again, as before, she thought she might have actually caused, and not prevented going into the Gospel story. Jamison thought she had control now. It seemed that perhaps she did; that was a problem.

———

Jamison paced his office trying to make sense of Lisa's most recent text message. Ever since she was twelve, she sent a text whenever she had a sleep episode. He was concerned since she had gone four months now with no episodes. He knew the therapy was working. He was thinking there may also have been some effect from the scare the last two events had on her. His theory was that her subconscious did have some control; he knew it did, that was why the hypnosis was effective. He was even halfway through preparing a final article to summarize and conclude the effectiveness of hypnosis for sleep disorders using Lisa's case.

His greatest concern, one he had for some time, was that Lisa did not wish to exercise control. She must accept the truth and reality about her dreams so she could give them up and live a normal life. And what did she mean Gideon was with her?

Lisa came in the office with Gideon. Ginny dropped them off and Lisa had walked him around the block before coming up. They were both a little damp from the rain. He took her coat, and gave Gideon the obligatory pat on the head. As usual, Lisa pulled off her shoes before making herself comfortable in the large red chair. Gideon sat at her feet. They talked about the usual things, her school and family and friends. She always asked about the uncles and he would give her news if any. Since they had been meeting weekly for Gideon's training since the first part of January, they had less conversation than when meeting every three weeks.

Jamison started the serious conversation. "Are you ready to tell me about your latest experience?" He still would not use the word adventure just as she would not use the word dream.

"It was Saturday morning, Valentine's Day. You got my text with the time. I was alone in the house as my parents were at a funeral out of town for the day. Ginny was at a garden club meeting, then a lunch date. When we are alone I let Gideon up on the sofa. This time he was quite close to me, my arm around him and he had his head on my lap as I was reading. Something was different this time Jamison. I know you will not be happy with me. I think I had a choice this time. Not a choice of if I should go into the story when it called to me. It was more than that. I was reading about Jesus miracle of healing a man with a withered hand. I thought to myself that I really did wish to see that and I wished I could be there. I purposefully read the part about that three times. Then I was there."

Jamison was more than disappointed; he was concerned. He thought to himself. Oh Lisa, Lisa, what are you doing? However, he said nothing. Lisa continued.

"I knew I was in Capernaum because I could see the lake from where I was standing, and I have been there before. There were quite a few people walking around. I looked for Jesus because he was always nearby. I saw him walking up the hill from the village. I recognized James and Peter and Andrew with him. There were a few others with him that I didn't know. I also recognized a few men as Pharisees since they dress a little differently. Jesus once pointed them out to me. Other more wealthier men wore more colorful clothing and sometimes of nicer weave, like linen instead of the more common wool. Everyone seemed to be headed toward the building I was near. I guessed the building was a synagogue since that is where this story takes place. Jesus walked directly to me and gave me the wonderful smile he always did. He said, 'Welcome back Lisa. Is all well with you?'

"I smiled at him and shrugged my shoulders. I could tell by the look of concern in his eyes that perhaps he knew about my disagreement with Josh. Maybe? Just then James walked over and took him by the arm and began leading him toward the synagogue. I followed close behind. When we got to the door he stopped and turned to me and said, 'You cannot come in here Lisa.' I asked him why. Jamison, he had this smirk on his face, really, he did, and he asked, 'are you a Jew?' then before I could open my mouth, he followed that with, 'I do not think so.' It was like he was being humorous. Now I can laugh at what he said, but then I wanted to go into the synagogue and see him heal a man with a withered hand since that was the story I was reading. I reminded him that no one could see me. He said he could and he was here to fulfill the laws not to break them. Then I told him if this is a dream, then I would not really be there. He asked me if that was what I really believed, then he went inside with James."

Lisa sighed and reached down and patted Gideon. "I sat on a wooden bench outside the building when a couple of women vacated it to go inside. I was happy when Gideon approached. When he got close I noticed he had on a red collar, with dog tags. I leaned over and petted him. It was not Andrew's Gideon, who generally smelled like fish. It was my Gideon with a collar who smelled clean and spicy. I realized my Gideon is also larger than Andrew's."

Jamison remained quiet and as usual tried not to show any reaction so she could focus on what she was saying. Comments and reaction of a listener usually have an effect of some kind on memory recall.

"Gideon had a very bewildered look on his face, almost fearful. I didn't blame him. He didn't have Jesus there to reassure him. I motioned for him to get up on the bench by me and I wrapped my arms around him. His body was very tense and I did wish he wasn't there as I didn't want any harm to come to him. And I didn't like seeing him frightened. I wondered if he had been near me all the time and I hadn't noticed, or if he had just arrived, or arrived a little away from me and just found me. We sat together and watched the children playing. Most looked to be five to ten years of age. They played together, boys and girls. One group was hitting a round stone with sticks, some form of hockey. Others were running around like kids do. They were surprisingly quiet with their games. I guess they knew what was inside and had learned to play quietly.

"It didn't seem long before I heard a commotion from inside and a group of people came out of the synagogue. They all looked very excited. I stood on the bench to see better. One man scooped up two little girls who ran to the group. He put the girls down and was waiving both of his arms above his head. I heard someone comment that it had been over ten years he had no use of it.

"Then Gideon and I were on the sofa. Gideon was still sitting very close to me. He licked my face, wagged his tail and climbed off the sofa. He seemed excited and ran in circles, then dashed out of the room, then in a few minutes back to the library. I sat on the floor and hugged him; I was so happy he was home safe with me. I think he was also happy to be home. Then after twenty minutes, I pulled myself together and sent you the text that I had an adventure."

Jamison turned the recorder off. "Interesting that Gideon did not wake you from this adventure. He did when you fell asleep over your biology book. I know you said that was a regular tired sleep and not a sleep event as you had no memories from it."

"He couldn't Jamison. He was with me."

Jamison sighed and wiped his hand across his forehead. "Lisa, I understand Gideon was in your dream. But I am concerned that he was not able to wake you. I felt confident all our training was working."

Lisa pulled the paper out of her pocket and handed it to him. "I knew you wouldn't believe Gideon was there. I even wrote what you would say."

He took it but didn't open the folded paper. He sat quiet for quite a while. "We will continue working on his training Lisa." He sighed, "This is good Lisa. I hadn't thought of it. You and Gideon are close. If he is part of your dream, then a bark would not mean anything because it would only be natural for him to do so in the dream. We need to work on a different signal. I will talk to George. Although a warning bark would be useful if someone was around, we need Gideon to learn to wake you if you are alone."

She started to say something but he gave her the signal of his raised hand that he would rather she did not. Jamison mused that at least he had Lisa partially trained.

"Now tell me about how this experience was different besides having Gideon there."

"Like I said, I wanted to be there even before I was invited. Like it was not a surprise."

"You think you had control?"

"I think I did."

He said nothing. He knew she knew what he would say.

They then worked on the hypnotherapy. Gideon stood alert when he heard the tape replay his warning bark as part of her therapy. He appeared very curious, but was quiet. Jamison was sure he knew it was his own voice and the reason for the bark. He began thinking Gideon was a smart dog; but why had he not done his job for this last episode?

———

When Lisa and Gideon left, Jamison made his usual notes for her hypnotherapy sessions. This took a little time since it was her first event since October. These notes included the name of the book she was reading when the event occurred. In keeping with his promise to keep her secret he did not include anything about her dreams. The team consisted of behaviorist and not Freudians, thus they had not inquired about her dreams. He was especially concerned and as a professional he knew his duty was to include a note that Lisa may have initiated this sleep event with the purpose of experiencing a dream. He had to do it.

Jamison then took the tape into his study where he would make another copy and hand write his notes from their meeting. It was nearly four, not quite too late to call his uncles. Lisa had not been the major topic of their phone calls for three months now. He would mail the tape in the morning as he would not make it to the post office by the time he made the call to the uncles.

He wrote up his notes that he would send with the tape and sealed the package. He dialed the number and did hope one of them would be up even though it was a bit late. He got his usual response when his Uncle Glen heard his voice.

"It be a wee bit late Branden, needless to say, we were expecting to hear from you today."

"Good evening Uncle Glen; my call is about Lisa."

"We were expecting that."

Jamison shook his head. It seemed Uncle Glen seldom admitted to unexpected news.

"Ryan will be back in a bit. We were having a wee sip before bed and he had to fetch another bottle from the cellar. Ye know, we keep them there so as to not to have too many wee sips." He chuckled.

Jamison knew they kept too many bottles of the good stuff in the basement, but brought only one up at a time. He really never figured the logic of how that might diminish the amounts of wee sips of their stock of Jameson Irish Whisky. Their only complaint was that the name was spelled wrong. He heard a loud clank he imagined as his Uncle Glen dropped the phone to the table. He also heard voices as his Uncle Glen said, 'It be Branden, the lass is at it again Ryan. Then he heard the clank of glasses and a sigh from one of his uncles.

"Hello Branden. Glen says the lass has begun her adventures again."

"She had a sleep episode last week; another one where she dreamed that she was in a Gospel story."

"How long has it been since the last?"

Jamison sighed, "Four months. I will mail the tape in the morning, express as usual. Can you have Uncle Glen go to the extension?"

He heard laughing at the other end. "We are together now. We are up to date Branden; we have a speaker phone. We just push the button and you can hear us together." He then heard the voice of his uncle Glen. "And we don't need hands to hold on to speak, so we can sit and sip as if you were here with us."

The voice of Uncle Glen added, "Tell us about it, Laddie."

Jamison decided to be brief. "I have a fear she may have caused this sleep event. She told me she wanted to see this specific story. It was when Jesus cured a man with a withered hand in the Synagogue. She said she wanted to be there and she read that part of the story over three times and was there. In the past she always said the book called to her. She would be reading and then be in the book she was reading, but not have decided it."

Jamison felt that when he talked to his uncles, he generally found logical answers in the process of saying the words out loud. "That she caused it may have been part of the dream experience."

He got no response so proceeded. "The other thing in this event was that she claims she took the dog with her. She said he was by her with his head on her lap. In the dream she said he came up to her and it was her Gideon, with his dog collar and tags on; and not the dog in her former dreams."

"Andrew's dog?" asked Father Ryan.

"I need to tell you more as you will hear it from her on the tape. She said the dog looked frightened and she had to comfort him and hold him. Then when the dream was over and she was herself at home, she claimed the dog was excited and ran all over the house like he had been gone and wanted to be sure of where he was. That is her opinion of his actions. Perhaps her idea of the dog's action after she woke was also part of the dream..."

He heard the voice of his uncle Father Ryan talking to Uncle Glen. "What do you think, hard to buy that one?"

Uncle Glen's voice was next as he moved closer to the speaker. "The girl is clever, but it would take a lot of imagination to talk about the dog seeming frightened."

Father Ryan's voice interrupted, "The dog's reaction of it when it felt it was home from someplace, by exploring the house. Sounds real to me, like that is what a dog would do."

Jamison was upset, "We all know she didn't go anywhere. The dog could not know what she was dreaming. Think about it. You may pick up something I missed when you hear the tape. I only heard it a second time as I made the copy for you." Then he added, "Lisa does indeed have a great imagination."

"Father Ryan, why have her dreams moved to only these Gospel stories? She still reads extensively many books. Her reading list is with the tape."

"I am thinking she is looking for him?"

"Him?

"Jesus; her imagination is her own private world, and her sleep episodes is how she explores that world. I am thinking she is looking for him there, in her world."

Jamison bid the uncles good night, locked the office and headed home. His Uncle Father Ryan's last words were on his mind, "I am thinking she is looking for him."

Chapter 10

"You would not have called to me unless I had been calling to you," said the Lion." [C. S. LEWIS, *The Silver Chair*]

LISA WAS UP earlier than usual for a Saturday. She quickly dressed and in her haste from her bedroom met face to face with a huge bunch of balloons in front of her door. She should have expected that. Her father had done this same thing ever since she could remember, adding one more balloon every year. She didn't need to count; she knew there would be sixteen. She grabbed the lead string that held them together and headed downstairs with Gideon at her heels. She looked over the banister and for a brief instant thought it would be fun to simply float down instead of taking the steps one at a time.

Ginny looked up at her as she came into the kitchen, "Good morning birthday girl." She walked over to her and gave her a kiss on the forehead.

Lisa responded with a hug to Ginny and walked to the back door to let Gideon out for his morning business. "Where's the family?"

"The Dean is golfing. No rain for the first time in weeks. Your mother hasn't come down yet, and you and she have appointments at Mister Blake's at ten this morning."

"Oh, I almost forgot. I did forget. Thanks Ginny."

Gideon did his 'let me in' bark, so she opened the door for him. She poured his kibbles into his dish and refilled his water bowl. "What's for breakfast?"

"Busy dear, it is a DYO, do your own, today."

"On my special day?"

"Who is getting a special day party ready?"

"Sorry Ginny," Lisa walked over and gave her a hug. "Thanks. What can I do?"

Ginny poured two cups of coffee and pointed to a paper on the table that looked like a list, and sat down at the table.

Lisa helped herself to some granola, sliced a banana into it, and filled the bowl with milk. Then she looked at Ginny. "Have you eaten yet?"

Ginny nodded that she had. Lisa joined her at the table. "Thanks for the coffee." She picked up the list with columns of names, which included everyone except for her dad and Gideon, and their respective chores for the party.

This would be her first dinner party, not as formal as her parent's usually gave, but a real grown up party. She chose blue and white for the color scheme. She resented sharing her birthday with Saint Patrick, and the need to flaunt the color green. She liked green, and probably would have liked him; but it was her day. She and Ginny, mostly Ginny, selected the meal that would not include corned beef or cabbage. Her birthday cake was cheesecake with blueberries, and blue candles. Her guests had all responded, so she would have everyone she loved to celebrate with her. Even Jamison had accepted the invitation; there would be twelve guests for dinner.

She wandered into the dining room. The table had already been spread with a white cloth. New periwinkle blue placemats and napkins arrived a few days ago, and two table flower arrangements in blue and white were on the table. A beautiful bouquet of blue hydrangeas sat on the sideboard. She looked at it and hoped no one would ask about it. Ginny said everyone, except those who knew, would think they were part of the decor. The flowers were from George; she hadn't gotten any from her boyfriend Josh. She knew George knew she and Josh were a couple. She resented the flowers even while she thought it was terribly sweet of him to have sent them.

She had seen George every day during the holidays to help with Gideon since she couldn't walk him then. Then he came nearly every weekend in January and February to help train Gideon to bark a certain kind of bark if he saw her asleep.

Ginny was probably right when she warned Lisa that George had intentions more than acting as Gideon's trainer. Lisa had been so into Josh she brushed aside such comments, after all George was five years older than she was. Sure, he was incredibly handsome, but he wasn't book people. He was logical, not like Jamison; there was no one like Jamison. Logical, more like her father. She thought—no her father was book people and not logical. Regardless she was sure George was not her type.

Ginny's voice interrupted her reverie, "What are you doing in here girl? The list, the list, we all have things to do. The table can be done later."

Lisa's parents and Ginny gave her birthday gifts in the late afternoon before the party and the arrival of the caterers. Jamison had sent a gift ahead, so she opened it with the family gifts. She remembered telling Jamison before her thirteenth birthday that friends remembered friend's birthdays with gifts. He had remembered since then. She was delighted with his gift of a small book in Gaelic and a Gaelic Dictionary. His birthday was a few days before Christmas, and he was usually in Ireland then. She usually found a unique book, sometimes a suggestion from her father, for Jamison's combination birthday and Christmas gift. After all they were book people.

She wore the new blue dress, the gift from her mom, and coordinating earrings, from Ginny. Her dad's gift was a beautiful sapphire ring. The dinner was lovely. Josh gave her a lovely bracelet. Gideon gave her a new leash with rhinestones.

That night after the party, Lisa felt loved as she curled up in bed with Gideon lying at her feet. She wondered why she felt so awkward, or so something, when she noticed Josh glaring at George that evening. He even made a couple of remarks about why it took so long to train the dog. Lisa was uncomfortable with those remarks as she wondered if they were aimed at Gideon, or at George. She could understand he might be jealous of George; but there was no excuse to put down Gideon's intelligence.

Jamison was troubled when he got the text message that next Monday morning from Lisa. "Adventure in Jericho with Gideon." They didn't schedule a special debrief meeting since they had retained weekly hypnotherapy sessions on Fridays since her episode a month ago. Then Thursday another text, "Another adventure, no Gideon." He wondered what he had missed. Lisa had months with no episodes, then the one a month ago, now two. Unlike the past two years, her recent sleep episodes all came from her reading the Bible, instead of a random book she was reading. She told him she thought these were more real because they were true. He mumbled to himself, "Oh, Lisa, I still wonder what is going on inside that head of yours."

Just then a chime sounded indicating someone was at the office door. Jamison let Lisa and Gideon in. He set up the tape recorder, while Lisa and Gideon were making themselves comfortable. She handed him her reading list, it now contained less than half the number of books she read a year ago. He looked at his young patient who was looking at him as though she had not a care.

"Are you ready to go?"

Lisa began, "Sunday night, after my Birthday dinner. And thank you again for the lovely book."

"You are again welcome. You were saying?"

"I was reading in my room. I was on my bed with Gideon leaning against me. I wasn't even reading the Bible this time. I was looking at a Bible commentary I got at the library. I do understand that the Gospels, or even the Bible is not intended as history and I don't expect that. I was curious about the times he went to Jericho since that is a story in books for Children about the walls falling down. I think I even heard a song about that from the Sunday School kids once when I was helping out. Another kid song was about Zacchaeus climbing a tree that took place in Jericho. This commentary also mentioned a man Jesus healed in Jericho. His name is Bartimaeus, and it even gives his father's name, but I don't remember what it was. I sometimes wonder about people who were healed, when some have their names in the Gospels, and other people are referred to as just a man or two blind men. I personally think maybe the ones with names were part of the early church and shared their own stories about Jesus. It could be.

Jamison gave Lisa a slight nod, and a look that usually meant, let's move along.

"I was reading the commentary account of Bartimaeus, and I was there, and so was Gideon. I know last time I had an adventure I told you I wanted to go. But this was like in old days and unexpected. Gideon was walking so close he almost tripped me. It was very hot with the sun directly overhead. We were on the outskirts of a large crowd that was moving very slowly. It wasn't only a crowd of people, as some were leading goats or sheep and donkeys heavy with bundles. I was guessing that like Jesus, they had come from long distances and this was the way to Jerusalem for Passover.

"I looked into the crowd for Jesus but didn't see him right away. The road was wide, maybe twenty to thirty feet. It was dusty like hard packed dirt, and some of it was large flat rocks. It wasn't at all like the little streets I had seen before even in the countryside. Then I saw Jesus and tried to get near but that was very hard. Since no one could see me I got bumped into several times. For some reason these people don't have the space requirements we do in our time. They don't mind physically touching and bumping into one another in crowds. Maybe that made it easier because when someone bumped into me, they didn't even look around.

"My biggest concern was about losing Gideon. I tried to pick him up even though he weighs close to forty pounds. That didn't work. Andrew's Gideon weighs less. I moved out to the edge of the crowd so he could keep near me, and he did, almost between my legs. I still didn't see Jesus. I decided to run ahead of the crowd and look for a safe view point. There was a wide area uphill a short way from this main road with merchants mostly selling some kind of bread, fruit and cups of water. Even there it was crowded. I snatched a small gourd of water from a boy who was selling drinks by the gourd. I sat it on the ground and Gideon got most of it before the boy, with a puzzled look, retrieved it refilled it and sat it with the others for sale. Probably cleaner from Gideon's germs than some of the ones who were drinking and replacing the gourds for the next customer.

"Not everyone on the larger road below came up to this mini market place. I watched the crowds of people and their sheep and goats. The donkeys or mules generally were carrying large bundles; a few were carrying people. Another thing Doctor Jamison about being there; you have to watch where you step. And then there are the smells of animals and unwashed people. Then I saw Jesus and the disciples coming. He was walking close to a donkey with a woman on it. She was completely covered so I didn't see who she was. I wondered if it was Mary. John was leading the donkey. While I was trying to figure things out from where I was I heard a large commotion and yelling, more than the generally commotion of the setting. Someone was leading a man who stumbled along. They led him to Jesus. The crowd had stopped and all attention was directed to where Jesus was. I couldn't hear anything, but could see fairly well since the mini market place was higher than this main road. Then the man began jumping up and down and many of the people began singing and shouting. The gist of most of the words were praises, and some songs about praise to God.

"Then we were home. Gideon didn't act like he did the time before. He jumped down, walked around my room, then back on the bed and sat close to me again."

Jamison turned off the recorder.

Lisa let out a large sigh and stood up disturbing Gideon. He followed her to the water cooler where she poured herself a cup of cold water. She held a cup towards Doctor Jamison and he nodded his head and she brought one to him. She drank two of the little paper cups, then refilled it again and offered it to Gideon. He politely took a few laps.

"Are you ready to tell me about your experience yesterday?"

———

Lisa walked around the room, then back to the window. "Jamison, I am tired and I am hungry."

"Then let's get something to eat, and we can finish after. Would you like that?"

Lisa nodded.

"Call home and tell them I will take you home so Ginny won't have to make another trip."

Lisa stared out the window and the clear blue sky as she called Ginny. She thought the sky seemed bluer here on the ninth floor than it seemed from windows at home, maybe the trees had something to do with it. "Hi, Ginny, Doctor Jamison and I are going to get burgers and fries, then need another session. He will drive me home. I don't have homework tonight." She grinned at Jamison who definitely showed an emotion when she said burger and fries. "Things are fine Ginny; I got a little long winded and we still have some things to talk about."

Lisa closed her phone and turned to Jamison. "She understands the hypnotism part of our meetings, but doesn't understand what we could possibly talk about that you would be interested in. Ginny and I do talk a lot as you know; I tell her all the things I tell you; well most all. You know how you do sometimes suggest I share less with you. Of course, you know I never tell her or my parents about my adventures."

She knew the sign from Jamison when she tended to go on, as he was already at the door to leave. They walked down the street to a little restaurant known for great hamburgers. Gideon was allowed in since he is a service dog. Jamison had a salad, Lisa a double patty hamburger. The second patty went to Gideon. They chatted more about school and a little about Josh and George. She confided to him about her feelings for Josh and how she wanted him to believe her version, that she really went into a story and it was not a false memory. She also had much to say about George and their weekends working with Gideon. When Jamison mentioned something about a relationship, she protested that he was making assumptions like Ginny. George was a good friend, not competition with Josh.

Lunch over, Lisa took Gideon for his necessary walk around the block and met Jamison standing in front of his building holding two Starbucks coffees. He handed her one and they went up together. She took a long sip of her latte. "Thanks again Jamison for the lunch and now the coffee."

They went in the office, and as usual Lisa removed her shoes and pulled her feet up under her in the large red leather chair. This time Gideon was more relaxed as he stretched out at her feet, instead of sitting alert and upright.

Jamison put a new tape in and turned the recorder on.

Lisa began, "Gideon did not go with me this time. It was Thursday night and I was ready for bed. I sometimes read in bed, but generally poetry or something that doesn't take a lot of thought as that helps me sleep. Another flaw in our plans, Jamison; Gideon was at the foot of my bed, but that is the one time he learned to not bark, because it is a normal sleep time. I am usually sitting at my desk when I read my Bible, but I was curious about the Jericho story and if the blind Bartimaeus incident was the same day or trip in Jericho as was the story of Zacchaeus. I got out of bed and retrieved my Bible to look the story up again to see if that was the case. I got to the story of Zacchaeus, and then suddenly I was there. I know I was quite curious about the story, but not like I did that one time and wished I could be there. I didn't have the premonition I sometimes have that cue me in to set my timer. There was no time. Since Gideon wasn't touching me; he didn't go this time."

She turned and looked out the window. "It was hot again, but earlier in the day from the look of the sun. When I had been in Jerico before; when he healed the blind man, I was only on this wide road and didn't see anything of the city or surroundings. That time my adventure was only a road that was ascending through desert like area. I wouldn't have known this was the same place. Now I was in a city. I had the impression that it was a very old city. This is the second time I was in an adventure and didn't immediately see Jesus."

"The city, what I could see from the narrow street I was on, looked beautiful to me. Maybe because there were gardens and the palm trees, colorful flowers in the gardens. I peeked over a low wall into a courtyard that had a fountain and statues, like I imagine were in Greece or Rome, from old paintings and stuff I have seen. I wandered a few streets, again wondering why Jesus wasn't close by as he had been before. There were a lot of people around, but not what I would consider a crowd. I was frightened when I saw about twenty Roman soldiers heading down a street toward me and was glad that they couldn't see me. People ran and scattered to give the soldiers plenty of room on the street. I found an unoccupied doorway and scrunched myself in it hoping no one else wanted that space. The soldiers were in formation, not just wandering like the other time. A fairly strong hot wind was blowing between the buildings. Where I stood, most of the buildings were two or three stories high, most had gardens on their roofs.

"Then I heard the noise of a crowd of people headed in my direction. I moved out on a wider street and realized this part of the city was on a hill, with even more streets and buildings below. The streets looked quite narrow in the lower part of the town. From there I could see the country-side. Below were orchards and fields like those I saw when I was there before. I recognized olive trees by their blue-grey color. Then I guessed that the oncoming crowd might be around Jesus so I headed that way. It seemed the equivalent of two blocks to me, but the streets there weren't nice and straight and block like. I came into what seemed like a town square, a large open area with palm trees. Most of it was paved with colored stones in a circular pattern; and there were three fountains and benches and some statues, which surprised me for a Jewish city. This square was packed with people. Once I got close, I couldn't see Jesus because of the crowd around him. I climbed into a window alcove about three feet up. The building's stones were rough and easy to climb. Thankfully I had my slippers on with textured soles. And no, I had not worn them to bed. But I was in my pajamas. Just as I got a look at Jesus in the middle of the crowd; I was sure I saw Zacchaeus, because I saw someone climb one of the trees in the courtyard. It was only like twenty-feet from where I was standing.

"Jesus walked to the tree and said, 'Zacchaeus, come down. I would like to come to your house.' He did and I saw that he was indeed a small man, his head came up maybe to Jesus shoulder. He was dressed in very colorful robes, and the turban on his head must have been silk, a deep green color. They walked by me and Jesus stopped again, looked up at me and said, 'Come down Lisa, come with us.' I did and there seemed to be room without the bumping into people for me to walk right beside Jesus, with Zacchaeus on the other side of him."

Lisa stopped and sipped on her coffee. "The group of us, me and Jesus and his disciples, went back up the streets I came down earlier. As we went higher there were fewer buildings. They evolved into what seemed like mansions, each with its own wall and gates. I noticed earlier there were about five or six Pharisees in the group, but as we got higher it seemed they dropped out. I wasn't sure if it was voluntary or they hadn't been invited. Soon it seems there was only Jesus, Zacchaeus and some of his disciples. I knew Andrew and Peter and James and John and Phillip and Thomas. I think I had seen many of the others, but not known who they were. As we were going up the hill into this nicer area, some young men came running to Zacchaeus. I heard him give them orders to prepare for a feast. They sure could run fast. He told a couple of others to get some people he knew. He named about five or six, I don't remember them as they were foreign to me. The whole party going up with Zacchaeus seemed to be in a festive mood with laughter and smiling around.

"We got to his house, really quite a mansion even in our times. An ornately carved wooden gate was already open and what I guessed were servants came out welcoming everyone in the party. It looked like there were nearly thirty of us that finally arrived. We were all led into a smaller inner courtyard. This one had a large pool, about ten or more palm trees, pomegranates, and what looked like dates. Jesus was led to a large stone bench and someone had water and was washing his feet in minutes. The servants were busy about washing every one. When they had also poured water over people's hands, they began passing around baskets of fruit and little cakes and nuts and some cold meats.

"I was impressed Jamison because all this food appeared within half an hour of our getting there. They then came with wine and poured it into metal or wood goblets from leather looking containers and metal pitchers. I wandered around this house then I came back out to where Jesus was and sat next to him where John had been sitting. I haven't talked to Jesus very often, just been there. I asked him about what was happening. He said I could stay if I wished. The meal would not be served for six or seven hours. I looked at him with question and he added, 'It takes time to kill and roast the fatted calf.' He handed me some little cakes he was holding. They were like an energy bar with lots of nuts and raisins and other dried fruits. I sat taking in all the bustle and conversation. People seem to talk about the same things, such as the weather and economy. No one mentioned politics here. When a platter of what looked like meat pies came by, Jesus took two and handed me one. Then I had to get up because Peter came to sit where I was. Before he sat down Jesus asked me if

I wanted to stay for the meal. I shook my head and suddenly I was in my bed with my face plopped in the middle of my Bible. Gideon was still asleep at the foot of my bed. I didn't even have time to taste the little meat pie, but I felt the delicious aroma had followed me. Jamison, I do wish I had more control over my adventures, because I would have tasted it before I returned if I did.

"This was such a lovely adventure. The city and trees and the food were all so different from in Galilee. The farmland around Jericho seemed more extensive than in the Galilee area. Everything was beautiful there. Also this was the first time it seemed I had some choice of when to come back, since he asked if I wanted to stay."

Jamison turned off the recorder. "You do have choices Lisa."

———

Jamison and Lisa both sat looking out the window as the sky turned into a mixture of gold and pink. As usual Jamison felt some kind of bonding between them when Lisa related her dreams. Perhaps they were soulmates of some kind, whatever that meant. He knew his uncles were right and the relationship was no longer that of a therapist and patient. He did more research on imagination and children with overactive imaginations. That fit Lisa somehow, but still he wondered how she came up with some of the details from her dreams, even with her extensive reading.

"Are you ready?" He asked as he removed the second tape and put it into his briefcase with the one he recorded earlier. He got his and Lisa's coats from the rack by the door and waited while she put her shoes on and attached Gideon's new rhinestone leash. He thought she looked as weary as he felt. Now was not the time to remind Lisa of the importance that she gain control over her life. In the last year they had made excellent progress. He needed to understand why, after months of no episodes, she would suddenly relapse. Lisa was still in danger even though the last three episodes since October did not seem to involve sleepwalking.

They took the elevator to the basement parking garage. Jamison picked Gideon up and carefully put him in the back. He didn't want dog claw marks on the car or leather interior. Gideon dutifully laid on the small back seat of the Porsche as if it had been made for him. He was glad Gideon was on the small side for his breed. Lisa got in, then complained when Jamison started to put the top up. He humored her and left it down. He guessed she would change her mind when they were on the highway with the cool March evening air whipping around her at fifty miles per hour.

She spent half of the time on the drive home searching for radio stations and resetting most of the preset buttons as she did so. He was proud of her, as she didn't even attempt or ask that he roll the windows up as some of his passengers often did when the top was down. With the radio and the wind it was difficult to talk much in the twenty-minute drive to her house.

When they arrived at the Longford residence Lisa got out and Gideon allowed Jamison to gently guide him out of the back. Jamison noticed Lisa's cheeks were pink and her eyes were sparkling from the open-air experience.

"Thank you Jamison for everything, for being here for me, it seems all most all of my life."

He was concerned when he saw the sparkle cloud up with moisture.

She went on, "I don't know what I would do without you, how I would survive. Sometimes I think I would just go crazy and they would lock me up or put me on drugs. You are my knight Jamison, my dearest knight."

For a moment he feared she was about to throw her arms around him and give him a kiss on the cheek, something she had done several times in the past when feeling emotional. Instead she took his hand, squeezed it, then led Gideon to the house, "Good night, Jamison."

Jamison drove home with the top still down hoping some of the cool March evening wind whipping through his hair would clear his mind of troubling thoughts. Being a knight would be an easy task, they only had to fight dragons without; Lisa's dragons were inside and he still couldn't get in her head, even though that was his task. Instead he had to battle Lisa. It seemed the battle was with words, but words had great power. After all these years she still would refer to what happened during a sleep episode as an adventure and not as a dream even with his logical explanation of how the dream went to her memory as a false memory, something that did not really happen. Why could she not accept the truth?

His mind drifted off into his philosophy of words. He felt if people even knew what they were saying and were precise with the words they used; then perhaps they could get along better—perhaps? Like the word love, which has more meanings than most. That reminded him of Lisa's term of soulmates for their relationship. When she defined what she meant by the word he did not object to her use of it. And that was the problem; Lisa did know the meaning of the words she used most of the time. Because of that she refused to say dream instead of adventure. They had a number of discussions about the word adventure and its meaning. Adventure - a verb, to engage in hazardous and exciting activity, especially the exploration of unknown territory. Jamison knew adventures were dangerous things.

The wind only blew the thoughts around in circles inside his head instead of clearing them. He was home in a few minutes. He pulled into the garage and retrieved his briefcase. He needed to make copies to send to his uncles and to make notes from their meeting while it was fresh in his mind. He reheated leftovers, made a pot of coffee and began copying the tape and creating notes for Lisa's file and for his uncles. It was too late to call them; he would wait until morning.

He pondered the question highest in his mind. Why now Lisa, after our success with the hypnotherapy? And why were these dreams only from her reading the Gospels? The whole theory that her sleep episodes were caused by her eyes moving over the lines of the book she was reading creating a self-hypnosis that put her into the sleep episode might not apply now when she was only reading bits of a story. Much of Lisa had to do with her highly active imagination. His uncle Father Ryan last suggested Lisa may be looking for him, for Jesus, in these dreams. Mixing religion into Lisa's complicated life was something he wasn't sure he wanted to get into.

The next Monday morning Lisa got to sleep in. It was a school in-service day, no school. After letting Gideon out, she looked for Ginny. She found her doing laundry.

"Good morning Lisa, did you enjoy sleeping in?"

"Yes, but I do have homework. Teachers reminded us today would be a good day to get caught up on any missing homework assignments or ahead on projects coming up. Nothing missing, but I do have that English report due in a few weeks."

"Is that your plan for the day?"

Lisa hesitated, "Maybe? I would like to go to the mall with Jane and Grace, if that is okay?"

"Only after your laundry is done, and later we do need to make plans for the Dean's birthday, and since your mother is out of town, it is up to us. Will you want a ride?"

"I will check. Jane has her license, and gets the car sometimes."

She went back to the kitchen to let Gideon in, then back to Ginny and make the phone call. She called the girls who said yes to the mall, and that they also had chores. Jane could pick her up and they could have lunch and do shopping, or whatever.

She fed Gideon then helped herself to some cold cereal. Sometimes Ginny didn't make breakfasts on laundry day, which generally was Mondays. As she ate she thought about what homework she had to do and how long it might take. She wasn't concerned. Her parents sometimes thought she should get better grades, being their child and all that, but she did okay. She didn't have to worry about scholarships or ability to get into the college of her choice. She had no choice; she would attend the University where her parents taught. She thought even if she had terrible grades, they would let her in. Still she had some pride and kept them up to a high B average.

Jane's mother picked Lisa up before twelve and dropped them at the mall with pickup time at four. When Lisa thanked her, she said it was her turn since Ginny seemed to be chauffeuring the girls most of the time. For lunch, the three headed for their favorite with a wonderful Mexican cuisine.

"Still it was great for your Mother to drive us today," Lisa said.

Grace agreed, "Yes, thanks Jane. Great when we can all drive ourselves."

Jane grinned at her, "Sixteen in three weeks. My parents said I could get my license that week. Only of course, still need the family car—not totally independent."

Grace looked at the two of them, "Six more months for me."

Jane responded, "That's what happens when you are smart and skip a grade, and hang out with your elders."

They both looked at Lisa. She grimaced, and held up her wrist to reveal the medical bracelet with the epilepsy symbol. "I guess whenever I convince Doctor Jamison that I am all better." Her parents and Ginny knew she had two recent sleep episodes after three months of none. She decided she would tell her friends. "I was doing great, three months with no episodes, then recently two of them."

The girls changed the subject. Grace began, "You have to tell us what is going on with you and Josh and George."

"What?"

Jane added, "And your Doctor Jamison, like wow Lisa he is incredibly good looking, even for someone older."

Grace grinned, "He and Ginny look good together."

"Ginny is seeing Walt; Doctor Jamison has a friend in Ireland."

Grace conceded, "What we really want to know as your BFF's is about you and Josh and George. Are you and Josh like having issues. Like we saw how he glared at George. He even asked me after the party if you were seeing George. I said no; that George was only helping with your therapy and with Gideon." Lisa looked down when Grace mentioned Gideon. There was no Gideon. Although he was allowed at the mall being a medical service dog, she could go places without him as long as she was with family or close friends. She missed him.

Lisa felt uncomfortable that Josh was questioning her friendship with George. Then she remembered his Christmas gift, the heart necklace. She accepted it only with condition there were no strings attached; she hadn't been ready for a commitment then. Perhaps Josh had a reason to question their relationship. Although she didn't always wear the necklace, she had it on.

"Remember at Christmas when Josh gave me this?" She pulled the necklace out from behind her sweater. "Remember I told you we had no commitments, and I told him I would accept it only on that basis. Maybe I haven't been fair to him?"

Grace and Jane looked at her. Jane asked, "So, you like Josh."

"Ah, well yes, I do. I think everyone thinks of us as a couple; I guess I have been thinking that too."

"And George."

"What?"

"Maybe your friends see you and Josh that way. Does George?"

Suddenly Lisa felt confused. Jane had hit a sore spot. She didn't want to make a choice; but after all Josh was her boyfriend and George was..."

Just then their waiter brought their tabs. The girls each pulled out cash, as did Lisa. Normally she would use her credit card. But her 16-year-old friends did not have credit cards. She had to be careful when shopping with them; they had allowances and looked at price tags. She had taken money for granted until she had real friends and realized her family was not really normal in that regard. She had no idea what her family's income was, though her father said she had some kind of annuity from her father's great uncle, the past president of the University. They never questioned her book purchases and once she became interested in clothes and shoes, had not questioned any of that shopping.

The topic stayed on boys a bit longer. Jane and Dave had been an item for a couple of years, and Grace just started dating Logan a few months ago. Jane seemed to be content with her relationship with Dave. After three hours of shopping the only purchases were three pairs of socks. The girls thought wearing the same goofy socks would be fun.

Lisa thought no more about her last two adventures until later in the evening at home. The shopping and lunch with Jane and Grace was a needed diversion. She seemed to feel good after being with these two friends. She and Ginny made her father's birthday celebration easy by making reservations at his favorite restaurant. Florence already purchased and wrapped an original autograph copy of a C. S. Lewis book he had his eye on. All year Lisa and Ginny also kept a look out for books he would like. They had good luck last summer and their gifts were wrapped a week ago.

Before he left that morning, her dad said she could invite George for the dinner if she wished. She suggested Josh and he said that would be all right too. She wasn't sure if he meant invite both Josh and George, but decided that would not be a good plan. Walt had been invited. He seemed to be around more frequently since the engagement. Since Ginny was part of the family that made Walt also part. Lisa loved it that her father and mother accepted Walt the landscaper as equal to any of the professors or the president of the University. Later when she told him she hadn't invited George, he suggested they invite Doctor Jamison. He said something about him also seeming part of the family. Lisa realized sometimes she really didn't know what her father was thinking.

The family had a quiet dinner that evening. She was surprised when her father said he had indeed invited the doctor, and that he had accepted the invitation for tomorrow. Lisa loved it that her family loved celebrating sometimes the smallest things, but especially birthdays. Her father's enthusiasm was rubbing off and she decided she was looking forward to the next day and the birthday celebration.

She said good night to her father and to Ginny and took Gideon to her room. It was the first time she had been alone all day, the first time to think about what was heavy on her mind that morning, Josh and Gideon. Gideon had gone with her on two adventures. She realized that he had been laying very close, even touching her those times. The other time he was at the foot of the bed and she had an adventure, he didn't go. Could that have had something to do with touching?

If Josh could go with her like Gideon did, then he would have to believe her and trust her like Gideon did. She would like it if he believed her anyway; but then again it would be exciting to share an adventure with someone you cared about. The more she thought of it, the more she decided that would be an excellent idea. Then they both could report the experience to Jamison and he would finally accept she was somewhere else, somewhere in a story and not dreaming.

Chapter 11

"The truth." Dumbledore sighed. "It is a beautiful and terrible thing, and should therefore be treated with great caution."
[J. K. ROWLING, *Harry Potter and the Sorcerer's Stone*]

THURSDAY LISA ASKED Josh to come over so they could do some reading together for youth group; they were going through the book of John. He agreed and had dinner with Lisa, Ginny and Walt, since the Dean was at a dinner meeting and her mom was still at a conference out of town.

They had an early dinner. Josh and Lisa headed for the library, while Ginny and Walt went to her sitting room to watch a basketball game.

Lisa felt uncomfortable about what she was going to propose; but wanted to get to the point. "Josh, I want to be honest with you, can we talk again about my experiences before we do our reading?"

"Sure, what do you want to talk about Lisa?"

In the library they sat together on the small sofa. Lisa was close to him and he responded with an arm around her. She put one leg over his and he responded by folding her into his arms. "Josh I want to be serious."

He laughed, "So do I." And kissed her.

"Josh, we were going to talk about my experiences." He released her. "Okay Lisa let's talk."

"If you could go with me Josh, would you want to do it?"

His laugh seemed nervous. "What — go where?"

"Say for instance that Doctor Jamison is wrong and your idea of what can and can't happen is wrong, and say for instance that I am right and not dreaming and that I can and do go into the story I am reading." He started to say something but she put her fingers gently on his lips. "Then say for instance, that by holding onto me someone can go with me into what we are reading together. If that could possibly be true, would you be willing to experiment and go?"

He gulped, "Sure, why not."

She thought that would have to do. She snuggled closer to him and suggested they read the words together out loud beginning with John chapter four. They read only to where Jesus arrived at Jacob's well when she felt, no this time she knew, she was going into the story.

Josh left fifteen minutes later.

Ginny was on her way downstairs to get coffee for herself and Walt when she heard loud voices. She rushed to the hallway and saw Josh headed to the front door shouting at Lisa. "You are a freak, Lisa, a freak!" as he rushed out the door.

Ginny went over to Lisa and put her arms around her to comfort her. She was a wise woman and knew now was not the time to talk. "Want some coffee dear, I just made some?" Then she added, "I thought I heard Gideon's bark."

Lisa felt too angry to cry, but she knew her face was red and probably looked like it. "Where is Walt?"

"Watching the game; I was making coffee—decaf. Do you want company dear? You can watch the game with us? Don't have to think watching basketball."

Lisa followed Ginny to the kitchen and poured herself a cup. "Thanks, maybe later."

Ginny left with two coffees. Lisa sat on the floor wrapping her arms around Gideon. He looked bewildered about what had just happened. She also needed to tell him what a good dog he was for his bark and for pulling on her sleeve. She gave him the words of affirmation George taught her, and gave him two doggie treats.

She usually sent Jamison a text when she had a sleep experience, but this was not really one. Maybe it was, she had gone into a Gospel story with Josh; but they were back within minutes with Gideon's bark and his tugging on her sleeve and pushing the Bible onto the floor. The new training included his tugging on her clothing in addition to the special bark. Gideon certainly was a good dog. She needed Jamison and George to know how he had done. But maybe not George; she didn't know how to explain Josh. She could leave out Josh's presence, but not for Jamison, their relationship was built on trust. She could never deceive him even a little.

Lisa mumbled to herself, "There is something about being overly honest." She thought, there might be. She knew her parents or Ginny would attribute her secret as an overactive imagination and side with Jamison, that she was dreaming and not really there. Dreams were okay, but as Jamison said, adventures were dangerous; and had been dangerous this evening. She knew Josh would not want to have anything to do with her now. Then the tears came as she stumbled up to her room and plopped on her bed. Gideon climbed beside her, gave her a kiss and lay next to her. He knew the truth.

She knew Jamison would be concerned when she finally sent a text about ten o'clock, "Bad experience." She was right. She immediately got a message from him.

"Need help now?"

"No."

"Tomorrow afternoon?"

"Yes, regular time is okay."

Sleep did not come easy. For some reason Gideon knew she needed him so he slept close to her instead at the foot of the bed that night.

That next morning Lisa woke with a headache. When she saw her eyes were bloodshot from the crying off and on during the night, she decided she didn't want to go to school. She stumbled down to the kitchen and let Gideon out.

"Lisa, what's happening dear?"

"I don't feel like school Ginny. I didn't get much sleep." She sat down and picked up the coffee Ginny put in front of her. "Josh and I had a thing last night, kinda serious. I don't want to deal with it at school."

Even before she finished talking Ginny was on the phone calling the school to say that Lisa was ill.

"Do you want something to eat dear? I can fix whatever you like. The Dean left early this morning. Your mom will be back late this afternoon. He will pick her up at the airport, so I'm free if you need to see Doctor Jamison."

Lisa let Gideon in and filled his bowls. She sat at the table and accepted the toast and jam Ginny handed her.

"He called earlier this morning and asked me to have you call him when you were up."

Lisa looked up. "I guess I can do that."

Ginny added, "He was rather insistent, asked me if things were okay. I didn't say anything about you and Josh last night dear." She then sat by her and picked up her coffee. "I am always here you know."

"Thanks Ginny. We had this bad quarrel. I wanted us to be close so I told him about my sleep thing. He knew a little, but has been asking why George is here and all that. I'm confused Ginny. How do you know about love?" She wanted to tell Ginny as much as she could. "Do you tell Walt everything about yourself, little things?"

"Of course not dear. We are two different people. I don't keep important things from him, but we are each our own unique individual person loving each other. I don't expect him to understand my quirks, but simply to accept them. That is enough."

"Thanks Ginny." As Lisa stood, Ginny kissed her on the head. Lisa said, "I will get dressed."

"You didn't eat dear."

"Later."

"Call Doctor Jamison."

Lisa and Gideon headed upstairs. "I will."

She called Jamison and arranged to meet him at two thirty, the time for their regular session. She decided being busy was a good idea. She tidied her room, took Gideon for a long walk; then finished a novel she had been reading for nearly two weeks. She didn't really want to think of what to say to Jamison or what he would say about what she had deliberately done.

She was anxious when she and Gideon got there. She thought she knew what he would say to her; but this time she had proof. She would have him talk to Josh and he would tell Jamison that it was all real.

Jamison met them at the door. They chatted a few minutes about the dinner that previous Tuesday evening for her father's birthday. "Are you ready to tell me about last night?"

Lisa nodded and he got the recorder. Once she asked him why he didn't have it ready when he knew they would be talking about her adventures. She loved his honesty when he said getting it out and setting it up gave her a few minutes to pull her thoughts together and be more relaxed. She loved Jamison's consideration for her.

He turned the recorder on. She wasn't sure how to start, so began with her idea.

"Remember when I told you weeks ago about the time Gideon went with me into a Gospel adventure, and then the next time when we went to Jericho. Those times Gideon was sitting by me with his head on my lap. The last time I went he was with me, as usual, but didn't go into the book with me because he was at the foot of my bed. He thought I was doing normal sleep; so don't blame him for letting me go. I seldom read in bed, so I'm not sure why I did then. I wasn't trying to trick him Jamison. I wasn't thinking.

"Later I got the idea that if I could take Gideon with me two times because he was touching me, then maybe I could take Josh. Don't ask why I would want to take Josh. I told you that he didn't believe me when I explained to him I was in a story when I had a sleep episode. He took your side Jamison; that it was a dream. I wanted him to believe me, to trust me." She hesitated and was almost ready to not tell Jamison, not all the truth. She sighed and continued; trust was the basis of their friendship.

"I told Josh I wanted to experiment to see if he could go with me into a book. He said okay, and I trusted that he might be serious and believe me. And then I told him I had no control if or when I went to a story, so probably nothing would happen. When I explained we had to be very close he complied and we had our arms around each other and I put my leg over his. Like as close as we could decently be."

She stopped; suddenly feeling awkward explaining some of the details, but as usual was open and honest with Jamison. She went on, "He was trying to kiss me, but I told him to be serious, this was an experiment to take him to Samaria. That was the story we were going to read in the Gospel of John, where Jesus meets a Samaritan woman at a well. We both started reading the story together out loud and we were there Jamison; Josh and me together."

Jamison waited in silence. Lisa listened to the whirl of the recorder, recording silence.

"He was scared; I was excited. Jamison, I saw the look in his eyes, he really was frightened. I tried to reassure him and I pointed to the scene in front of us. About half a block, maybe not that far, we could see a structure and a man sitting there. I knew it was Jesus. In the distance was a village. I was so excited that he could meet Jesus in person. I grabbed him by the hand and told him to come on and see Jesus. He just stood there and screamed at me. 'What did you do to me Lisa? Stop it. Stop what you are doing.'

"I grabbed his hands and tried to pull him toward Jesus. I told him. 'If you just see him, talk to him you will know he is real, that this is real. Come Josh.' He wouldn't move. I was getting angrier by the minute and almost left him there but remembered that Gideon had been disoriented when he went with me before. Only I couldn't talk to Gideon. Then I heard the barking and barking and felt jerks on my sleeve. My head, which was in the middle of the Bible, fell over and the Bible fell on the floor. That was Gideon's doing; waking me.

"We were both on the sofa in the library and Gideon was standing in front of me doing his special bark to wake me. We hadn't been gone more than a few minutes. Josh got up. He was red in the face and very angry. He accused me of hypnotizing him to see weird things and that you had taught me to do that and..." Lisa broke down in tears. Jamison handed her the box of tissue.

"I don't know how to do that and I wouldn't do such a thing." It was a few minutes before she could talk again. "He called me a freak and headed out the door and before he slammed it, or tried to, he said again 'you are a freak Lisa, a freak,' and left."

Jamison turned the recorder off.

"Gideon barked and woke you?"

She nodded. "Not just barked, he also pulled on my clothes. I didn't go to school today. I didn't want to see Josh. Maybe he reacted like he did because he was scared, what do you think? Will you talk to Josh?"

"I don't think it is a good idea for me to attempt to talk to Josh. I don't know what happened with you two. I do believe what you told me about it Lisa. I do. There may be a reasonable explanation, perhaps not reasonable to some people, but a realistic one. I need to do some research, but I have read instances where people can share dreams."

Jamison didn't think Lisa heard him, or rather heard what she always seemed to as she translated his word 'dreams' into her word 'adventures.'

She said, "I hurt Josh, and maybe Gideon by taking them somewhere they—somewhere they couldn't or shouldn't be. Gideon couldn't protect me there, and that is his job. I am so sorry." She snuffled into the tissue, then slid out of the chair and wrapped her arms around Gideon and whispered into his fur, "So sorry Gideon."

———

Jamison completed his two sets of notes; one for Lisa's treatment file, and the other set for her dream analysis. He was pleased to include a note that the training for Gideon was successful for her most recent sleep episode. However, he also had to include that Lisa said she knew when she felt she was about to experience the sleep episode, and she did not want to stop it even if she could.

He copied the tape and packaged it for the mail. It was early enough for a call to his uncles. He smiled knowing they would say they were expecting his call. His uncles would be up since they seldom retired before midnight. Uncle Ryan answered the phone.

"Branden Laddie, we knew you would be calling," even before he said anything.

He heard him put the phone on speaker and call to his brother. He thought they must have it set up to pick up every sound in the room. Then he heard Uncle Ryan say, "The laddie is on the phone, just like you said he would be." He heard shuffling and the chair scraping the floor as his Uncle Glen pulled it to the table next to the phone, then his voice.

"Branden, good evening Laddie. We knew ye would be a calling tonight."

"Good evening Uncle Glen, Uncle Ryan."

"It must be about Lisa since we talked only two days ago."

"Yes."

He clearly heard sounds of the clanking of glasses and liquid pouring. The uncles had their wee bit generally sometime between eleven and twelve before retiring.

"Tell us what we need to know."

"I believe she again had a choice of starting a dream, not random like in the past."

"Was it a Gospel story?" asked his priest uncle Ryan.

"Almost Uncle; she said she was not alone. Remember when she claimed she took the dog Gideon with her. Now I am talking like her. When she dreamed she took the dog with her."

He heard chuckling from one of the uncles, but continued, "She got the idea this happened because the dog was by her, with his head on her lap. Since she dreamed this happened twice, she had the idea she could take her boyfriend, Josh, if he was touching her."

"Hum, very interesting." He wasn't sure which uncle said it, but imagined the other nodding his head. They were like that, in agreement half the time, disagreement the other half.

"Her story, which is on the tape you will be getting, is that they sat close and began reading the story she wanted to get into."

Uncle Ryan asked. "What was the story Laddie?"

"Samaria, about meeting a woman at a well."

"Oh such a great story Branden, one of many where Jesus went to those who would least expect him."

"Yes Father." Jamison used his uncle's formal title whenever he began talking his faith.

"Go on Laddie."

"Lisa says, you will hear, that she and the boyfriend were there and saw people. She thought she saw Jesus in the distance. Then she said the boy appeared very frightened and told her to quit whatever she was doing. At the same time Gideon was barking and pulling on her clothing and pushed her head so she woke up as did the boyfriend. She said he was very angry; he said she had done something to him. Lisa said he claimed she had hypnotized him since she learned how to from her shrink. Lisa was upset and tells me that he is no longer her boyfriend, even if he wanted to be."

"She was distressed from this experience?"

"Yes, very much so; and I forgot, she asked me to talk to the boyfriend and get him to tell me what happened. I told her I would not do that."

Uncle Glen said, "Good decision Branden, unless he comes to you of course."

Uncle Ryan added, "Branden, if this was an elaborate dream from her imagination; why do you think she didn't simply keep him in it and have him part of the story she was experiencing?"

Jamison responded, "What? Like I said, they were together. She said Gideon's bark brought her out of her sleep episode after only one or two minutes. You know she has always been honest with me. She isn't telling stories, or she could have done that."

He clearly heard his Uncle Glen muttering in the background. "Maybe a shared dream?"

Jamison spoke up, "Uncle Glen, did you say something about shared dreams?"

Uncle Glenn said, "Yes, you know I have done extensive research on that phenomenon. If Lisa and this Josh have an intimate relationship, a dream could be shared."

"I gave it a thought Uncle Glen, about shared dreams; after all I do read your work. She shares details of her life with me. I don't think their relationship is intimate. I know she would have told me if they were intimate sexually. She once told me she is sometimes uncomfortable with some of his caresses. She often shares details of her life that I have no need or desire to know."

Uncle Ryan asked, "What are the other logical ideas Branden?"

Jamison didn't respond. He chatted a few more minutes with the uncles. Like himself, he knew they would want to listen to Lisa's story themselves before offering opinions.

The next few weeks the Josh thing made lunches and other times the group got together awkward for Lisa. Neither of them had to say anything for everyone to know they were no longer a couple. Jane knew they had a disagreement, and went out of her way to be kind.

Josh immediately started dating a cheerleader named Diane. After a couple of weeks of snide remarks from some of the group like, "Get a room;" Jane told Josh in front of everyone. "Josh, we don't know what you are trying to prove, but the sexual innuendo stuff in front of all of us just isn't cool. Just grow up!"

Lisa was thankful for the Diane thing, it got her off the hook with her friends for an explanation as to why the break up. They all assumed it was due to Diane; and Josh was willing to let everyone accept that as the reason he dumped Lisa. Even so she still felt guilty for what she did to him.

The next day when Jane picked Lisa up for youth night she said, "Josh is acting like a jerk because he lost the hottest girl in school, so he is trying to prove something with this Diane stuff."

"What?"

"Lisa you are. It has only been a few weeks since you became free, but the guys will be lining up, even though you are shy. A girl who looks like you doesn't go without a boyfriend for long; looks are almost everything you know."

Lisa was surprised at what Jane said since she still felt like a freak, regardless of what she looked like. She never learned how to flirt, and it took six months before she and Josh got together. Then only because she thought Jane had a hand in it. Lisa thought Jane was the hottest girl, her blond hair would do anything she wanted, and her clothes were delightful. Lisa still dressed toward the conservative side due to her mother's influence.

"Lisa, are you here?"

"Hottest, Jane that is you. I am not interested in boys right now with just three weeks of school left."

"Josh isn't worth it Lisa."

They were silent a few minutes as they were both enjoying the song on the radio. Jane was introducing Lisa to her favorites. Then Jane surprised her with. "There is always that gorgeous George friend of yours."

"George? Jane he is twenty-one, five years older than me."

"Lisa he is a hunk, and why do you think he keeps seeing you."

"He comes to see Gideon and work with his training."

Jane laughed and laughed.

"Shut up and drive."

Lisa was distracted at youth that evening. She began thinking about George, how his hair was curly and he had dimples when he smiled. He was just a friend, but maybe Jane was right, just maybe he had an interest in being more than a friend. She swore to herself that if she and George got together, she would never tell him the truth about her freak secret.

Although Lisa expected to have more time for her own reading choices now that school was out, she knew now having friends would continue to cut into her reading time. She and Gideon were reading in the library when her father came in and sat by her. At least Gideon was on the floor instead of by her side. Her father sat on the sofa across from her; said he had something they needed to discuss.

Lisa frowned, "What?"

"I had an interesting conversation with George yesterday. He called and came to my office."

Lisa put her book down and gave her father her full attention.

"He told me he understood that you and Josh are no longer seeing each other. Is this true?"

Lisa nodded her head.

"Josh was a nice boy, and your age." Her father was quiet for a few moments and Lisa thought he was done and picked her book up again. He was not.

"George came to see me to ask if he could date you. He told me it was not for an old-fashioned reason, but that he thought your mother and I might have some concerns since you are only sixteen and he is twenty-one." He looked at her intently and continued, "Have you and George been going out?"

Lisa was surprised. "No, the only time I have seen him is here at the house when he is here to train Gideon, or we go out to walk Gideon. Sometimes he will stop by just to see how Gideon is doing." She smiled at her father, "We always have things to talk about besides Gideon." Then she gave a frown. "Besides, Josh was like sort of my boyfriend for the last year."

"Do you like George?"

"I don't know Dad; how do you know something like that? I consider him a good friend."

"If he wanted to take you to dinner on a date; is that something you want?"

"I guess I do like spending time with him, so sure."

"Good, that is what I thought. I like George. I told him it was up to you, of course. And I also told him I would keep my eye on him, and there would be a strict curfew."

"Dad!"

"Like I said, I like George. Treat him right Lisa."

"What?"

"He is starting his junior year and has six more years of school; you have six more years."

"Dad!" Lisa felt more shocked with her father's comment about six more years, than with the idea that George wanted to date her and had even asked permission.

He stood and walked over and kissed her on the forehead. Then changed the subject, and they talked about the family three-week road trip starting on Saturday. Lisa always loved the annual road trip; however, this year she would miss time with her friends; perhaps miss George.

Just as he left the room he added, "Did you know he got a job this summer training two dogs for the police department? He says training the handlers is more work than training the dogs, which is easy."

"George?"

"Sure, who else have we been talking about."

Lisa was not sure what dating George would mean. Everyone seemed to already have put her and George together. Jamison even had inferred she might have some feelings there. She liked George but wasn't sure she was ready for something other than continuing the friendship they already had.

Jamison was expecting Lisa in a few minutes. Although he received a number of text messages from her during the family road trip only one was that she had the beginning of an episode, which she prevented with her timer, combined with Gideon. Lisa only had three sleep episodes, including the one last week, in the last three months since what she referred to as the Josh affair. She had been in control in all three. He decided to extend his upcoming trip to Ireland to six weeks instead of the four planned. Lisa really didn't need him, she had matured and now had many interests and friends.

Lisa bounced into his office and gave him a hug. "I have missed you Jamison!" She was wearing shorts and a white cotton shirt. At sixteen, she could have passed as twenty today. She took her sandals off and curled up in the chair with Gideon in his usual position on the floor at her feet. "It was a wonderful trip. Gideon was a great traveler and with his service dog coat he was welcome everywhere. I do have to tell people, especially children not to pet him. I say, 'He is not a pet, he is a working dog, please do not distract him.' Then curious ones can't resist but ask what he is doing. So, my response is that 'I have a medical condition, he protects me.' Rude people try to ask more but I ignore them and generally my parents will also intervene."

Jamison said, "Thank you for the texts and sharing the pictures. How did you like the South in the summer?"

"Ugh! My mom didn't say anything to my dad, just gave him looks. As you know Ginny didn't go with us because she said no way was she going to Georgia in July. But mostly we were in hotels or the car. Not much outdoor time even for evenings. The heat seems to hang around all night." She shrugged her shoulders and added, "Everywhere is air conditioned, we were all right most of the time; only it was a bit hard on Gideon."

Then she handed him her book list with only four books for the three-week trip.

Jamison decided to get to business. "Do you think you did not have many experiences because you are not reading as much, or do you think you are gaining control over them?"

"Honestly, I think both. The last few times when I felt a book calling me, I did push the timer, but felt that I could say no and not go in even without doing that."

Jamison smiled at her response; then asked, "What are your plans for the rest of the summer?"

Lisa's face showed a slight blush as she whispered, "I might be spending more time with George, maybe."

"George?"

"Did I tell you that Dad said he asked him if he could date me?" She was grinning now. "He said he likes George and it was okay even though he is so much older than I am. He is twenty-one, yes still is in school. He has six more years. But so do I."

Jamison thought to himself the five-year difference was one only a sixteen-year-old would consider as much older. "What are some of the plans you and George have?

"Not really plans Jamison. Only I hope to spend some time with him. I think we are already friends, like more than just as Gideon's trainer." She then giggled, "Obviously, more than friends, since he wants to date me. I think I like him Jamison."

Jamison did not want any more details, especially since she had provided so much with the Josh breakup. He simply smiled and nodded.

"Don't give me the doctor look Jamison. You and I will always be an item since we are soulmates."

Jamison sighed inwardly. "Lisa, you know…"

She stopped him with a teasing smile, "You are my first and true love Jamison; but I do think I would like to marry George."

Jamison diverted the conversation back to why she was there and they proceeded with her hypnotherapy session. She moaned when he told her he would be in Ireland the next six weeks. He reminded her she would be busy getting to know George.

He did the paperwork for her therapy files. If the number of Lisa's episodes continued to decrease and her control continued, he would write his final article and close her case. He did have to admit he may only have been responsible for some of her success, growing up and finding herself may also have accounted forpart of her success. He knew he would miss the delightful Lisa Longford.

Chapter 12

"If you would be a real seeker after truth, it is necessary that at least once in your life you doubt, as far as possible, all things." [RENE DESCARTES]

JAMISON LOOKED FORWARD to meeting with Lisa on his return from his six-weeks in Ireland. She only had two episodes during the six weeks. As usual, she sent him a text, among many others, when they happened. She had control and did not go into the story she was reading in either of the episodes. They met the week before school started.

The beginning of the session involved talking about what they each had been doing the last six weeks. As usual Lisa wanted to know about Ireland, Jamison's uncles, and as much as he would tell her about the village they lived in. He humored her, except that he left out his growing relationship with Colleen, a young widow recently returned to the village.

Lisa complained, "Our sessions would be much shorter if you kept me updated at least every week like I do you. And the pictures you promised. I only got a few. I send you updates and pictures of what I have been up to." She gave him a charming smile.

He reminded her. "Certainly, I need to know what was happening in your life Lisa. But you might limit communication to significant things. You do understand Lisa?"

She responded, "I know, I know Jamison. Then you already know George and I are now dating. But at least I didn't text you about my concerns about how much he cares about me. I know George has been working all summer helping train the new police dogs and taking an on-line class. We don't see enough of each other, in my opinion. Am I asking too much?"

When Jamison was not willing to answer that question, she continued with an update on her family. Ginny and Walt finally set a date and would be married the first week of December. Since she had no episodes, the session was for the hypnotherapy. They also worked with Gideon to see how Gideon was doing in waking her with his special bark. He had her feign falling asleep. Within a minute Gideon responded appropriately and was given praise and treats.

She gave him her reading list for the six weeks he had been gone. He looked at it and noticed it was about the equivalent to a week's worth of reading from two years ago. He asked her, "Are you still reading in the Gospels?"

"Some; the Gospels really don't have that many stories when you consider all of books. Much of the writing is Jesus' teaching and the parables and things like that. I have read Acts twice. Now that book has a number of stories I would love to visit." She stopped when she saw his eyebrows rise slightly. She went on, "I would love to see Paul and some of the wonderful adventures he experienced. I have had no invitations to those stories."

"Lisa, I thought you were going to change your thinking and not encourage your brain to go there."

"I know, and see how well my efforts are working."

He laughed, "And did a busy summer and George assist you in those efforts?"

"Yeah, I guess, I think this summer I read fewer books than I generally do in the summer break from school." She glanced at the list and added, "The kinds of books I'm reading now also are different. Remember how I loved to roam through castles and mansions a few years ago. Now I read more books in contemporary settings. Maybe some of it is like you said, that now I am not curious about the story settings."

"Like you were curious about the settings for the Gospel stories?"

She was quiet for a moment, then added, "Interesting, yes that might be it. But then there always is Jesus."

Jamison decided it was time to bring up what he knew would be a difficult subject for Lisa... that she may no longer need their therapy sessions. "Lisa since you are doing so very well and gaining control over your life, I believe six weeks might be a better interval between sessions." He watched as she clearly reacted to his statement as she stared at the floor. Before she could respond he pulled out one of what he considered two of his trump cards for helping her accept their eventual separation. "I contacted your care team and they have agreed to remove medical restrictions." He pointed to her medical alert bracelet.

"Like I can drive?"

He nodded.

Lisa climbed out of her chair and wrapped her arms around Jamison nearly knocking him over as the desk chair went rolling backward.

"What do you think?"

"Wonderful."

"Then we can get together in six weeks; and I will expect that you will let me know about any changes or when you have an episode."

She moved to the window and stared out. "I don't know how I shall do without you Jamison. Remember we are soul-mates."

He gave an inward sigh. "Is six weeks so long?"

"Yes."

He added his second trump card. "Remember when we talked about your contributing to the next article about your case? We can begin on that."

She turned to him and her eyes brightened.

"I need your parent's consent for you to work with me."

"I am sure they will." She gave him with one of her confident grins.

Jamison suddenly felt relaxed about the situation. He wasn't sure if Lisa really realized the six-week thing would be leading to a three-month interval and so on.

The bell from the outer office signaled someone was there, probably Lisa's ride. Jamison stood. "It must be Ginny here for you."

"No, George brought me."

They walked to the door. Gideon's tail went wild at the sight of George, even though he quietly and obediently remained at Lisa's side.

When they left Jamison completed his clinical notes in Lisa's file; along with the recommendation that her medical restrictions be removed. He then took her reading list into his study where he kept her other file with details of her dreams. They had not talked about her regular night dreams this time and hadn't for some time. Over the years those did not seem to have any correlation with her dreams during her sleep episodes.

Even though she had no dreams from the two sleep episodes over the last six weeks, he would send the book list to his uncles. The list usually had the book or story circled that was part of or the cause for a sleep episode. Jamison knew it was time to close both of Lisa's files. He was relieved, yet somehow disappointed that her dreams of experiencing Jesus in the Gospel stories had ended. He knew his own return to his faith had been restored because of the dreams of her adventures in the Gospels. He should have told her, and he would. It was important she know he might not believe she was there, but her descriptions from her wonderful, and perhaps inspired imaginative dreams brought the truth and reality of Jesus back into his life.

Jamison had been impressed when Lisa said the Gospel stories were more real to her because they were so very short. In his practice he knew the more words a person used the less truthful they tended to be. It seemed to him when his clients took time to carefully think out what they were telling him and chose their words carefully, that they came closer to the truth. Perhaps that was why when he read the example Jesus used about prayer, "Lord have mercy on me a sinner;" Jamison had fallen on his knees and repeated that prayer. He hadn't been to confession in years and wondered then if it would take hours, or if the priest would accept that simple confession.

———

Lisa had no sleep episodes or even potential episodes in the next three weeks from her last meeting with Jamison. She was meeting him today to start on the article they were writing together about her case. When she and Gideon arrived at his office, he led them past the sofas and small table to a door at the far end of the room. As he opened the door, he turned to her, "We will work in my study." He gestured around the office. "The office is for consulting and therapy meetings."

They went in. Lisa looked around the study; the walls were floor to ceiling with bookshelves except the windowed wall. Then she saw two large red leather chairs, copies of the one in his office. Her eyes grew large as she stared, then walked around and lovingly caressed each chair. She looked at Jamison, "You have been holding out on me four years."

"What?"

"Why didn't you tell me you had more of these? You told me you bought mine, well the other one, in Italy and it was handmade for you. Now you have three?"

"The subject didn't come up Lisa, why?"

"I don't know. All these years we could have been meeting in here, each of us in one of these wonderful chairs. Maybe..." she said with a soft smile, "Because we are soulmates, we could each have been more comfortable in here together." Then she frowned, "Instead of you on that rolling office chair." She chose one and sank down into the familiar softness of the leather and looked around the cozy study full of books.

Jamison went to a closet, which opened into a small coffee bar, complete with real espresso machine. "What is your pleasure Lisa?"

She asked for a cappuccino then stood again and perused the bookshelves. She walked around the room scanning the titles that included a variety subjects including many classics. "These are not all professional books. Do you have more at home?"

"Well—yes, I have a library at home. You know how libraries tend to expand."

She smiled and remembered when she had proudly shown him their family library, and her father had shown him his personal library in the basement. Obviously, they were soulmates; Jamison was book people.

They chatted while he made their drinks. He handed her a large cup with her cappuccino, complete with the resemblance of a dog's head in the cream. She took it and returned to the red chair where Gideon had remained while she did her little tour of books. She looked into her cup. "How did you do that?"

"A lot of practice."

"Am I here to see what a great barista you are?"

He smiled as he placed a bowl of water down for Gideon. Then sat in the other red chair opposite Lisa. "That—and also to get started on our article."

Lisa was distracted by the comfort and beauty of Jamison's study. She looked around and began noticing small art pieces on the shelves among the books. She wanted to simply be there and perhaps talk about books and stories with Jamison. She was not in a mood to begin doing anything that sounded like work. She sipped her cappuccino and watched as the creamy dog's head morphed in to a cloud whisper.

"Lisa?" Jamison brought her out of her reverie. "What I wish to do is to add more details about your experiences, but only if you approve. As with the other three published papers about your case, you are an anonymous patient."

Lisa appreciated it that Jamison seemed to consider them a team, just as she thought of them as soulmates.

"For this paper we will use your input, your side versus my side, as you sometimes like to call it. I believe the paper I am proposing will be published based on my reputation; otherwise no reputable journal will take what I am proposing. The paper will be my side of our case, and equal space to be your side. Your side, as the patient, needs to be written so no one can guess the gender or age of the patient in this case. Similar to the way these cases are presented." He stood and retrieved a small handful of professional journals with yellow bookmarks for selected pages. He handed them to her and sat again.

She sipped her cappuccino, then replied, "You knew I decided a few months ago my career of choice would be as a writer. To hide my identity, age, and gender will be a good exercise for me." She relaxed and smiled. "I am looking forward to doing this Jamison."

"Your school work is priority. My agreement with your parents was to obtain their approval of our article before I submit it for publication. Lisa there is a risk to you. So far you are not sharing details about your experiences with your parents."

"I know, I didn't and still don't want them to think of me as a freak." She hesitated and added, "Like Josh."

"Lisa it is up to you entirely what you wish to disclose. My recommendation is that you, as the patient in the case, not as the real you, agree with my diagnosis of dreams. The amount of reality the patient, you, experience in the dreams is up to you."

He stopped and Lisa thought he looked troubled as he added. "If you wish to share our opinion differences regarding experiences, of adventure versus dream; then I will write my part of the article with that perspective. I would like you to begin and set the tone, I will follow with the therapist's side that matches events you decide to include."

Lisa said, "What you mean is that I can write as a patient who has vivid dreams during a sleep episode, the therapy is to give him or her ability to control the dreams and thus the duration or existence of the sleep episode."

Jamison seemed to respect her moment of thought and silence. She continued, "Or I can show the patient as a person who believes he or she is really there inside the book experiencing adventures from unwritten pages. The person who disagrees with the doctor."

"Needless to say, we will both be truthful, but truthful on a need to know basis. Withholding intimate details from others not involved is not being untruthful. Few people share their dreams, other than with intimate friends. Our article should be more about our experience and about us working as a team, not especially the content of your dreams. Does that make sense?"

Lisa nodded in relief. She had no problems disclosing she had a sleep disorder; she did have a problem disclosing to anyone other than Jamison that she was a freak, that she really was there in the story. That didn't work out very well with Josh who supposedly had cared about her.

They talked about the writing process. They would exchange drafts by email and plan on talking by phone when necessary. He reminded her again that school was her priority. As they were wrapping up, Jamison said he had something to share with her, not as her therapist, but as a friend. He told her that he began reading the Gospels to better understand her dreams, and confessed her faith and way of seeing Jesus in her dreams was a significant influence on his return to his faith. He had not been to Mass for years, except when in Ireland with his uncles. He wanted her to know that her desire to see Jesus had awakened in him such a desire. With his faith restored he was now attending Mass regularly. He even commented that his uncle Father Ryan told him he needed to share the renewal of his faith with Lisa.

Lisa did not get much writing done for her article with Jamison. She apologized several times and gave up. Her life was simply too complicated. The few spare minutes she had were devoted to George. Also she was taking several extra classes her school offered that would provide college credits. Those along with her other classes, resulted in a full schedule, in addition to her being editor of the school paper. Then there was Ginny's wedding scheduled for the first of December. Even though Ginny was doing all the planning and work, Lisa and her mother acted as her consultants, even though Ginny did not request their approval on every detail. Even Gideon was suffering from lack of attention and walks. She was surprised when her dad began taking him out for nearly an hour every morning.

A few weeks after Lisa got her driver's license, she decided to take Jane and Grace out for shopping and lunch to celebrate her independence. She had also been neglecting them, because she now attended George's church instead of theirs. After the first excited greetings and congratulations for her license, the girls began with what they called boy talk. Jane made the first announcement.

"Look." She held out her arm with a small gold bracelet.

Grace in the back leaned over the seat to see. "Very nice."

"It is a steady bracelet. When Dave gave it to me, he was so cute. He said rings were more serious, then added that he was serious, but a bracelet was like a larger ring ,like his affection for me."

Grace asked, "Affection?"

"We are not at the stage for the word love yet."

Grace added, "That's nice. Affection is a nice word, better than like."

The three girls giggled. They arrived at the Mexican restaurant for lunch and continued the boy talk once lunch was ordered. They all were able to admire the bracelet more closely than in the car. Grace brought up George. "Are you and George like steady?"

She had to admit to them, "We haven't talked about it."

Grace added, "Exclusive?"

Jane said, "That's the same thing."

Grace went on, "You need to use the words; helps prevent making assumptions like I did with Ron. I assumed we were dating exclusive, he didn't."

The other two just looked at her but didn't say anything. Lisa knew they all had known about Ron; but assumed Grace also knew, so they didn't say anything to her. They probably wouldn't have anyway. No one wants to tell a girlfriend her guy is two or three timing her. Lisa's friends seemed to be very interested in Ginny's wedding. She thought they couldn't help it, since she talked about it often enough.

Jane asked, "Where is Ginny going to live when they get married?"

"She bought a house only two blocks from us. She is still going to take care of us, supervise the cleaning lady, do shopping and help with meals, but go to her own house with Walt at night."

"So Walt must have a lot of money to buy a house in your neighborhood."

Lisa replied, "I don't know. I think Ginny has enough. She bought her new car for cash and Dad helps her with her investments. He said Walt was marrying Ginny for her money. I think he was joking."

"Wasn't she like, the help?"

"No, she is family, but I do think my parents paid her. She will still manage the house." She sighed, "I don't know about money stuff. I need to learn."

Jane laughed, "We know. You still don't look at price tags."

Lisa felt a little embarrassed. At least she knew better than to tell her friends Ginny was paid as a nurse for the fifteen years she lived with them, and only had to spend money on clothes and personal things. She heard her father tell Ginny to take out a mortgage on the house instead of paying cash as her investments were earning more than the mortgage interest. Lisa was glad George planned on becoming a stockbroker or banker or something like that. Then she still wouldn't have to think about money.

The shopping trip was to find costumes for a Halloween party they were all attending. Lisa and George were going as space aliens. She wanted green tights and some green face paint for her and George. He said no to tights for himself; she thought he would look pretty good in them. When she got home she tried on her costume without the green paint part. She read something in a book once where the author thought maybe what people in ancient days thought of as demons were really visiting aliens. She talked to pastor about it and he walked her through the scriptures about what they really were. She knew Americans didn't believe in demons any more than they did space aliens.

She went to the kitchen to talk to Ginny and show off her costume.

Ginny grinned at her, "You are too cute to be an alien dear."

"My face will be green to go with the rest of the costume."

"I am happy you are getting out more."

Lisa sighed, "Only when George is in town. I do miss him. Hum, something smells good."

"Dinner is in the crockpot. I am meeting Walt at our house, we have some painting to finish before we can move in some of his stuff."

Lisa saw a gleam and glow coming from Ginny as she continued. "Only four weeks before the wedding, we have a lot of work to do. But he needs to move in next week since his house sold much more quickly than he expected. Never mind Lisa, you know all this. I seem to be babbling lately." She gave Lisa a hug as she left. "See you tonight dear. I won't be too late. You can feed the Dean and your mom."

Lisa walked to the crockpot, lifted the lid and responded, "Sure. I will hand them a plate and..."

Ginny was gone before she could continue her smart remark.

Lisa opened a can of dog food for Gideon and sat and drank a cup of coffee while he was eating. She watched him eat and decided he was gentleman dog who eats nicely, not gulping his food down like some dogs do. She was startled when the phone rang. It was her mom calling to say she and the Dean would not be home until late. Lisa turned the slow cooker off, took the roast and potatoes out onto a bowl to cool before putting them into the refrigerator. She decided she wasn't hungry so headed to the library with Gideon.

They curled up on the sofa. Lisa began to feel lonely so complained to Gideon. "No Ginny, no parents, no George except on weekends. Next month, Ginny will go home every night to her own house. It's just going to be you and me Gideon." She held him closer.

———

Jamison got a confusing phone call from Lisa about seven.

"Jamison, I need to see you now! I had an adventure, but it was all different. I'm scared Jamison. Can you come over?"

"Is your family home Lisa?"

"No, only Gideon and me."

"We can meet for coffee at The Cabos, it is close to your house."

"Now?"

"I can be there in five minutes."

They arrived at the door at the same time. Gideon could go in places since he was a service dog and was wearing his blue coat. Her favorite barista greeted them, "Good evening Lisa and Gideon."

Jamison tried to sound light, "You and Gideon are known here?"

"Yes, it is a University hangout. But mostly because of Henry, George's friend, so we come here sometimes."

When Henry brought their coffee, Lisa took a sip and looked around the busy coffee shop. "Can we sit somewhere more private Jamison?"

"We can." He stood and took their coffees to the counter and asked for them to go. They walked outside. He settled Gideon into the small backseat of his Porsche and apologized to Lisa that the car did not have cup holders.

"We could have taken my car, well my Mom's. Ginny went with Walt to do more painting on her house, or maybe it is their house. I don't know."

When he didn't start the car she asked, "Where are we going?"

"Here, you wanted a private place to talk."

She silently sipped her coffee as the windows fogged up, Gideon whined. It seemed he thought when someone was in a car it should be moving. She reached her hand back and patted him on the head. "It is okay Gideon. We are here to talk."

She finally turned to look at Jamison and began. "I had an adventure into a Gospel story. But, Jamison I did not plan on going there. Not that I ever do plan, but like I have told you usually I am reading the story and thinking about it. And yes, sometimes I want to go into a story to see a miracle, to see Jesus; not this time."

"Tell me what happened."

"I went shopping with Jane and Grace to get a costume for a..."

"Give me the short version."

"Ginny was with Walt to work on their house. After next month she will leave every evening to go home, to her own house. Mom called and said she and Dad would be home late."

He noticed a change in her voice. "I only see George on weekends. I was feeling alone and—and grumpy," she took a deep sigh, "I had put on my costume, a green alien costume to show Ginny, who wasn't interested. Anyway, I changed my clothes. Okay the short version. Gideon and I were in the library. I was going to read for my world history class. I don't let him sit by me anymore if I am reading. See Jamison, I do listen to you and know Gideon needs to protect me. But I wasn't paying attention. I remember that Gideon did have his muzzle on my feet, but I didn't think about it then."

"I picked up my history book and turned to a page with a picture of a Chinese parade with the large colorful dragons and other characters in strange masks. My history book suggests that people in ancient times came up with all sorts of superstitions as a way of making sense of things they did not understand. The scene made me think about my alien costume and about aliens. I had a meeting a couple of months ago with pastor to talk about aliens because I once read something about maybe ancient people thought aliens were demons. He said he didn't think there were aliens. He had several theories about the use of the word 'demon' in the Bible, suggesting it referred to mental illnesses that could not otherwise be explained."

Jamison had ignored his coffee and sat with his eyes closed thinking, 'the short version Lisa,' but knew this probably was the short version.

"Jamison, are you listening?"

"I am Lisa, go on."

"Then with the idea of aliens and demons in my head, I thought about the time I rescued Andrew's Gideon in the boat on the lake and got soaked. I remember back then I wanted to go into that particular story because Jesus would cast out demons from someone when they got to the other side of the lake. After that storm I was home..." She emphasized the word 'soaked.'

"That is all I was thinking, and then it happened Jamison. I was there in Galilee in that story of the man with demons. I didn't have my Bible and wasn't reading. I was thinking about the experience in the boat and about where they were going, but wasn't really wishing I could be there. What frightened me Jamison is that my adventures were always from the story I was reading; and sometimes when I was curious and wondering what if... This time not; it was like the Pevensie kids in Narnia; I was there unexpectedly. I wasn't completely frightened until I got home again."

"Do you have any idea how long the dream was?"

"I was there about an hour. Then I called you when I was back home."

"Oh Lisa, how long has it been?" He answered his own question. "About seven months since you had an event."

"Jamison, I couldn't stop it because it happened so fast. And ..."

"Was the dream frightening, the demon part?"

"No, I didn't see anything frightening. I think they were just crazy men and Jesus healed them and gave them back their sound minds."

He was silent for a while, then said, "Lisa, do you know why Gideon did not wake you?"

"Jamison, he was there with me. I just didn't pay attention to him touching my feet."

"Do you wish to hear what happened?"

The car windows were completely fogged over and it was getting chilly. Gideon made a few more plaintive whining sounds. "I do. Are you feeling better right now, still frightened?"

Lisa was silent as she drank her coffee. "I am okay now, and yes I can tell you the details later."

"Can you come to the office tomorrow after school."

Lisa's voice quivered. "It is not Gideon's fault. I am sorry Jamison that I disappointed you."

He reached over and patted her shoulder. "No, I am sorry Lisa. You have been doing so very well. I should not have said that about Gideon. I am proud of your accomplishments." Only he wondered if like Gideon, he was too close to Lisa to protect her.

Jamison walked Lisa and Gideon over to her car. After she left, he drove home. He was sure she was telling the truth. The article they were working on would have to be abandoned, since now after this incident, she may now have even less control over her sleep episodes. Worse yet, what she told him meant he would have to share the event with her care team. Before, the diagnosis had always been that she was possibly suffering from self-hypnosis as she was reading. According to Lisa this event did not involve reading. He mused. Then again, she said she had her history book open. Maybe her episode dreams were not directly related to the story she was reading. Maybe? He was confused. He would call his uncles when he got home. He didn't. He wanted to hear Lisa's story the next day first.

———

Jamison paced the floor in his study. He had missed something, some clue. His uncle Glen had his opinion; now Jamison wondered why he had not listened to him. He knew why. He was a man of science, a seeker of truth. His uncle, Professor Glen Jamison, studied and researched paranormal events over forty years. Most of his research related to dreams and sleep disorders. Both of his uncles did warn him Lisa was vulnerable and at risk of getting lost. Lost where? He reached for a bottle of Jameson on a shelf in his coffee bar and poured it into a small glass. He sat in one of the large comfortable red chairs to consider what he would say to Lisa. His conscience would not let him ignore what she told him last night. Now, if she could slip into a sleep episode without a book? If she could, then his hypothesis that she was hypnotizing herself as her eyes moved over the printed lines was a false one.

However, his treatment had been successful. With the hypnotherapy she had gone from several episodes a week, down to several a month and to none for the last seven months. He poured another whisky, he thought he needed one before he could face Lisa. He mused to himself. Both the uncles suggested he get Lisa to Ireland as soon as possible. What they referred to as a land of mystery and faith, where the earth and trees and every living thing could communicate with the human soul. Their solution was opposite of his; they thought mystery led to truth. He thought instead that truth dispelled mystery. The problem was that the uncles both seemed to believe what Lisa said. Jamison also knew she was telling the truth, that was his gift, or curse. "Where do you go Lisa? How can I get to you, how to keep you here with your family, and yes, my dear soulmate, to keep you safe and happy with George?"

He heard a soft ding from his computer monitor; he looked to the screen and saw Lisa getting off the elevator and walking toward his office. All the offices on the ninth floor had these security systems. She was a beautiful young woman. He smiled to himself. Whisk her to Ireland? He knew for certain she would have her bag packed in the morning with even the whisper of such an idea, even with her growing love for George. Ireland was not going to happen.

Jamison opened the office door to Lisa and Gideon.

"Good afternoon Lisa," He bent down and patted Gideon who licked his hand. "We will meet in my study today." He went to the office desk and retrieved the tape recorder and led them into his study.

"Cappuccino?"

"Yes, please."

Lisa made herself comfortable in one of the leather chairs. Gideon sat at her feet. They talked about the weather and her family while he made her a coffee and one for himself. It took a few minutes to find a good spot for the recorder and accessible plug. Then he sat in the red chair opposite her.

"Ready to tell me about your dream?"

"My adventure," she countered. "Like I told you last night, it started as I was thinking about demons and remembering when I was on the lake in the storm and trying to save Gideon and got soaked. Suddenly I was there only a few feet from our boat with its broken mast, and the larger fishing boat with the disciples." He quickly made a mental note, Lisa referred to it as 'our boat.' She was still taking her dreams much too seriously. His focus returned to Lisa's story.

"The disciples had two large fires going. On one they were roasting fish. It seemed the other larger fire was being used to dry clothing and fishing nets that were propped up on nearby branches. Jesus was further away, alone facing the lake. The sun was high in the sky, like at noon; clouds from the storm were completely gone. I felt Gideon close by me and realized it was my Gideon. I looked around and didn't see Andrew's Gideon. I walked toward Jesus, and he greeted me, 'Welcome back Lisa. You decided to come back to see the end of this, ah, this adventure.'

"I didn't know what to say to him. He looked at me intently, smiled at me and said, 'It all shall be well Lisa.' Just then Andrew's Gideon ran up to us. He and my Gideon did the dog get acquainted thing, then ran back to where the disciples were mending the broken mast. Jesus looked back at me. 'It was kind of you to help Gideon in the storm. I would not have let him come to harm, but you comforted him in his troubled time. Even before he was sent to live with you.'"

She finished her coffee and sat the cup down. "He really did say that Jamison, like he knew about Gideon." She continued, "I didn't know what to say. It was the first time he had talked with me like this, and to mention that I had been kind. I was almost in tears. So, I smiled at him and reached down and petted Gideon who had not run off with the other Gideon. I was proud of my Gideon; he is a good dog."

"Then Jesus was talking again. 'You came to see what your people might refer to as a mentally ill person, and as I remember it, perhaps to see pigs cliff-dive into the lake.' I relaxed and laughed with him. He knew all and I didn't need to ask any more questions. He said it would be well. He used those exact words Jamison."

Gideon stood and walked to the door as a clue he needed a break. Jamison turned the recorder off and waited for them to come back. It was raining by then, so when they returned they needed to spend a few minutes wiping Gideon's feet with paper towels. Jamison made two more coffees, gave Gideon a bowl of water, and turned the recorder on again.

Lisa seemed thoughtful, then she began her narrative again. "Jesus and I walked back to where the disciples were at various tasks and the two dogs went romping into the shallows of the lake. Jesus said something like, 'The boys are about to be in for a surprise. I know the stories are not clear if there was more than one troubled man. There were two, twins like your sons, but so alike no one could tell one from the other, and both afflicted and tormented. They will be here shortly.' He then suggested I walk down the shore in the other direction as the men would not be wearing clothing and that might disturb me. He pointed to a cliff and said that would be where the pigs would do what I had referred to as cliff-diving."

"Remember way back then that was one of the reasons I wanted to go in the boat. I was younger then." She paused and gave a tentative smile, "He did say, 'twins like your sons,' I don't know Jamison what that was about. Back to my adventure. Then Jesus told me to come back when I saw the twins sitting with them by the fire. It did get a little scary then when I heard screaming and a large commotion so I headed down the shoreline in the direction Jesus had indicated. Both dogs were right at my heels. The sound of the men's yells frightened them as it did me. I did not turn to look. I did see the pigs in the distance, they were large, but not as large as those I have seen at our county fair. I guessed maybe at least twenty or more, it was hard to tell. I never did know why pigs since Jewish people did not eat them. They must have been raising them for the Romans and others living among them. I stopped when I heard the loud squealing of the pigs. Both dogs stood, one on each side of me. The noise was even worse than the sounds coming from the crazy men. And they did indeed run off the cliff into the water. At first I was afraid some of them would swim to shore, but none did. The dogs and I stood there until all was quiet, then we turned back and walked toward the fires and the group of disciples."

"Andrew called to his Gideon and he went to him. My Gideon stayed by me. The two men had blankets wrapped around them and were talking with Jesus. Their hair and beards were matted and I could smell a horrid stench I knew was coming from them. I looked closely at their faces and could see their eyes. The feeling I got from their eyes was one of gentleness. Jesus looked up at me and smiled. Then I was back home in the library. Again Gideon seemed confused and I was so sorry about him having to go with me. He has been rather clingy since then, or I guess you would say protective."

As usual he waited until she was finished before asking many questions. "Last night you said something about reading history. Did you have your book open and had you been reading before you were thinking, like you said, about demons?"

She mused a few moments. "I did. I remember that is why I thought about demons. I was looking at a picture of a Chinese parade with one of the long dragons and people with masks of creatures. Yes, the book is what got me to thinking about ancient people's interest in demons and protecting themselves from them." She held out her cup. "More?" Then she added. "And no, I did not have my Bible open then, or reading that story. That was what was so strange about this adventure."

He asked as he began making another cappuccino, "Then you were reading about the Chinese?"

"Yes, but my mind wanders as it sometimes does when I am reading boring parts of a book. I'm not saying the Gospels are boring, the stories are short and for those I simply wondered what it might have been like to be there, wondering not wandering."

They talked while they finished their coffees. Before Lisa left, he told her he had to let her care team know she had her first sleep episode after seven months. He said he didn't think they would revoke her driving privileges. He would tell them he thought it was still due to her reading and self-hypnosis. However, now he was not quite so sure himself. He copied the recording to take to the post office on his way home. He left early as his mind was not amenable for working on several articles he had on his schedule. He also dreaded the phone call to his uncles knowing what they would have to say. He could not, or rather would not, consider a possibility where imagination could become a reality.

———

Jamison got home with time for a long run since the rain had stopped. The air was crisp and the golds and reds of the early autumn leaves contrasted with the blue of the sky. He thought the blue seemed more intense after a rain. Running was the one time he trained his brain to go on autopilot, just think about the feet and pavement, one foot after another. Once home from the run, all the thoughts of Lisa poured back into his head. The girl had gotten to him from the first sparkling smile years ago, the girl who declared herself a freak and liked herself. For the last four years he watched, more than watched, he was part of her life as she evolved from child to woman. Maybe Lisa was right, maybe they were soulmates, whatever that meant. He honestly did not know.

He made the call and got his usual response.

"Hello Branden," came the chorus of his uncle voices.

Uncle Glenn added, "We knew it was ye Laddie."

Jamison smiled at the familiar greeting. They had ceased asking if he was calling about the lassie, since he had nothing to report about Lisa's dreams for seven months now.

He got to the point, "Good evening uncles. I am calling about Lisa."

He heard a collective sigh from the other end of the line in Ireland. They waited for him to speak.

"She had a sleep event yesterday. The tape is on the way to you."

"Still from the Gospels?" Asked Uncle Ryan.

"Yes, only this time she was reading a history textbook, not her Bible."

"Go on."

"She said she was looking at a picture of a Chinese parade with the great dragons and masks of other creatures. She said she knew many of the symbols were superstitious protection against demons. She said she then thought about Gospel stories mentioning demons, then said she remembered when she was there in a story." He paused and realized he was using Lisa's words. He changed. "When she dreamed that she was in the story where Jesus quieted the storm, that in the rest of that story Jesus healed a man with demons. She thought it would be interesting to see that happen; especially the part about the pigs."

Uncle Ryan, then Glenn commented, "Aye, we know the story."

"That is the story, or the dream she was in, she had, yesterday. Also, she said her dog Gideon with her."

He heard nothing but imagined them both shaking their heads together. He thought he could guess what they would say next, and they did.

"Ye need to get the lass here Branden. We need to see her and talk to her."

"You know I can't do that."

"And why not? Surely she would have some time with school holidays coming up. She could stay with us or with your Colleen."

"It is only October; she doesn't have school holidays until December."

"It is important enough she could be excused."

"That is not the point Uncle Glenn. Even if I wanted to, which I don't, how could I bring a young sixteen-year-old girl with me to Ireland?"

"Tell her parents how important that she get treatment here. It is the only place for what you and we know would save her."

"I don't know that. Uncle Glenn, Uncle Ryan, we don't need to go over it again. I believe in truth and facts."

Uncle Glenn spoke, "Do ye now? That is not your heritage Laddie. Here in the land, we see all the truths, all the world, all the worlds. The idea of practical facts makes those in your country blind and their blindness creeps to the rest of the world. You come from a family of mystics Branden. That is what you are, who you are."

Uncle Ryan added, "Ye know that is truth Laddie."

"I cannot bring Lisa to Ireland." He hesitated then added, "If you think you have something useful for her, I will let you talk to her."

His uncles were quiet for what seemed minutes. Jamison wondered why silence always seemed so powerful in that it distorted time. He broke the silence. "Call me when you have listened to her story."

He heard mumbles in the background then Uncle Ryan surprised him with, "How about we make a visit to you. You have said you wished Colleen to visit. The three of us could come. Say nothing now Laddie, think about it. We could come next month for a few weeks and still be home for Christmas."

Before he hung up he said he would consider it. They had played a trump card suggesting Colleen visit. They said their farewells and Jamison reached for a bottle. A little early for a drink, but after all he was a Jamison, maybe he was learning.

Chapter 13

"Though the Witch knew the Deep Magic, there is a magic deeper still which she did not know. Her knowledge goes back only to the dawn of Time." [C. S. LEWIS, *The Lion, The Witch and The Wardrobe*]

IT WAS AN early snow for the first week of November so Lisa's father drove her to Doctor Jamison's office. He said he would return for her and Gideon in a couple of hours. She knew her parents were concerned since they, as well as Jamison, thought her sleep episodes were over after seven months of no incidents; now two only a week apart. Her reading time over the last few months had been reduced because she was taking an extra class in school, and then Ginny's wedding in a few weeks, also she and George had been spending more time together. She wondered herself, why now?

The adventures had been wonderful. But she was a bit frightened since these last two adventures into Gospel stories happened without her actually reading the story they were in. Always in the past a book would call to her as she read and thought about the story she was reading, wondering what was behind the story. However, these episodes happened suddenly. Today she could honestly tell Jamison she had no control. She held back a tear as she pushed the elevator button for the ninth floor. She felt confused and a little frightened. Maybe Jamison could tell her why things had changed, now after seven months.

Lisa met Jamison with the usual greetings as she made herself comfortable in her usual chair. He set up the recorder once Lisa and Gideon were settled in, "Ready to tell me what happened?"

Lisa thought he looked tired or perhaps stressed. She wondered if it was her fault; and thought perhaps that it was. After all they were soulmates and she was sure he did love her, at least in his way. "I have distressed you and George and my family. I am so sorry Jamison, but I swear I did not plan or really want to go this time either." She swallowed hard. "I don't think I did Jamison." Her eyes became misty. "I am sorry Jamison. I am frightened."

He nodded in his understanding doctor's way. "Nothing to be sorry about Lisa."

She sniffled back the emotion that had been creeping up on her. "As you know I have been busy with school, and George, and Ginny and Walt's wedding."

He finally smiled with the soft twinkle in his blue eyes he often gave her.

Lisa continued, "Here is what happened. Yesterday I was sitting on the sofa in the library addressing the rest of the wedding invitations for Ginny, as they had to go out that afternoon. There were not very many to finish. Ginny brought me a cup of tea and some cookies. We chatted and she thanked me for the help and left with the invitations I had finished. When she left, she said she would be out as she was headed for the post office. Mom and dad were at work and I was alone. I know I was already feeling, maybe a bit sad and lonely since Ginny is leaving us in a few weeks. She will keep on doing what she has always done; only she will go home at night, to her own home."

She reached down and patted Gideon on the head. "I know Jamison, you want to know where Gideon was and why he didn't wake me." She sighed deeply and looked into Jamison's blue-grey eyes. "As you know, sometimes I ask Gideon to sit by me when no one else is around, and honestly Jamison, I have been careful not to have him by me when I read. In fact, I now do all my reading in the chair, not the sofa so there is no room for him to be by me. He is such a dear Jamison even though he doesn't understand why."

Lisa noticed the look she got from Jamison when she thought he gave her when he wanted the short version. "When Ginny left, I motioned for Gideon to come up and sit by me. He climbed up and put his head on my lap. I sipped my tea and munched on the cookies. I was thinking about Ginny's wedding, about the food and music and all the preparations involved in a wedding. Then I thought about and wondered about the wedding mentioned in the Gospels. I wasn't reading my Bible and did not have a book by me. I was about to tell you there were no books around, but obviously I was surrounded by books, since I was in the library."

"Then I was there, walking with a group I recognized; Jesus, Peter, Andrew, James, John, and Zebedee. A woman was with Zebedee, and I guessed she was his wife. Peter's wife was also there as I recognized her from my one time at their house. Gideon was at my heels and I reached down and patted his head. I wished I had put the leash on him, but of course, I didn't expect to be there; honestly, Jamison. Jesus was near the back of the group and walked over to me and smiled. He welcomed me, 'Welcome Lisa, I am pleased you decided to visit again.' I was overcome and almost burst into tears. He put his hand on my shoulder. He repeated what he said the last time I was there. 'It shall be well Lisa.'

"Although I didn't cry, I believe a few tears leaked out. I relaxed and smiled at him. I was not sure how it worked but the others were all intent in conversation and as usual didn't notice him talking to me. They never do. I noticed he looked so very young compared to when I had seen him last. Only smile lines, not the heavy darkness under his eyes. Jesus explained, 'the bride is Philip's sister. My mother is second cousin and very close to the mother of the bridegroom. She spent a few days here helping with the preparations as weddings are very important to our people.'"

Lisa smiled at Jamison. "Jesus was considerate to me, an outsider to his world and time. I was almost in tears again because he had given me the background of the event. I followed the group as we neared a village on a hillside. We walked up to a fairly large house, larger than others around it. There were colorful awnings on one side of the house that provided shade for couches and other seating underneath. I heard music coming from a group of men and women playing some kind of harp type instruments I am not familiar with, and some pipes that sounded like recorders."

"Servants came out with the pitchers of water, which they poured over the hands of all the guests as they arrived. I watched as the disciples began mingling with the other guests and for the most part seemed to know many of them. People were dressed better than what I had observed in other visits, they also smelled better. And the delicious aromas of the food are difficult to describe. Smoke and succulent scents came wafting from the back of the house where meat was roasting. Jesus was mingling and talking with others so I wandered back there and saw two goats or perhaps sheep, I couldn't tell from the shape, on spits over a fire pit. Gideon was right by my leg, almost touching me. I did notice his nose twitching over the delicious cooking aromas. Another fire pit had fowls and fish on racks and another with clay pans of some kind where servants were baking some kind of flat bread and putting them into baskets as they were done. This back courtyard from where the food was being prepared and served had almost as many people as the guests in the front.

"I wandered back to the front area and saw more people arriving. People were not paying any more attention to Jesus than to other guests and I remembered his public ministry had not really begun. Here he was just another guest, Mary's son. I remembered the crowds, the thousands of people, maybe some of these were there later when he fed over five thousand who had followed him to that remote area. It was not too crowded for me to walk around, but I still had to take care not to bump into anyone.

"Gideon stayed very close to my heels. I loved him then maybe more than any other time because he was so trusting to just be near me, he felt safe. I kept my eye on Jesus because I still didn't know which of the women was Mary, and guessed she would come and talk to him as she would have done in this story. I also kept my eye on John. He still would glance my way when I moved to a different part of the house or courtyard. I believed Jesus, that he couldn't see me; still it was uncanny. Three women found a seat near Jesus and sat and talked with him for a few minutes. Then he got up and left with one of the three women. They walked by me and I had the opportunity to see her close up. She was very beautiful, but seemed too young to be his mother. Somehow, I knew it was her.

"I wondered if this was the time for the miracle of water to wine so I got up and tried to follow them. Philip and Andrew were right behind him, as were John and Peter. They all went into a smaller room off the outdoor courtyard where we had been sitting. Several servants followed the group; there was no room for me to follow without getting bumped into. I stood near the door trying to hear what was happening inside. But I could not. About ten minutes later the group came out and everyone seemed to return to what they were doing. Two, who might have been the servants, left last and returned with several more men, all carrying huge clay jars. I guess that is what to call them. Then there was a great deal of coming and going from that room with men carrying the jars back and forth. I had to scurry to get out of their way so headed back to the pavilion and to what was going on inside. I was excited and felt sure they had been carrying water in and wine out.

"Other servants were passing around platters of meat, bread, fruit, and little cakes of dates, raisins and dried fruit. Most, except me of course, had a goblet or cup for wine. As I had seen before, sometimes they seem to share their wine cups or goblets. Something we certainly would never do. The servants began refilling these from the pitchers of wine. I also knew he had already turned the water to wine by the reaction of the guests who began comparing their drinks with one another. Jamison, here was another time in a Gospel story and I again missed actually seeing a miracle. I helped my self to a piece of meat and bread from a platter sitting on a table. The meat was a bit spicy, but wonderful. I knew better than offer it to Gideon; he has a strict diet.

"The music increased in volume and beat and people began dancing. The dancing wasn't in couples like we do. Most of the dancers were men; they were good with great footwork and even Peter looked graceful in the line. It seemed there was a pattern of some kind as they danced in a line or in groups. Some of the young women were in a group with tambourines, some wearing colorful shawls or scarfs.

"Then suddenly I was home in the library with Gideon beside me. He licked my face and arm and wagged his tail. I knew he was happy to be home. He didn't seem as distressed as when he had gone with me before."

Lisa let out a huge breath. "I couldn't have stopped it Jamison and lately I have been careful not to let Gideon touch me when I am reading. He notices because I won't even let him lay on my feet."

As Jamison turned the recorder off, Lisa added, "The wedding food was excellent Jamison. I wish you could have been there with me and Gideon."

Jamison talked a few minutes with Lisa's father when he came to pick her up. Her father was concerned. Jamison tried to assure him. "I am sure these recent sleep episodes are only a simple setback and that can happen. Her concerns with the changes in the family structure with Ginny's marriage in a month probably has been unsettling for Lisa." He cringed internally knowing his comment could be the truth, but suspected it was an outright lie.

Richard Longford nodded in assent. "Yes, things have been a bit confusing at home with Ginny's wedding a month away." He chuckled. "I wonder what it will be like when Lisa marries."

Jamison smiled reassuringly and continued, "I do think she will adjust to these changes very well. Except for and in spite of her medical sleep disorder, Lisa is a very well-adjusted young woman." He knew at least that statement was the truth.

Lisa hugged Jamison as she left. "Thank you, Jamison." They scheduled a hypnotherapy session for the next week.

Jamison took the tape from the recorder and took it to his study. He made a copy to send to his uncles for their interpretation. He wanted them to have it soon because of their upcoming trip to see him; so sent it express regardless of the cost. He was looking forward to his uncles and Colleen's visit in three weeks. They would all experience an American Thanksgiving; then the next week was Ginny's wedding. They all had been invited to the wedding, but declined invitations to the Longford Christmas events as Colleen and the uncles wished to be home for Christmas. Lisa had been excited about the uncles visit and seemed happy about meeting what she referred to as the mysterious Colleen.

Jamison finished his notes for both files. In her medical file he made notes that the changes in her family structure may have caused this second relapse of having another episode after seven months of control. Based on past experience he expected the next two months to be uneventful regarding Lisa's sleep episodes, as she would be busy with his uncles' visit, Ginny's Wedding, then Christmas events. And... George would be around more.

He sighed as he closed up the office. He knew any patient with any care program would have a slight relapse. Lisa would be fine. After all, hadn't Jesus told her all would be well. Jamison shook his head and mumbled to himself. He had already been drawn too deeply into the girl's dreams and was beginning to question himself. He often wondered why he had brought the uncles into Lisa's case. He thought his analysis might have taken a different turn without their input and advice. He was distressed that their concerns had rubbed off on him and caused him doubts. He respected their expertise, but after all he was a man of science and a seeker of truth. "Aye, there's the rub," he said out loud to himself as he locked the office door.

———

The Longford household was in the usual holiday season uproar with the addition of Ginny's wedding the first week of December. Lisa regretted Jamison's timing for his uncles and the mysterious Colleen's visit when she would not have the time she wanted to spend with them. She had spoken to both uncles a couple of times by phone, and was eager to see them in person. Although the party from Ireland arrived in time for Thanksgiving, Lisa didn't get to meet them until two days before the wedding. She was delighted with the uncles, but disappointed with Colleen. She had seen a few pictures of her, but still had a romantic idea of meeting a quaint looking Irish girl from a small village. Instead, Colleen was a beautiful young woman, very sophisticated and classy looking, much like Lisa's mother, who took to her immediately.

Father Ryan Jamison and Professor Glen Jamison fit in with Longfords quickly. Lisa had expected them to be something like Jamison, but they were not. She remarked to him, "Jamison, I thought all Irish were quiet and reserved like you. But your uncles seem like they could easily be the life of the party."

"They often are, Lisa. In fact, our village would be a quiet country village if it were not for those two always finding a reason for the village to celebrate one thing or another. I sometimes think they have fabricated much of the ancient history for the village."

With that she saw Colleen and Jamison give each other knowing looks.

Uncle Glenn made sure both Ginny and Walt knew that Walt would not have had a chance if he had the opportunity of meeting the charming and beautiful lass first.

The day after the wedding, the Irish guests had brunch at the Longford's, and Lisa had a few minutes to get to know Colleen better. She was surprised as she and Colleen sat in the library and Colleen commented on the number of books. "I am surprised about American's and their books. Branden's home is full of them, like a library, and..." She looked around the room with books from floor to ceiling. "Your home also, with so very many volumes."

"We are book people."

"All Americans?"

Lisa didn't want to indicate all Americans, so said, "Not all, I guess some of us."

Just then Jamison walked in with her father.

Lisa said, "I was just telling Colleen that we don't represent our country very well—as regarding collecting books.

Jamison laughed, "No, probably not; many people rely on their local libraries, and now often read electronic copies of books."

Her father added, "Brunch is ready. Can you believe it, Ginny baked a ham and left salads and baked muffins for our brunch? Not sure how we will do without her for three weeks."

Lisa wanted to add she was not sure how she was going to do without Jamison for six weeks as he was returning to Ireland until mid-January.

Lisa had no additional sleep episodes in the seven weeks Jamison was in Ireland. As usual she kept him informed of what was happing in her life with several text messages a week. One generally was that she missed him terribly. She did send a message that she felt one instance when she thought a book was calling her, but she said no — and didn't even need to set her wrist alarm.

On New Years Day she texted him that George finally actually told her he loved her. "He used the word love." Then the next day he got another text message. "Jamison, you and I will always be soulmates, always. But I will marry George because I do so love him."

When Jamison returned, he was subjected to Lisa's usual enthusiasm she exhibited when she had not seen him for a while. He accepted her hugs and the kiss on the cheek. Gideon even seemed glad to see him as evidenced by what Jamison thought was extra tail wagging. He suggested they could meet monthly for a hypnotherapy session until the end of the school year; then do a reassessment. She was distressed because she knew the reassessment meant that she might no longer need to see Jamison for therapy.

The uncles were surprised that Lisa had no more incidents after the last two in the fall. Jamison assured them he trusted Lisa's honesty and suggested her emotions and involvement with George may have set her on the right course without their intervention.

Then he got the phone call the week before Easter.

George was home from school the week before Easter. Lisa did feel better with him near. She knew, when being honest, that her concern about Jamison abandoning her was because of all people, she wanted Jamison's approval. She had George's; and after all she and Jamison were soulmates.

That week she and George attended the Maundy Thursday service at his church. She found it to be very moving. When she got home and curled up in bed she found her Bible and wanted to read the story of the crucifixion again herself; she used the version in John's Gospel.

Jamison got a call from Richard Longford at two in the morning. "Doctor Jamison, I am so very sorry to bother you. Lisa has had an episode or some kind of emotional breakdown. She is asking for you. Again, so sorry, is there any way you can come talk to her. Please."

When Jamison got there, Florence met him at the door and ushered him in. she asked, "Would you like coffee?"

"Yes, please; will you tell me what happened?"

They led him to the kitchen and poured him a cup. They all sat at the kitchen table. Richard began, "It was about eleven thirty and we were headed for bed. We heard Gideon barking. Florence was already in bed. I went to the hall to see what was happening. As you know he doesn't bark without a reason. I was only halfway down the hall when I saw Lisa crouched on the floor. She was vomiting and shaking and crying hysterically. I called Florence who came immediately. It took both of us to help her up to the bathroom, where she vomited again. Florence got her cleaned up, and I cleaned the floor."

Jamison remained silent. Florence continued the account, "We both thought she was suffering from food poisoning since she had been fine earlier and had gone to some church service with George. Once we got her cleaned up and into bed her sobs subsided. I convinced Richard we didn't need to rush her to emergency."

Richard looked at them both and shrugged, then he added, "Because I was concerned about food poisoning, I called George to see if he had the same symptoms and to ask what she had eaten with him. He said they both had a hamburger and that he was fine. He wanted to come over. By then it was close to twelve. I told him to call in the morning."

Jamison looked at the two concerned faces. "Why did you call me?"

Florence's eyes misted. "She asked for you, no begged we would ask you to come. Doctor Jamison, Lisa's isn't just crying; she has been sobbing, heart breaking sobs. She said she needed Jamison."

He followed Lisa's parents upstairs. Her bedroom door was open. Richard spoke up, "Doctor Jamison is here." The three of them went into her room. Gideon was curled up next to Lisa who was half sitting propped up with pillows.

Lisa's eyes were red and bloodshot from the heavy tears. She gave them all a feeble smile. "Thank you."

Jamison smiled back at her and sat in the chair Richard moved toward him. Richard and Florence sat on the edge of her bed.

She looked at them and asked, "May I talk to Jamison alone for a few minutes?"

They nodded and left the room.

Jamison pulled the chair closer to the bed. "Bad dream?"

Tears rolled down her cheeks and she shook her head.

"I take it you want to tell me about it now, right?"

She nodded her head again.

Gideon looked up at him as if to say, "I am doing my job doctor, not to worry."

"Was Gideon with you?"

"No, I was here in bed. He thought I was in a normal sleep so didn't bark."

They were both quiet for a few minutes. Finally, Lisa began, "I was there at the crucifixion Jamison."

He sighed.

"George and I went to church for the Maundy Thursday service. When I got home and was in bed I wanted to read about it all. I knew I shouldn't do that, but got my Bible and looked up the story in the Gospel of John. I read the account twice, and I did say or wonder what it might have been like to be there. And I was.

"I found myself shivering even though the air was heavy and oppressive. It was almost dark caused by black clouds that surrounded the place. I saw lightning in the distance and heard what seemed like a steady roll of thunder. I was standing only ten feet from a small group of people. I looked at them first. They had their backs to me, but then I realized John and several women were there. John turned and looked my way. Like usual he looked but did not see.

"My next sensation was the sounds and smells. I didn't want to look, but I looked beyond them and saw the crosses. There were three. They were maybe a two hundred feet or more away. Some soldiers carried torches because of the darkness. Not like night, but a heavy darkness they could feel; I could feel. I had thought the idea of the smell of death was a literary concept. It is not. Maybe it is the smell of blood that makes it the smell of death.

"It was not so dark that I couldn't see him. If I didn't know where I was and who he was I would not have known him. I could not see much of his face because his head was dropped down on his chest. I felt like I knew he was already dead. I looked at the crowd around the crosses. There were about thirty or forty people, mostly Roman soldiers. Some of these were shoving other people back. The man on the cross to the right was screaming in pain. I watched as one of the soldiers walked to him and slammed the butt of his spear into his mouth. The screams stopped with a gurgling sound, then moans through the blood pouring from his mouth.

"I did not want to look at Jesus again, but I did. What I could see of his face was dark black streaks, blood? My eyes went down and I saw the blood from his side still flowing a little into the pool at the foot of the cross. I so wanted to get out of there, to run. Instead for some reason I moved closer to the group I was near. When I saw Mary standing near, I began to cry. The pain in her beautiful face was unbearable. I told myself I wanted to be anywhere else, but I remained there, frozen, almost close enough to touch her. She walked a couple of steps to me and looked me in the eyes. Not like I think John does. She saw me. She spoke to me, 'It shall be well Lisa.' Then she gave me a smile and softly touched my forehead with her finger.

"With that Jamison, I was back home. I sat up in bed with my heart pounding. Gideon was at the foot of my bed whimpering softly. I guess you know the rest of how sick I was." The tears began flowing and she gulped back a sob. "The darkness, the horrid smells, and then her touch. All so real Jamison, so real. I know I was there."

They were both quiet some minutes then he said, "I think we need to tell your parents Lisa. You need to tell them you had a vivid dream and what it was about. They will understand."

She sobbed out, "Okay."

Jamison went to the door and called for them. They came in and he told them Lisa had a very vivid dream. He said that sometimes in her sleep episodes her dreams can seem very real to her. He told them she was reading the story of the crucifixion in the Bible after being in church and hearing about it.

Then Lisa repeated to her parents what she just told Jamison. With this second telling he ended up with tears, as did her parents. Florence said she would come in and sleep with Lisa if Gideon would move over. Lisa said she would like that. Jamison left the house about three-thirty that morning.

Chapter 14

*"The most beautiful thing we can experience is the mysterious.
It is the source of all true art and all science. He to whom this
emotion is a stranger, who can no longer pause to wonder and
stand rapt in awe, is as good as dead: his eyes are closed."*
[Albert Einstein]

Lisa missed a few days of school getting her strength back
from not eating for three days. She was surprised she lost two
pounds, just from three days. Then again some of it may have
been water loss, she had heard that one before from dieting
friends. She thought that was a not good way to lose weight.
She had a meeting with Jamison on Friday afternoon. She
guessed they would be talking about her experience. She repeated it three times already, once to him, then to her parents,
and later to George. But he needed to record it, so knew she
would need to repeat it again. This time she hoped she would
remember the details. This was one experience she was trying
to forget, unlike the others when she concentrated on remembering.

Jamison met Lisa and Gideon at the door and led them into his study instead of the patient meeting office. She flopped her coat on a chair and removed Gideon's service dog jacket. Jamison collected both and put them in a closet. He looked different today. He was wearing jeans, a blue sweatshirt, and even regular guy shoes and not the dad type. She had never seen him dressed casually, except when he came to her house late that night when she was terrified. Lisa was also in jeans with a new pale blue wool sweater.

"Coffee?"

"Oh yes, cappuccino, please."

She curled up in one of the soft red leather chairs and Gideon lay at her feet.

Jamison prepared the cappuccinos then sat across from her. They were silent a few minutes each concentrating on their coffee. Lisa took a few sips and thought they were excellent.

"Why are we here? Don't you wish to record my experience?"

"Later."

She felt nervous because he was staring at her, somehow looking at her differently, not just the 'waiting for you to talk' look. "What?"

"Lisa, I have been doing more research on your," he paused, "your experiences." Then he stood and began pacing the room. Lisa became even more nervous since he seemed to be...perhaps to be nervous.

He sat down again. "And she touched you?"

Lisa asked, "What?"

"Mary."

She raised her hand and placed a finger in the middle of her forehead to indicate where Mary had touched her, "She did."

He stared out the window at the blue sky instead of looking at her. "Lisa, I want to do something very unprofessional, and it scares the shit out of me."

Lisa sat upright. She had never heard Jamison use that word before. She asked, "What?"

"I want to encourage you to have one of your experiences, to have one here."

She stared out the window in shock, then turned and grinned at him. "You gonna put electrodes on my head and see what is going on in there?"

He laughed. "I have wish I could have for the last five years; no, this maybe worse."

She frowned and said it again. "What?"

"I wish to test something about shared dreams, to see if I can share yours."

The whole idea unnerved Lisa and she spilled her drink. He jumped up and grabbed a towel from the little coffee bar and handed it to her. She wiped the coffee off herself and the chair. Gideon got up and walked around as though he sensed the tension on the room. When Lisa sat back down, he again lay at her feet.

"I would like to test something; just if, perhaps—if and how Josh might have been with you in your experience. Shared your dream Lisa." He said it almost like a question, like a request.

Lisa's thoughts took off in a whirl. She wanted Jamison to believe her. Was he teasing? No, she trusted him; he had always been honest. Then she wondered if it could happen. Josh went with her. He didn't believe her and had his own explanation of the adventure in the Bible.

"Jamison, you know I don't really control the experience of going into a story. Sometimes it doesn't happen."

"That is okay, we have the afternoon scheduled."

"Did you have someplace or time in mind?"

"I do. After your experience two weeks ago, I believe it would be good to see the risen Christ."

"The what?"

"The Gospel story of when Jesus met the disciples in the early morning and had fish for them."

Lisa smiled at him and clapped her hands. "Oh my yes, that is a favorite of mine—yes."

He went on like he had been planning this for weeks. "Gideon would need to go with us, otherwise he will wake you and it would be over before it started."

She laughed at him.

"I also have a timer we will set. It has your wake-up signal. I was thinking we might try for two or three hours before it wakes you or maybe us."

"Us?"

"Us, if I am part of your dream."

"Adventure," she added firmly.

He got up again and walked to his desk and picked up a little clock like device and a small card. "And Lisa, here is a phone number of someone you can trust in the event I react like Josh, or if I don't wake when you do, or if something goes wrong." He walked over to her with the little clock and a card, which he handed to her. The name on the card was Father Ryan Jamison with an international phone number.

Lisa closed her eyes; he was serious. "When do you wish to do this test?"

He laughed softly, "Now. But I need to use the gents room first." He left before she could respond.

Lisa got up and paced the room wondering what possibly could happen. Her honest guess was that nothing would happen. When he returned, she decided to do the same and headed out the office door. Lisa thought for one brief minute she should head for the elevator, but knew this is what she desperately wanted; Jamison to believe in her. She used the ladies room and returned. She had to knock on the office door several times before he came to the door.

Gideon gave her his normal happy greeting and walked about the room on her heels. For some reason she wanted to make it happen. She was frightened, what if Jamison had been right all the time? What if she had this incredible imagination that could come up with something as terrifying as what she saw two weeks ago? Maybe this test really was for her, to prove to her that was the case, and not because he believed her after all.

He broke the silence of her thoughts. "I promise not to react like Josh." He chuckled. He seemed to be in a good mood and here in his private study let her see his emotions. Here in his study he was Jamison, and not so much Doctor Jamison.

Lisa threw her hands up in the air. "Okay, let's do this test thing."

He retrieved Gideon's jacket and leash and handed them to her. While she was putting them on Gideon, he picked up the timer clock, sat on the floor and set it in front of him. He patted the floor beside him and Lisa sat down by him. He seemed to be directing things, so she decided to let him continue. "What next?" He asked.

The ball was in her court. "We need a Bible."

He stood and retrieved one from his desk and returned to her side on the floor. He held it and opened it for her while she scanned through to the Gospel of John, then to the twenty-first chapter. They scanned the page together and looked at one another. This was the story.

He asked again, "What next?"

"We need to be close, very close to each other and Gideon. I think we should read the words together, out loud at the same time."

He pulled her close to him, their sides touching. Lisa pulled Gideon onto her lap. He put his left arm around her and she put her right arm around him. They laid the open Bible on the floor in front of them. He pulled Gideon closer so he was touching both of them and placed one hand on Gideon; Lisa did the same. He gave her what she thought was a somewhat a tentative smile and looked down at the Bible.

"I thought we might read it several times wait a little, then try this test some other day." Together they began reading the account of the story. When they finished, they began to read again, but said only a few words and were there.

———

Jamison blinked in the cold and darkness and then whispered, "Lisa?" He felt her hand touch his and turned and grabbed her. He pulled her around and held her tight and whispered, "Is this really happening?"

They were in the dark. He wasn't sure what to think. Maybe the power went out. Then shook his head knowing that could not be true. Not with huge windows and blue sky a moment ago. No! Something happened, they did not seem to be there in his office. But where? Once his eyes adjusted, he could see better. They were outside, it was chilly, and the sky was dark but seemed to be turning to the pale grey of early dawn. He let go of his embrace and instead clasped her hand. They both stood silent facing what Jamison realized was water, a large lake. He looked around, still clinging to Lisa and asked. "Where is Gideon?"

They both called and Gideon came up to them dragging his leash behind. Lisa stooped to pick it up Jamison said, "Is that him?"

Before she could answer, they saw a man walking toward them. Jamison suddenly felt overwhelmed. He guessed based on Lisa's other dreams; this must be Jesus. They stood still in anticipation. But when he approached, he knew simply by the presence of the man that it was indeed Jesus, at least how he imagined he would be, not so much from the physical looks, but a presence.

Jesus spoke. "Welcome Doctor. I am pleased to see you today." He reached out and touched Jamison's shoulder, then turned to Lisa and added. "Welcome back Lisa."

Jamison felt his heart pounding as though it wanted to escape his chest. The dawn's soft light was approaching quickly and now he could see more clearly. He noticed Lisa had tears in her eyes. She stammered. "It is you. You are alive!"

Jesus smiled and spoke again; then motioned and simply said, "We need more wood." He pointed to the shoreline and walked in that direction. Lisa and Jamison followed and began doing what he was doing, picking up pieces of wood. They followed him to a place where he dumped his wood into a rather large stack already accumulated.

The sky continued brightening, lighting the bluish greenish color of the lake. Jesus piled some of the wood into what appeared to be an ongoing fire pit surrounded by stones. Lisa and Jamison began handing him smaller pieces of the wood. Jesus arranged the wood to his liking, and broke the silence, "Now we need fire."

Jamison was surprised at Lisa's boldness when she said. "But can't you just," and made a motion with her hand. She had been with him before. Perhaps their relationship would allow for such a comment.

Jesus responded, "We have no need to call for fire from heaven Lisa, we have no Baal worshipers to impress."

Jamison knew the reference to a story in the Bible about the prophet Elijah.

Jesus picked up a long stick and headed down the shore several hundred feet away, to where a large fire was blazing. Jamison noticed there were five or six of these campfires scattered in the distance. The dawn was light enough they could now see a number of boats heading for the shore. Jamison guessed the other campfires were the families waiting for their fishermen to return to shore.

Lisa and Jamison followed and stood close enough to hear Jesus ask for fire and watched him stand there talking about the weather as the end of his stick began to glow. Jamison realized they were obviously invisible to everyone except Jesus. They all walked back and he laid the fire to his pile. It became a rather large blaze in minutes. Jamison thought to himself that he hadn't seen a campfire start up that quickly, even if there were no Baal worshipers.

"Fish!" Jesus said as he looked at the two of them. "Come."

They both obediently followed him to the shore. He pulled his outer garment up and somehow tied it around himself. He then waded into the lake up to his knees. Lisa stayed on the shore, but Jamison wadded out with him into the water, as did Gideon who was splashing and dog paddling around them both. Jamison watched Jesus peer into the water, reach in with both hands and grab a squirming fish. He tossed the fish toward Lisa on the shore where it splashed water and mud on her jeans. Gideon splashed toward the fish as if it were a game of catch, getting her even wetter. Gideon looked up as another one came landing in the shallows close to Lisa; then bounded back into the lake dog paddling to get back to Jesus.

Jamison moved a little closer to Jesus, the water nearly to his knees and decided to give it a try. The fish were slippery and he marveled as he watched Jesus grab two more and fling them towards Lisa's feet. Jamison was excited when he finally snagged a medium sized fish. He did not want to lose this one, so instead of tossing it he splashed back through the water and proudly presented it to Lisa.

He didn't go back out as Jesus was returning to shore with a very large one in his arms. Jesus handed it over to Lisa. She absently reached out and accepted the fish. She frowned at the wet smelly thing that had soaked her sweater and almost dropped it. She didn't.

Jamison picked up a couple of the larger fish on the shore. He was already soaked from his fishing experience so didn't seem to notice. Jesus picked up two more fish and placed them in Lisa's arms. When Jamison saw how Jesus was scooping up the smaller ones into a makeshift carrier from his robe, he did the same by tucking a few into his already soaked sweatshirt. They all went back to the fire and dumped their load on the ground.

Jesus asked, "Doctor, do you have a knife?"

Jamison reached in his pocket and pulled out a pocket-knife. He opened the blade and handed it to Jesus, who used it to sharpen a couple of smaller sticks. He put three smaller fish on one and laid it across the fire, then did the same for three more. He cut slits in two of the larger fish and put them also on sticks. He wiped the blade on his clothes and handed it back to Jamison. "Thank you Doctor."

"Now we need bread." Jesus said as he looked toward a woman lumbering toward them carrying a large basket. She neared the fire and put her hands out to warm them. She turned to Jesus. "Sir, would you trade a fish for some bread?" She reached into her basket and pulled out a cloth bulging with lumps what appeared to be bread. They could even smell the freshness of it. He picked up two large fish and put them in her basket. She thanked him and walked away.

He turned to Jamison and Lisa. "I don't make bread from stones, but I can make bread from fish." He laughed and Jamison was sure he knew the reference was to the 'temptation' story.

"Come." Jesus motioned as he pulled one of the skewers with the smaller fish from the fire. He pulled the skin back from the fish and pulled at the flesh. He pulled his hand away and blew on his fingers, then reached in again and pulled a chuck of fish out and put it in his mouth. He smiled. "Ready." He reached into the basket and pulled out a piece of bread. It was soft and flat like pita bread. He pulled off a chunk of fish and wrapped it in the bread and handed it to Lisa. "Eat." Then he did the same with another piece of the fish and handed it to Jamison. "Here Doctor, not the one you pulled out, that was our bread, but just as good." They both stood, trying to take it all in.

Jesus repeated again, "Eat, eat."

He made a fish sandwich for himself, took several bites, and then he looked up. "Looks like the boys are back!" He turned and gave them both a grin and added, "Watch the rest of the fish." Then he headed back toward the shore of the lake. They did not follow this time and stood staring at the fish on the fire. Jamison tasted his fish sandwich and watched as Lisa began on hers.

"What are we supposed to do with the fish on the fire?" She asked looking up at Jamison.

Jamison was not sure if he had ever felt so free, or light, or whatever the word might be. He laughed and laughed, "Watch them."

Instead they both stared out at the lake forgetting their fish sandwiches. Jesus was shouting something at the boat as the men were rowing to shore. They then rowed back out and tossed their net into the water. They heard the shouts as they began dragging it up to the boat.

Some of the men were leaning into the net tossing fish into the boat while the others were trying to pull the net up. The sounds and action brought people out from the other camp fires. It was dawn now and all could see the predicament the Zebedee ship was in. They began rowing to shore towing their net of fish. Some of them climbed out of the boat and began tugging at the net. Men on shore ran to help and soon there were at least twenty working on pulling the net to shore.

When it looked like the boat was grounded and all could see the number and size of the fish, their helpers left them running. They took off and began pushing their own boats back into the water. Jamison and Lisa stayed by the fire. They were both cold and very wet, and after all Jesus told them to watch the fish. Jamison's jeans were soaked from wading into the lake, and his sweatshirt from his reaching into the water to grab a fish. Lisa hadn't wadded out, but Gideon splashed her and she dutifully carried three good-sized fish in her arms. Cold wet smelly fish. They were surprised how quickly the news of the fish spread as they saw several coming toward the lake down a path from the town. When they saw an older man and woman approach the fire Lisa told Jamison. "That is Zebedee and his wife."

Gideon, who was standing in attention by Lisa suddenly bolted with a bark and ran to what looked like his somewhat smaller twin. Jamison watched in amazement as the two dogs sniffed each other, then began to romp and play. Gideon easily recognized by his blue service dog jacket and trailing leash.

Salome, Zebedee's wife came to the fire and began pulling cooked fish off the skewers, carefully removing tender chunks of flesh, and putting it into pieces of the bread. Jamison didn't realize how much bread was there, but it seemed she was making a lot of sandwiches.

Suddenly a lot of activity was going on around them. Someone came down to the shore with two donkeys with carts and they all began filling the carts with fish, under Zebedee's directions. Zebedee then moved towards the fire. He ate the sandwich his wife handed him then returned to supervise the rest of the loading of the catch.

Jamison moved close so he could listen to what was going on with the loading of the fish. He overheard comments about the need to get the fish to market quickly since there had been few fish for the last two weeks. The market would pay dearly. He did get bumped into a couple of times so watched more carefully where he stood. He saw that the other boats were now also catching fish not far from the shoreline. The Zebedee crew did not express concern since they said they would be in town first as the two carts moved away. Other men were carrying large baskets woven with rough branches with the rest of the fish toward the town. He wondered about the cooperation going on around him and if all these were related or only friends.

Jamison turned and saw Jesus talking with Lisa so remained where he was. He wondered what they were talking about. It was a short conversation so he moved toward Lisa and the fire. She began to name fishermen who were milling about with Jesus. Both of them had to move further and further away as the group crowded around warming themselves. She pointed out the brothers James and John. She said they looked different all wet. Some of them pulled off wet robes and were dressed only in short tunics. She said she thought one was Phillip, but surprised he would go fishing with them. Phillip came and sat on a log they had been using so they had to move further away again.

"That is Peter," she said of a man who had just scarfed down two large fish sandwiches. "And Thomas is the one who is making sandwiches." They watched him take the fish from the fire as they were done, and put some more on. He had a knife and began filleting sections putting them in the basket with the bread. Jamison thought there seemed to be a lot of bread as he watched him making the fish sandwiches. Jamison wondered that no one, other than the disciples, recognized Jesus. The other people around treated him like he belonged there, doing what he was doing. Jamison noticed Jesus motion to Peter, who followed him away from the fire and down the shoreline. John started to follow, but then turned back.

Andrew called to Gideon; two dogs responded. Lisa called for her Gideon and he left Andrew and the other Gideon and came to them. Jamison noticed Lisa was beginning to shiver, as was he. A wind had come up from the lake and their clothes were cold and soaking wet. The fire had done little to dry them. Now with the disciples around the fire there was no room for them to get any of its heat. He didn't know what it took to leave this place and really was not ready, not yet. He listened to snatches of conversation from those around the fire; some talking about the fish and Jesus and relating various stories about him, others questioning the future.

He looked at Lisa again. He thought she was about to turn blue. He put his arm around her to try to warm her. He would have approached Jesus but he was some ways away with Peter. He stooped and picked up Gideon's leash and decided to approach Jesus when he returned. He didn't want to go chasing Gideon if perhaps Jesus could send them home.

There was no time to approach Jesus because he heard the familiar buzzing of the timer. Jamison stooped down and picked up the wet Gideon and put his other arm around Lisa. She clung to him, and there they were standing dripping wet in his study.

Chapter 15

"By the truth we are undone. Life is a dream. 'Tis the waking that kills us. He who robs us of our dreams robs us of our life."
[Virginia Woolf, *Orlando*]

Lisa felt Jamison's arm clutching her and holding a wiggling Gideon. He dropped Gideon then pulled her lightly into his arms and held her a brief moment. He let go and sighed. They were both soaking wet. She looked down at her sweater. It was dirty and wet, not just from his wet hug. She heard him mumble to himself. "Let us be reasonable here Jamison. Look for facts."

Lisa stooped down and hugged Gideon who looked at the two of them. She guessed he might have enjoyed their adventure, at least his part of the adventure in the lake and with the other Gideon. Then she looked up at Jamison, "What did you say?"

Jamison and Lisa both looked at each other as they recognized the strong odor of wood smoke and fish in the room. Lisa thought she recognized a look of panic in his eyes that grew when he again felt at his wet clothes. His jeans were quite wet, as was his sweatshirt, and his shoes. She felt and then looked down at her muddy ruined sweater. Gideon's blue service coat was wet and he had a strong fishy smell about him. Perhaps the smell was coming from all of them. Jamison looked at Lisa and stated the obvious, "We both seem to be rather wet. I can't take you home like this. Call home and say I am taking you to dinner."

She looked at him, "Like this?"

He laughed. "No, I will take you to my house and we can get cleaned up." He added, "And have dinner."

He picked up the timer and the Bible and other things on the floor. When he noticed Lisa's chattering lips, he walked to a closet and pulled out a jacket. He put it over her shoulders. "Let's go."

At that hour the building was deserted. They walked to the elevator and rode it to the basement parking. His Porsche was the lone car in the garage. He took a minute to spread a blanket over the back seat then lifted Gideon in, then put the seat back into position for Lisa. She was amused at his comment that at least the wetness and fish scales were mostly on their fronts, not backs, and that hopefully the leather seats would dry just fine.

The drive was quiet except for the swishing of warm air from the heater. She had never been to his house, but knew where it was and had ridden her bike by it a number of times when she was younger. He drove the car into the garage. He again helped Gideon out of the small seat and the three went into the house.

Jamison said, "I will fix something to eat. You need to get dry." He stared at her a few minutes. "Come with me." He led her down a hall to a downstairs bedroom. She looked around; it was clearly a guest room. When he left, she noticed his shoes were squishing, like they were water soaked, which they were. He returned quickly and handed her a bathrobe and a neatly folded pair of what appeared to be his pajamas. "Towels are in the bath. A hot shower should warm you quicker than anything." He closed the door. She found a bathroom attached to the guest room fully equipped with towels. There were also soaps and even shampoos; which seemed to have been gathered from various hotels.

When she finished, she found Jamison and Gideon in the kitchen. He couldn't have had time to shower, but at least he had clean dry clothes on. She held out her wet dripping clothes in one hand and her shoes in the other. He pointed to a door. "You can put your clothes in the dryer. Here give me your shoes." She walked into the laundry room. Her sweater was ruined, but she could at least dry it with her underwear and jeans, which were all soaked. She felt uncomfortable here alone in Jamison's house wearing his pajamas. She totally trusted him to be a man of honor; still she wondered how someone would feel being in the presence of say the president, wearing only pajamas. Strange analogy she thought.

He had the oven door open and had both his and her shoes on a rack. Lisa asked, "What are you doing?"

He merely shrugged, "Might work."

Right now, she so wanted words from him. She wanted to know what he thought about their shared adventure. She had heard his theory about shared dreams. She knew that was what he was expecting, not this. Their soaked clothing, wet shoes, and the odor of smoke and fish clearly defied that theory. She heard the microwave heating something, and the drip sound from the coffee maker; then the aroma of coffee reached her. He had a bottle of whisky on the table with a half empty glass beside it. She looked toward the bottle and he shook his head. "Okay, I will have some coffee, thank you."

She sat at the table with her coffee. The silence was almost frightening for Lisa. She decided Jamison had to do the talking this time. He had to tell her about the experience; about the adventure that clearly was not a dream, and and he had to know they had not been sleepwalking. He had been there with her in a Gospel story. He saw Jesus. Her adventures, all of them, were true and real.

She looked at Gideon, who seemed content after eating whatever Jamison had put on the floor for him. Jamison had already removed his wet companion dog jacket and obviously had dried him with the towel tossed by the door. Gideon was curled up close to the open oven, seeming to enjoy the emanating warmth.

The microwave bell dinged and he got up to remove the contents. "Hungry?"

Lisa shook her head.

He smiled at her. "Home-made lasagna, I'm a fairly decent cook."

"Not hungry."

He smiled again, and sat the dish on the counter by the microwave and returned to the table.

A tear trickled down Lisa's cheek. "You were there with me Jamison, really there."

He looked very sober and responded quietly, "Yes."

She needed him to say the words. Words were important and she wanted him to say he was really there, that he had really seen Jesus.

"Tell me Jamison. Say the words." She knew he knew exactly what she meant.

He gulped down his drink, stood and walked to her side of the table. He reached for her hand and she stood facing him. He gently put his arms around her and kissed the top of her head. He whispered. "I was there with you Lisa. I saw Jesus." Then he quickly moved away.

Lisa brushed away the tears that suddenly appeared. She had no thoughts, only feelings. She felt a sense of contentment and relief. She was not imagining, or crazy, or dreaming. Lisa felt like all the parts of her life finally merged into one. She was a whole person now. She was not crazy, and Jamison believed her.

She moved closer to Jamison and tightly wrapped her arms around him. He moved her away. "You know you must not do this Lisa." She knew. She stammered, "Sorry Jamison. I shouldn't have done that."

He gave her what she thought was an understanding look. Thankfully they were startled with the sound of a ding from the dryer in the other room. He went in to the laundry room and got her clothes out. Lisa held the sweater up to her nose. The sweater was wool and obviously had shrunk, and the heat brought out the strong smoky and fishy smell from them. She held it up to him, and he frowned with a groan.

Lisa watched Jamison dash up the stairs, then back in a minute with one of his sweatshirts. "Here this will do. Are the other things okay, other than the odor?"

She nodded affirmative.

"I need to get you home."

Lisa frowned. "No, we have so very much to talk about." She did not want the adventure to end. She feared the reality of it all would also end.

He shook his head, "Tomorrow."

She reluctantly went to the guest room to dress. When she came out he had her shoes in a plastic bag, and handed her a pair of flip flops. They were several sizes too big, but better than her wet sneakers or barefoot. She realized he really was not going to talk about what happened, at least not that night.

Although she did not put Gideon's wet jacket back on him, he obediently followed them into the garage and Jamison's car. Lisa asked, "What time tomorrow can we get together to talk about everything." She gave a deep sigh before he responded and added. "Oh, I promised to go with George to a family re-union tomorrow. It is out of town and probably will take all day. I will call him first thing in the morning and cancel it." She saw his look of concern so rushed on. "We have much to talk about Jamison. Everything has changed today, everything."

Then he said what she expected. "Go tomorrow with George. We have plenty of time to think and talk."

―――――

At home, Lisa and Gideon sat on the front porch instead of going in. She waved for Jamison to go on. As he drove off, she whispered to herself, "I love you Jamison."

Lisa held her sweater up to her nose. It still had a strong fishy and smoky odor from the fire. All the contentment and relief she felt at Jamison's house seemed to be fading away. She now felt concern, not about the wonderful adventure with Jamison and Jesus; but about what happened at his house only a few minutes ago. How many times had Jamison said they were both seekers of truth? What was the truth now? What was their relationship now? They had always been soulmates. Now were they more than that?

Lisa knew a shared secret created a tight bond. She tried to share her secret with Josh and that drove him away; she had not been willing to share it with George. She thought she knew she loved George. She also knew if she lived with George fifty years, he would never really know her, not like Jamison did. She and Jamison had a bond perhaps stronger than the knot of love that ties a couple together; a knot that ties soul to soul. Perhaps she had not wanted to get better because she would lose Jamison, her soulmate. Her secret was part of her soul, the part she had shared with Jamison for five years.

Gideon whined and shivered. She sighed as she pulled the damp dog into her arms, "Just a minute Gideon, we will go in. I need some time to think." Finally, after another whimper from Gideon, she stood and went in the house and up to her bedroom.

She didn't think she had gotten get quite as soaked as Jamison, who had been to his knees in the water. Her jeans had gotten wet from fish being tossed near her, and more from Gideon's splashing and shaking his wet fur beside her. Her ruined sweater was soaked from carrying wet fish. Lisa put her jeans in the hamper, and found a plastic bag for the sweater. She wanted to keep the scent of smoke and fish that clung to it. She did not want to keep the scent of wet smelly dog, and got Gideon into the tub for a quick bubble bath.

Lisa was not sure if she would be able to sleep. She decided Gideon was finally dry enough to be on the bed and she would at least make an attempt for sleep. Before she climbed into bed, she opened the bag and inhaled the scents of wood smoke and fish. Could George ever believe or would he be like Josh if she tried a test like she and Jamison just shared. Tears came again, this time more and uncontrolled. She also knew she desperately loved George. Her head was full of happiness, but also concern. She and George had talked in the last few months about a future together. He declared his love for her and she for him. Now, how could she give up Jamison. More importantly, how could she give up her adventures; ones that only Jamison could share. Gideon snuggled up and licked her cheek. "Oh Gideon, I am happy and sad and confused. I don't know what to do. What would George say? He would say marry me. What would Jamison say? He would say use your mind Lisa, always be a seeker of truth. What is real Gideon?"

She remembered a philosophical conversation she and Jamison once had over a cup of coffee, not as doctor patient, but as friends. He said one had to be careful of the spoken word. Once it became sound it became hard like a rock; then you had to do something with it. She didn't remember the rest of the conversation or why that quote. But she had taken it to heart as she contemplated the word love in her relationship with Jamison. It was a word she dared not even think or say. For years she felt comfortable and happy with the idea of it, but she had never dared to put the definition of love to those feelings because she did not know what she would do with such a heavy rock. Now what was she to do?

Her thoughts went back to Jesus and of how he had welcomed her to the stories she visited. The tears continued. Gideon snuggled closer to her and licked her cheek again. There by the Sea of Galilee only a few hours ago Jesus told her she no longer needed to come there to find him. "Oh Gideon, that is what Aslan said to the Pevenise children in the Narnia books when he said they would have no more adventures." She remembered Jesus' words to her several times. "It shall be well." Finally, she slept.

Jamison looked in his rearview mirror at Lisa and Gideon sitting on her front porch. He felt a strong compulsion to go to his office to look at evidence, hard truthful evidence. He did. As he drove into the parking garage he was even hoping his lack of technical ability would have failed and there would be no recorded evidence. Before the experiment he had set up a video cam in his office. He didn't want Lisa to know; now he didn't want to know.

He also wondered if building security kept the recording of movement in the building hallways. His office had live access to the motion cams when anyone got off the elevators on his floor. Since their floor did not have a reception area, he and his office neighbors could be notified of when a client or customer was approaching.

He smiled at the night watchman when he entered the lobby. He had an idea and spoke to him, "Hi, Danny. Curious, how long do you keep the tapes from the security cameras in the hallways?"

"Good evening Doctor Jamison; why, suspect something?"

"No, I'm just curious."

He seemed to be searching something on one of his computer consoles then replied. "Looks like what I have available is only a couple of months. I think they are archived somewhere for a longer period."

"Is that a lot of data?"

"For the lobby seems a lot since the cameras are running all the time. Even recording us sitting here, unless we are motionless like a statue." He laughed. "But not much data for the hallways on the other floors since all the security cams are motion activated."

Jamison remembered that explanation when he moved into the building. He occasionally turned that feature on when he was expecting a patient or client since he did not have a receptionist and kept his office door locked.

Jamison was glad that Danny seemed happy to have someone to talk to and especially someone interested in what he did all night.

Danny asked, "Do you want to see some, maybe on your floor? Except the ninth is boring, not much goes on except for the attorneys, they do have some interesting looking clients."

"Could you show me this afternoon from 5:00 p.m. until maybe 9:00 p.m. I think that should cover when I left."

They watched as he sped the video to the motion of a man exit the elevator and go into the firm of Laciton Brokerage at 5:10 p.m. He asked, "About here?"

Jamison nodded. The next motion view was Jamison exiting his office and entrance to the restroom at 5:20 p.m., then again as Jamison exited and entered his office at 5:25 p.m. The next video shot was Lisa going to and from the restroom at 5:30 - 5:35 p.m. The video again showed the Laciton customer exiting at 6:00 p.m., then a customer in and out of the realtor's office with the realtor following. Danny commented. "Seen enough? Your floor doesn't have much action, especially on a Friday."

"Would you please run it until 9:00 p.m. or when I and my patient left the office."

Danny did and they watched a few of the ninth-floor employees exit their offices, then at 8:35 p.m. captured Jamison, Lisa, and Gideon leaving his office. Jamison was embarrassed because all three clearly looked bedraggled. Jamison's clothes even looked wet. Jamison said with a forced laugh. "Thanks for the show."

Danny gave him an uncomfortable grin, "No problem, any time I'm on duty."

Jamison muttered a thank you and went up to his office. He unlocked the door to his study and turned on the lights. One piece of evidence was that the three of them had not gone somewhere sleepwalking in their shared dream, managing to soak their clothes. He realized he had the coffee bar in the study. Perhaps they could have still gotten their clothing wet, and even Gideon. He walked around the room. There were wet spots on the carpet, some very wet ones. He remembered spilling water out of his shoes before putting them back on. The only way they could have gotten that wet was to take their clothes off and soak them in the tiny sink. "Not logical Jamison," he muttered to himself.

Based on many conversations with his uncles and some of the research they provided, he had expected the possibility of a shared dream with Lisa. That was the purpose of the experiment; could they share one of her dreams. The dream certainly felt real and he knew why Lisa claimed she was there in her dream adventures. He would have said the same, except he knew better. He walked over to the computer set up on a low table near where they all sat for what he called, 'the test.' A friend showed him how to set the computer up to record a meeting or a session; something he had only occasionally used, until that day. He wondered if the computer had successfully recorded anything, or if his technical ability had altogether failed.

He didn't want to know. It was evidence he did not want to acknowledge, because he did not know what to do with that kind of truth. He wanted to put the moment off, or destroy it without knowing. He stuffed the computer into his brief-case and walked around the room. He picked up the timer that brought Lisa out of her dream, and saw his pocket knife on the side table. He had put it there when he picked up his cell phone. He put the knife in his pocket. He remembered he had removed his cell phone before they did the dream test because he didn't want a call to wake Lisa before her time. Or maybe more likely to wake him since he had a premonition he would be sharing Lisa's dream. And he had.

He locked up and headed home. He needed to talk to the uncles. He needed to get to Ireland as soon as possible, away from Lisa and whatever might have happened that afternoon, he looked at the clock, happened yesterday, it was nearly two already.

When he got home, he knew he would get no sleep. He needed to make notes, call the uncles, and get the quickest flight possible to Ireland. Writing was the only way to think clearly for Jamison. He respected words, and in writing them on the computer or even in scribbled notes was a tool for revealing the truth for him. Once you put the thought into the right word it seemed to have substance. The substance often led to clarity and more truth. He retrieved his laptop from his study and headed for the kitchen. The aroma of wood smoke and fish still lingered in the kitchen making it easy to still feel the presence of Lisa and Gideon; more importantly the presence of Jesus himself.

He poured himself a drink and kicked his wet shoes out of the way. The oven had not been a good idea. The shoes were still soaked through and probably unsalvageable. Tonight, truth and reality had crashed. Tonight he knew what he did not want to know. He knew that truth and reality were not equal, they were not the same thing. He stared at the wet shoes on the floor. The truth was they had gotten wet from wading in the Sea of Galilee. Reality was that it couldn't happen, at least not the way it seemed it had happened. But truth was that it had.

He started to pour another glass of Jameson, then stopped. He needed a clear head. He began typing all he could remember about what happened. He had pages. When finished he read them over and remembered more details and added those. He did that three times before he finally thought he had most of it. Then he did a separate account of what he observed Lisa doing. Most of the time they were side by side, but not all of the time.

Jamison expected his research into shared dreams would have allowed him to accept almost anything; anything except the physical manifestations of wet clothes and shoes and the odors of the wood smoke and fish that still lingered. From his research into extra sensory perception he thought perhaps she might have been able to send strong enough mind waves and pictures to frighten Josh. His other theory was that she may have picked up on hypnosis techniques from their many sessions together and subconsciously hypnotized Josh into seeing what she wished him to see. Both theories were useless, unless all of this had been his own dream, the entire evening.

It was nearly four in the morning when he finished. He took one more swallow of the whisky and headed to bed. The call to the uncles could wait, the computer in his briefcase could wait. He needed sleep, and he hoped a dreamless one. He made a decision, a difficult one and wanted to sleep on it. He was awakened with his phone ringing, what seemed extra loud. His head hurt. He managed to pick up the receiver. Two concerned voices chimed in at once. "Are you hurt, are you well Laddie?" came from his Uncle Ryan and Uncle Glenn simultaneously.

He looked at the clock. It was nearly five, and he had been in bed only an hour. He knew there was no point in telling that to them. "I am okay. Why are you calling?"

Again, the two voices, "We were concerned about you. Something happened, and do not tell us it was naught."

Jamison climbed out of bed and put on a robe. He put his phone on speaker. Before he could talk again Uncle Glenn said, "It was the lassie, we know that much. Something has changed."

He knew after what happened last evening, he should not be surprised about anything. He planned on talking to the uncles as soon as he could with a clear head, "Yes, something."

He heard one of them say to the other, "I said it was so."

"Uncle Ryan and Uncle Glenn something did happen. I will email my notes to you in a few hours and you will know all. I will be there as soon as I can get a flight."

He was surprised they remained silent so long. Then Uncle Ryan asked. "Is the lassie well, she has not been injured?"

"She has not." He did not add that she had not yet been injured, but soon would be.

He was surprised that they accepted what he said without the usual questions and suggestions. All they said was that they would see him shortly and hung up. He knew now, he would not be able to sleep, so got up and worked on his plans. He emailed the notes about his time with Lisa to his uncles. He even thought about mailing his wet shoes, but knew they were not the ones that would want evidence, quite the contrary. He booked a flight to Ireland for early the next morning, grateful for the internet that allowed quick irrational decisions, even though at a substantial cost.

He did not know what he would tell Lisa. He did know when he told her he was leaving for Ireland she would be devastated. He knew she would want to talk about yesterday—in detail. That was something he could not do yet, because he did not know what had really happened. Or maybe it was because he did know.

Lisa had a difficult time getting up when her alarm rang. George was going to pick her up at seven. She wished she had ignored Jamison's suggestion that she should not cancel going with George. She and Jamison had so much to talk about, so very much. While she was deciding what to wear she glanced at Jamison's blue sweatshirt. She picked it up and slipped it over her head. It certainly was many sizes too large. She looked in the mirror. "This is how I used to dress Gideon," and smiled down at her dog who looked up when he heard his name. "It matches your jacket, so I think I will wear it."

George was already in the kitchen talking with her dad by the time she and Gideon got downstairs. She smiled at him. "Sorry, I'm running a bit late. She looked at both of them, Coffee?"

George suggested, "We can get some on the way, if that is okay with you."

She smiled, gave her dad a kiss, and asked, "Where is mom?"

"Not up yet, it is Saturday. I have a tee off in thirty minutes, so better also be going."

The four of them left the house together. Lisa and Gideon got into George's car and she waved at her dad as they watched him drive off. George turned to Lisa. "Is that a new shirt? I don't remember it."

"Sort of." She guessed he expected her to look more like herself. He told her several weeks ago he wanted her to meet his two cousins, who generally gave him a bad time about his lack of girlfriends. Lisa understood George and knew the so-called lack of girlfriends was because he had ideals and also school to focus on. "I'm ready for that coffee you promised."

Gideon settled on the back seat and George headed for the highway after stopping at a coffee drive-through. He chatted about a number of things, then on to the reunion. "Hope you like my family. I have six cousins close to my age who will be there, along with their younger siblings and my aunts and uncles. Our family is close. I am close to some of my cousins. Because of being an only child my parents made sure we had enough visits and interaction."

George told her earlier his parents were driving themselves because they planned on spending the night there, and expected George and Lisa would not wish to. The talk and reminiscences of his cousins took nearly an hour of the three-hour drive before silence settled in. George apologized to Liza, "Sorry for monopolizing the conversation. I wanted you to know a little about the family you are about to meet."

Lisa gave him a feeble smile when he turned to her. She didn't say anything and wondered how much of the family talk she actually heard. Her thoughts were somewhere else, with someone else. She took out her phone and asked George, "Okay if I send a quick text. I needed to reach Jamison, but he didn't respond this morning."

George shrugged, "Kind of early."

She sent a quick text message, "Jamison, we need to talk, please call me as soon as you can." She put her phone in her lap, hoping he would, but worried what she might say if he did.

After several more minutes of silence George spoke up, "Lisa, I have a lot to talk about, not the family, but about us. I was looking forward to this long uninterrupted drive to talk about our plans." He looked over at her with expectations.

Lisa was not ready for plans for herself with George. All of her thoughts and emotions were somewhere else; somewhere with Jamison. She remained silent.

George continued, "I know we are not officially engaged. But I believe both my parents and your parents are expecting that to happen. We couldn't be official with you in high school. You graduate next month and will begin your first term at the University, and I also graduate."

Lisa began choking up inside. She wanted to stop George, she had to stop George from saying things or asking things that would only cause him pain. How could she stop him? But George continued, "It takes a lot of time to plan a wedding, unless we elope." He chuckled and looked over at her. She did not laugh or even smile. "Lisa?"

"I know we talked about a lot of things, of our affection for each other and possibilities. I don't feel engaged."

George's look was one of surprise. "Affection? Lisa, what is going on. You know I have told you how much I love you, many times. You have repeated that word to me." George's voice rose to one of almost anger.

"I'm not ready to become officially engaged in the car just so you can show your cousins you did it." She wondered where that comment came from, especially when she saw the hurt in his eyes. "Sorry George, right now, today, is not the time for this talk. It can wait."

Lisa's phone beeped a text message notice. She looked at it. She looked at George. "It's Jane. Okay if I answer her." He didn't respond so she did anyway. Jane's message didn't surprise Lisa. She had been expecting it. Dave had asked her to marry him last night. Lisa didn't want to share that with George at this particular moment. Lisa typed in "congratulations; I know you will be very happy."

"How is Jane?"

"Fine."

A heavy silence hung in the air until Gideon made some whining noises. George found a good place to stop and took him out to do his business. Lisa wasn't even sure if Gideon had gotten breakfast that morning. While they were out Lisa sent Jamison another text message. She mused and imagined Jamison would again tell her to be patient. She thought perhaps last night Jesus might have suggested she be patient. Maybe she would pass that message to George.

When they returned to the car and were on the road again Lisa started the conversation, "Sorry George. I had a difficult day yesterday and sleepless night. Now is not a good time to talk."

Surprisingly he responded, "Do you want to talk about it. You can talk to me just like you do your Doctor Jamison."

Lisa did not tell him the truth; that she could not talk to him like she did to her Doctor Jamison. George did not know her secret. Jamison knew her secret. He knew and cared about her anyway. They were soulmates, but yesterday she had dropped the heavy rock when she whispered to herself that she loved him. How could she marry George if she loved Jamison? The thought was heavy. A tear snuck out and softly slid down her right cheek.

When she didn't respond he said, "I am listening; if you don't feel well, we could turn and go back home Lisa."

"Tired. I am sure I will be fine. Maybe we could stop for breakfast? I didn't have any."

They turned off the highway at a sign that read 'food,' and found a decent restaurant for a breakfast for Lisa, and a snack for George and Gideon. Lisa managed a smile and remembered if she wanted George to be patient with her, she needed to be patient with him. Everything would come out in the end. She remembered Jesus telling her one more time. "It shall be well." Lisa put on her best smile, even in the oversized sweatshirt, that smelled like Jamison.

When they got to the reunion, she relaxed and laughed with George and his cousins, and was charming to the aunts and uncles. They all treated her like family, and they all loved Gideon. People always have something to talk about with a dog or small child around. George looked happy, and Lisa was glad she had kept her new secret, the secret about her and Jamison. She found several opportunities to send texts to Jamison during the day, but got no responses until she and George were on their way home.

She finally got a text from him, it read, "Sorry Lisa, I am now on my way to Ireland. Will talk later, Jamison."

She gasped and cried out, "No, oh no, please."

George nearly swerved the car as he turned to her. "What is it Lisa? What has happened? Someone hurt?"

It was too dark for George to see the tears that began to flow. But he did hear her when she shuddered and began crying in earnest. He found a place to turn off the highway into a truck stop. Gideon stood and whined.

George pulled her into his arms the best he could in the car. "Is someone hurt Lisa? Tell me."

"No," she sobbed, "Yes, I mean no one hurt." She silently whispered to herself, "Only me."

"What has been going on? It has been all day. My parents even asked me if we had a quarrel." He let her go. The rest of the trip home was made in silence. At home, George opened the door for Gideon and Lisa. He patted Gideon and said, "Three hours in a car is a long trip for the dog, what a good dog you are Gideon."

Lisa realized she at least needed to be polite no matter how much she was hurting inside. She looked at George and realized she did love him, really love him. But she and Jamison were soulmates with an incredible experience that would bind them in some way. Not as lovers, like her feelings for George, but as, as what?

"How much longer are you going to give me the silent treatment Lisa? It isn't like you."

Gideon looked up at both of them and gave a slight whine; something he never did. Lisa realized she was having an impact on the two she loved most. She blurted out, "I am confused George about something that happened yesterday. I do love you George, no matter what happens. I need you to love me, to not ask, but to hold on to me." She looked into his face, he looked confused; perhaps as much as she was.

George pulled her into his arms and held her closely for several minutes. She kissed him and wrapped her arms around him and gently whispered in his ear. "I do love you George. It shall all be well."

Chapter 16

"Above all, don't lie to yourself. The man who lies to himself and listens to his own lie comes to a point that he cannot distinguish the truth within him, or around him, and so loses all respect for himself and for others. And having no respect he ceases to love." [FYODOR DOSTOYEVSKY, *The Brothers Karamozov*]

TWO YEARS HAD past since Lisa last saw Doctor Jamison. Their last day together was the most vivid and memorable day in her life. It took months for her to finally admit that his professional diagnosis had been correct. She did not meet with the psychiatrist he recommended, as she had no sleep episodes after that last one. Lisa reflected on all their years together with the conflict of words, adventure versus dream. He did admit to the test that last day. He said it had partially been successful, and he had seen some of the things she described in that dream. That is when she finally got to talk to him. He said the rest of it, about her clothes smelling like wood smoke and fish, the time at his house, had all been part of the dream.

Later her father told her that Doctor Jamison said Lisa did not need him any longer, and that she would be going through some serious adjustments. And that he was sure she would adjust; he had confidence in her. The story was that he had a family situation, which needed his immediate attention. The reason for such a hasty departure.

Now two years later Lisa thought she was ready to see Jamison. She was no longer the young girl infatuated with her psychiatrist. She had almost completed one year at the University, and she and George became officially engaged in December. She was not embarrassed, she read enough to understand her feelings for her psychiatrist, were not all that unusual—considering.

Now, Jamison was in town to finish packing and shipping personal items to Ireland. She found out from her father that he had returned a couple of times last year to close up his patients medical files, and permanently close his office as he was permanently moving to Ireland.

This visit would be with her parents and George and Ginny and Walt; all there for a wonderful Ginny dinner. Lisa already knew most of what Jamison would share with her family, she guessed so did her father as for some reason he had kept in touch with Doctor Jamison over the last two years.

Once the greetings were over and dinner began Jamison updated the rest of the family. "Colleen and I were married a year ago, and now are expecting a child."

She didn't know that last bit.

Ginny asked, "When?"

"Early December."

After all the congratulatory comments, he continued, "I will begin teaching a couple of classes at the University where my Uncle Glen has been made dean of his department. Helps to have influential relatives."

The family all laughed. They all remembered the Irish Uncles.

Walt and Ginny discussed their plans to visit the Jamisons in four months and got assurances from them that he and Colleen were looking forward to the visit, and the pregnancy certainly was not an issue to postpone the visit. Then University gossip was needed to update Jamison on some people he knew.

George brought up the wedding. Even though he denied it, she knew that George had been a little jealous of Jamison, not as a romantic rival; but that he saw and felt the deep connection the two had. "Lisa and I have moved up our wedding plans from a Christmas wedding to one in June, when I will be graduating."

Lisa tentatively asked, "Castle still open for a honeymoon?"

Jamison's response gave her pause to wonder. "Yes, of course, Ireland is magnificent in June."

Conversation again turned to travel. Ginny and Walt had joined the Longford's in their trip to Italy when Florence Longford got her doctorate. Only George had missed out as he was taking extra classes to complete his master's degree sooner. Lisa had begged him to join the family, but he said Gideon needed him, and getting out of school sooner, meant they could marry sooner. She was content with that.

Lisa had not felt as tense as she expected with Jamison's visit. Now she somehow felt he would always be a part of her life, just as he seemed to have become a part of her family over the years.

Lisa motioned George to stay when she walked Jamison out to his car after the little dinner party. She needed to ask Jamison again about the last time they saw each other. When they were together in his study and then at his house two years ago. She wanted to ask him in person so she could see his face. She knew he might put the 'doctor' face on that hid his feelings. Still she needed to ask. They had discussed it in emails and even on several lengthy phone calls over the last year. He always had the same answer. She thought perhaps now he could be honest with her if he had to look her in the eye. As she walked with him to his car she finally asked, "Jamison, two years ago in your study, then at your home, what really happened?"

"We have talked about this several times Lisa.

"You know it is all gone, everything is gone. The books have not called to me since that day." She blurted it all out even though she knew he well knew she had no more adventures into books, no more experiences, no more dreams, no more memories, real or false.

She saw his eyes darken, a sadness pass over his face. He looked tired. Then she added words, "I feel like Susan and Peter; when you are grown up you can never return to Narnia."

She noticed a painful look on his face. "Do you like the way this story is turning out?" He asked emphasizing the word 'this.'

"You mean that I marry George, have twin sons, and live happily ever after?"

"Is that what you wish Lisa?"

"I do love George." She looked up at him. "Jamison, could we have ever?"

He shook his head.

Lisa continued, "I know, I know, often patients think they are in love with their psychiatrists. But you have been my savior, my knight in shining armor. I am no longer a freak."

He gave her a warm smile.

"Someday you will understand that I am none of those things. However, you were right Lisa, we were soulmates. I hope we shall always be friends." He unlocked the car door, gave her a hug and a smile. "You know I look forward to that wedding invitation. The offer for a place to stay in Ireland is always open."

"I will, we will next year when George graduates." She took his hand as he climbed into his car. She could not let it go. "I know we both were there Jamison, you and me, by the Sea of Galilee. We talked to Jesus and caught fish and ate fish sandwiches."

George and Gideon approached them. Jamison closed the door with a nod to George and started the engine. George put his arm around Lisa and whispered in a comforting voice, "He has been more than your doctor. I think he has been, still is your friend. It's all well Lisa. I am sure we will see him from time to time. After all, we were invited to stay in his castle on our honeymoon."

Lisa quietly added, "Yes, It shall be well."

Jamison looked into his rearview window and watched Lisa and George wave at him, then walk into the house with Gideon at their heels. Being Lisa's doctor, her psychiatrist for five years he ought to feel great satisfaction over his success. He knew without a doubt Lisa and George would go on to lead a happy and normal life together. The key word was normal.

Being Lisa's soulmate, he felt an overwhelming sorrow for what she lost; from what he had taken from her. Her words cut deep into a place in his own soul, a place he did not know was there or rather had only just come into existence. Her words rang true when she said, "Like Susan and Peter, now that I've grown up I can never return to Narnia." The pain was all the greater because he knew back then, two years ago he had the power to hold the door open for her. He still did not know why he did not, since he himself stepped through that door. Then again, he knew he had to let her go, let her go to a normal life.

Back then he didn't know where that door would lead. Even now he was still vague about what it really meant. He could not have allowed her to come with him. He remembered his torment the day he made the decision. He hated himself for leaving without facing her. Then worse when finally confronted; he lied to her and told her they had experienced a shared dream, one that even seemed real to him. He refused to mention or talk about wet fishy smelling clothes, let alone the video of that day. The uncles still had the cam video he took that afternoon in his study. It took several weeks before he was willing to look at it. That afternoon he and Lisa were not asleep in his study sharing a dream, a dream from which they could not be waken. They had disappeared.

He wished he could beg her forgiveness for his cruelty. He could not because she did not know, perhaps would never know it was he who wielded the knife that severed the spark in her soul. She would never know the spark had already ignited one in his own. She must never know he was both her nemesis and her savior. At least Edmond eventually found redemption for his cruelty to Lucy in denying her Narnia. Would there be an opportunity for Jamison to find forgiveness for denying Lisa her adventures into books when they called to her. He had encouraged her for five years to seek truth and reality. Now he knew they were not the same thing.

Finding Peter Chapter 1 (sequel to Waking Lisa)

"All good books are alike in that they are truer than if they had really happened and after you are finished reading one you will feel that all that happened to you and afterwards it all belongs to you: the good and the bad, the ecstasy, the remorse and sorrow, the people and the places and how the weather was." [ERNEST HEMINGWAY]

GEORGE FELT A tug on his arm and felt around for the source. Another tug and he woke to realize one of his eight-year-old-sons was trying to wake him. He reached for the child and pulled him into the bed beside him. It was Andrew and he was crying. He whispered, "Hey son, bad dream?"

The tears turned into sobs. Lisa turned over, sat up and switched on the lamp.

He struggled free when the light came on and climbed over his father into his mother's arms. His sobs morphed into hysterics. Both his parents were now holding him. George asked again, "Bad dream? Want to talk about it?"

They saw in the light it was Andrew. Lisa kissed his forehead, then reached for a bottle of water sitting on the night-stand by her. "Here honey, have a drink, then we can talk." The act of drinking drowned the sobs to mere tears.

Andrew wiped his eyes with the sleeve of his pajamas and blurted out. "Peter is gone, he didn't come back because of me." He buried his face into the crook of his father's arm and sobbed out again. "Peter is gone."

George climbed out of bed and picked Andrew up into his arms. Lisa grabbed her robe and followed them down the hall to the boy's bedroom. The bedroom light was already on. Lisa called out as they entered the room, "Peter?"

Andrew let out another wail, "He is gone!"

George put Andrew down. He wished he could be angry because of this foolish trick the boys were playing, but the nine-year-old Andrew's distress was clearly not playacting. Lisa took Andrew's hand and led him into the hall and down-stairs to the kitchen. She would try to comfort him while George made the search.

She started the kettle to make hot cocoa for Andrew and the coffee pot for her and George. It was four and they would have been getting up in an hour anyway. The cocoa and coffee were ready by the time George joined them. He was completely dressed. He sat by Andrew. "Were you outside Andrew, you and Peter?"

"No, we were in a book."

Lisa dropped her cup spilling coffee over the table. She reached for a towel to mop up the spill. George asked him, "What are you talking about Andrew? I asked if you had gone outside? I need to know where to look for Peter. How long ago did Peter leave?"

Lisa poured more coffee and gently touched George's arm.

He turned to her. "What?" He turned back to Andrew who had begun sobbing again. "Were you playing hide and seek?"

"George!" She was more insistent. "Let Andrew tell us what happened, then we can ask questions."

She picked up Andrew's mug of untouched cocoa and her own coffee. "Let's go sit down more comfortable and Andrew can tell us what happened."

George picked up his own cup and followed them to the family room. Andrew sat between his parents. His sobbing had subsided and he took a sip of his cocoa. He blurted his story out so fast they could hardly understand him. "We went into the castle, but this time people could see us. They took us to see Peter the High King. He was nice. We were there a long time and ate and I said we needed to go home. Peter wouldn't so I was worried. Then I wished I could go home and I was, but Peter didn't come. I waited and waited and I couldn't go back to get him and he didn't come. I don't know what to do." More tears trickled down his cheek.

George asked, "You were playing a game about a castle, did you go outside in the game?"

"No, in the book."

George stood and began pacing. "I am going outside to look for him."

Lisa sent Andrew to his room to get dressed while she hurriedly pulled on jeans and sweater and combed her hair. They met in the hall and went down together back to the family room.

"Andrew, tell me from the start, what you meant about going into a book."

While George was outside for half an hour or so, Andrew told his mother how he and Peter wanted to go into Narnia like the kids in the story did. They tried lots of things but they never worked. Then one day they sat together and held hands and wanted to be in Narnia and they were. They were reading a Narnia story when it happened. They saw a unicorn that let them come up and pet it. He told her they were always together and when they wanted to be home, they were. But neither of them could go alone. Only when they were side by side and holding hands together did they have, what he called, the power to go into a book. When they wanted to go home, they both wished it and they were home. He said they had been doing this maybe ten times since Christmas. But this time he wished to be home because he was sleepy and tired. He didn't think about Peter and didn't plan on going home.

"And it is my fault because Peter can't come home without me and I can't go get Peter because I don't have the power."

George returned. "No luck, but I woke five dogs and two neighbors. Did Andrew explain yet what really happened?"

"George, you do remember why I got Gideon; because Jamison was concerned that I was sleep walking. Maybe Peter was sleep walking?"

He shook his head. "The doors were locked and bolted, I don't know how he could have gotten out after we tucked them both in last night." Then added, "Still it is the best we can come up with now. I am going to look inside again."

George and Lisa did another complete search of the house with Andrew following also looking and calling out for Peter. Lisa thought perhaps his parents' optimism relieved him of some of his fears and he finally fell asleep on the sofa in the family room.

It was now six and Lisa and George went to the kitchen for coffee refills and plan their next steps. George picked up his cell phone. "I will call the police and report a missing child." He then broke down in sobs. "Lisa, Lisa this can't be happening."

She sat at the kitchen table across from him and took his hands. "Before you call the police, I need to tell you more of what Andrew said, and then I have something I must tell you about myself." Her hand was shaking when she tried to pick up her coffee, so she sat it back down. Her emotions were too deep for tears. "Andrew told me he and Peter could go into a book they were reading." She held up her hand as she saw a look of anger in George's face. "Listen George, don't think."

He started to get up to go to the phone.

Lisa's voice was stern and commanding. "Sit down and listen to me George. Please."

He poured himself another cup of coffee before returning.

"Andrew said they have done this many times, but he could only remember six that he could tell me about. He said they can't go into a book alone, only when together and holding hands, then they have the power. He said they can come back home when they wish. Last night Andrew was tired and sleepy and wished to be home. He said it was an accident and he didn't realize it before he was home without Peter. He thought Peter would be along any time and waited for him for hours."

George sipped his coffee, "What an imagination."

Lisa was quiet for minutes and when George stood to resume making the call she held up her hand. "Now for the confession; when I was a child, younger than our twins, I could do the same. I went into books and wandered through gardens and mansions. My sleep disorder, when I couldn't be awakened for hours, was when I was in a book. In grade school I was considered a freak, and considered myself one until, maybe until I met you. A doctor who knew of Jamison's work told him about me. You know he doesn't practice psychiatry. He does research and lectures and teaches because of his work with hypnotism. It was his working with me three years before I could sometimes stop myself going into a book by setting a timer which beeped to wake me based on post hypnotic suggestions we worked on regularly. Then after the sleepwalking incident I got Gideon and you. I found by accident I could take Gideon into a story with me when he was on my lap. I tried it with Josh, who couldn't deal with the experience. Then I took Jamison with me."

George just shook his head.

"After our experience he quit his consulting and began research for any cases like mine, for explanations and possibilities. That is why he now lives in Ireland for his research. He knows even if he finds evidence of reality of what I experienced and the one time he was with me, that he cannot publish it. Even so he is driven to know the truth."

George now stood. "I can't believe this Lisa, what you are telling me!"

"I know. George, for me and for your sons, can we please call Jamison first; talk to him. Then call the police."

"The time difference?"

"Use my phone. If he sees it is from me at this hour he will answer."

Lisa found her phone on the kitchen cabinet and looked up Jamison in contacts. She pushed the button and waited. When there was no answer, she repeated the step. Again, no answer. Just as George picked up his phone to call the police, Lisa's phone rang.

"Jamison, thank you." She put the phone on speaker. "Jamison, I put you on speaker. George is here with me. Peter is missing."

"What happened?"

George responded, "Andrew woke us quite early this morning saying Peter was gone. He told Lisa he and Peter had gone into a book. He came home but Peter didn't. He told her they can go if together because they don't have power to go alone. He said he was tired, wished to be home, but Peter stayed. He blames himself. He claims he can't go back to get Peter alone, and Peter can't come home alone. Lisa tells me you might know something about this, about this nonsense."

Silence. Then Jamison said. "I am sure you have made a thorough search. Have you called authorities yet?"

"No, Lisa insisted I talk to you first. She told me what she said was her 'great secret' for the first time since I have known her."

"Would you have believed her before?"

"I am not sure I do now."

"George, the first thing essential in getting Peter back, is by protecting Andrew."

Silence again, and Lisa and George thought they had lost connection.

Jamison repeated, "We need to protect Andrew if we are to get Peter back. If he gets confused or loses his faith in what he and Peter can do." He paused a moment then continued. "He simply must not. George, tell the police you suspect he was sleep walking, that his mother has a history of it when she was a child. Do whatever you can to keep the police from talking to Andrew. Lisa and George, you must, I repeat it, must convince Andrew you believe him, even if you don't. Where is he now?"

"Fell asleep finally, I don't think he slept all night."

"I want to talk to him, again with all of us. We need him to be secretive but not lie. Call me when he is awake. And yes do call the police. Maybe he did sleep walk and you will have him back in an hour. Even if you do find him, we have a serious situation. I will be on the first flight I can get and should see you hopefully in less than two days." He paused, then added. "I may bring my son, Dylan, if I can; might be helpful for Andrew. He doesn't know about books yet Lisa. Colleen and I need to talk and decide if he is ready. I don't want him to stumble into one by accident — as you well know."

"Can't you say more?"

"Not now, need to get a flight to the United States. It is a matter of life and death. I have two godsons who need me."

They heard the dial tone and looked at each other.

George stood and paced the kitchen. "All of this is too much Lisa. You and Jamison? He is a reputable doctor. Lisa you have known him most of your life. I believed and trusted him as a friend, enough to trust our boys to him as their god-father."

George called the police and reported his son missing. Meanwhile Andrew talked with Jamison when he woke. He provided details enough to almost convince his dad that he had really been there. Andrew did understand that the police would be looking for Peter here in our world and that they would not believe Andrew if he told them where he and Peter had gone. He was not to make up any stories. Only that he was to say he went to bed and then saw Peter wasn't there and that he waited for him to come back and he was scared and told his parents. All that made sense to Andrew.

The rest of the day was hectic. Andrew slept half the day, then clung to Lisa or George's side the rest of the day. Jamison told them they must not keep secrets from Andrew, something about the truth being a great force, that Andrew should be included in all conversations about Peter. They had Peter and Andrew excused from school for the next two weeks and also cancelled all of their business and personal obligations.

After a late dinner of soup and sandwiches, they went to the family room with their coffees for what George referred to as Lisa's secret childhood secret revealed. Lisa spent a couple of hours thinking through how much and what to tell George; especially since Jamison insisted Andrew know the entire story. Lisa sat in one of their two large red leather chairs, a wedding gift from Jamison. George sat on the sofa with Andrew curled next to him.

She sipped the hot brew and began, "Andrew before I tell you and daddy about myself as a little girl I would like you to tell me why you and Peter did not tell us about your adventures into books?"

He hung his head a little and said, "You would not believe us. We agreed together to keep it a secret because you would just laugh at us."

"Why did you think that?"

"We thought we were weird that we could do this because other people couldn't."

"Now you can understand what I am going to tell you and daddy. I was younger than you are when I could go into books. Like the children in the Narnia stories I didn't decide to go, I just suddenly found myself there. I couldn't decide to go or to come back like you tell me you and Peter can do."

They saw a tear starting to trickle down Andrew's cheek and George pulled him up into his lap.

Lisa continued, "Like you, I knew other people didn't go into books. I thought I was a freak, that's another word for weird. When I was in a story, people around thought I was asleep, only they couldn't wake me up like you can for anyone who is asleep. I would be reading a book at school and looked like I was asleep. Other kids thought I was weird and called me names. I didn't have any friends."

Andrew climbed off his father's lap and lay on the sofa with his head on his lap. Lisa continued. "I met Doctor Jamison when I was twelve. He used hypnotism to help me know when I was going into a story before it happened; like you and Peter know you are going before you do. It took several years with Doctor Jamison for me to recognize what was about to happen and to be able to choose to not go. When I was in high school, I began to have many friends, like Jane, Clara's mom, and Grace, who got married at Christmas. Then I went into some stories about Jesus and his disciples from the Gospels, because I didn't want to say no to those stories."

Andrew looked up. "Do you mean we could go see Jesus?"

Lisa swallowed hard. "I don't know dear. I don't think so. Your daddy and I have told you all about him. You know he is here and present with us all the time. When I was growing up no one told me about him. Grama and Grampa Longford know Jesus now, but they didn't then. Going into the stories was the way I got to see and know Jesus. Now I see and know him everywhere."

Andrew's face scrunched up in disbelief.

Lisa went on, "Once when I was holding my dog Gideon."

Andrew interrupted again, "The dog painting over the fireplace."

"Yes that Gideon, I went into a story and Gideon came with me. It was then I found that like you and Peter, by touching someone they could also go to the book."

Lisa looked across the room and saw that Andrew's face was eager with acceptance of what she was saying. George had the opposite look on his. She wondered if he was thinking she was telling stories to make Andrew feel better. She decided to finish quickly.

"One day Doctor Jamison and I went into a Gospel story together. Only when I wanted to talk about it, he said it was a dream we shared; so I no longer believed. The books and stories no longer called to me, and I never went into one again. Doctor Jamison knows much about the rare people who can go into stories and he will be here tomorrow night and we will work on a plan to bring Peter back."

George picked Andrew up. "Bed time son."

"I'm scared."

"You can sleep with us. Come on and get your teeth brushed and pajamas on." He took Andrew by the hand and led him upstairs. "I will be back when I get him tucked in."

Lisa knew George was not satisfied. She hoped she had been truthful enough for Andrew. Her mind flew back to when she was twelve and first met Jamison and the time she suggested he was her savior or her nemesis. Years later he admitted to her what he had done, that he finally believed her and that he had indeed been both her savior and her nemesis. He told her he closed the door on her gift, that he could have held it open for her, but did not and went inside himself. He had to exclude her from other worlds as it was the only way for Lisa and George to have a life together. She loved her life here with George and their sons; but sometimes wondered what if, what if she had told him she loved him, would he have believed her and let her go with him?

She sighed, she knew back then George would have been like Josh and declared her a freak. Did he believe her now, would he trust and believe Jamison? She realized why Jamison insisted the truth was essential right now for Andrew since truth and reality were tied together, but not the same thing.

Acknowledgements

I FIND IT difficult to begin to list the wonderful friends who have been beta readers, encouragers and fans, and most of all helpful editors. If I had an agent, I would acknowledge that person. My list of names is in alphabetical order since I valued each person for their unique contribution in creation of my novel.

I acknowledge with my gratitude to: Beverly Kolosseus, Carol Johnson, Jeanne O'Connor, Joan Spencer, Katheryn Pagh, Lin Willett, Pam Rigdon, Susann Smith, and the wonderful Starbucks baristas who kept the coffee coming.

Author Note

A NOTE ABOUT myself: My favorite book genres relate to speculative fiction, which for me include science fiction and some fantasy. Science fiction stories, in the truest sense of the word, because they represent possibilities. I love some fantasy stories because they are the origin of my early reading and love for "fairytales," even the "Grimm" kind. Our earliest stories, myths and legends, generally included magic and powers beyond our mere human abilities.

The ideas of truth and reality are a part of my story, *Waking Lisa*. I wanted to show that Lisa's experience in the Gospel stories were different from her experience in other stories because she believed these stories were true.

According to G. K. Chesterton; "As long as you have mystery you have health; when you destroy mystery you create morbidity. The ordinary man has always been sane because the ordinary man has always been a mystic. He has permitted the twilight. He has always had one foot in earth and the other in fairyland. He has always left himself free to doubt his gods; but (unlike the agnostic of to-day) free also to believe in them.

He has always cared more for truth than for consistency."

[Quote from his book *Orthodoxy*]